USA Today Bestselling Author
TRUDY STILES

Copyright © 2015 by Trudy Stiles.
Trudy Stiles, LLC Copyright ©
First published in 2015.
All rights reserved.
ISBN: 978-0-9911054-7-2

No part of this book may be reproduced or transmitted in any form or by any means, electronic or mechanical, including photocopying, recording, or by any information storage and retrieval system without the written permission of the author, except for the use of brief quotations in a book review.

This book is a work of fiction. Names, characters, places, and incidents either are the product of the author's imagination or are used fictitiously. Any resemblance to actual, locations or persons, living or dead, is entirely coincidental.

All rights reserved. Except as permitted under the U.S. Copyright Act of 1976, no part of this publication may be reproduced, distributed, or transmitted in any form or by any means, or stored in a database or retrieval system, without the prior express, written consent of the author.

This book is intended for mature adults only. It is not suitable for anyone under the age of 18.

Cover Art by Stephanie White of Steph's Cover Design
Cover Photography by Mandy Hollis of MHP Photography
Editing by Kathryn Crane
Editing by Murphy Rae of Indie Solutions
www.murphyrae.net
Interior Design and Formatting by Elaine York of Allusion Graphics, LLC/Publishing & Book Formatting
www.allusiongraphics.com

Editorial Reviews

Trudy Stiles' first two novels, *Dear Emily* and *Dear Tabitha*, received stunning praise from the indie community. Read these books before you read Dear Juliet and see what these incredible bloggers, reviewers and authors all saw in Trudy's work.

Dear Emily Reviews

Natasha Tomic, Natasha is a Book Junkie: "This book has the power of touching the reader so deeply by giving us unique and very precious insight into the world of child adoption, from both viewpoints of the birth mother as well as the adoptive parents. I walked away at the end of this book feeling like my heart had grown tenfold, overflowing with so many emotions, and desperately hoping that fiction, in this case, had found its roots in real life."

Mollie Kay Harper, Tough Critic Book Reviews: "I was blown away by the story's originality. I was blown away by the romance and passion. I was blown away by the heartache and pain. I was blown away that I whole heartedly invested my emotions into the lives of these two women."

Gitte & Jenny, Totally Booked: "What a truly breath-taking, compelling and beautifully stirring debut from Trudy Stiles. The writing was truly beautiful and the story which shows the past as well as the present was so raw and gripping my heart was so full of cracks by the time I'd finished."

Chris' Book Blog Emporium: "I love when a book can grip you right from the first few pages, pull you in and not let you go until the very last page. Trudy has written a page turner. Her debut novel knocked my socks off and she is definitely an author to check out."

Nic Farrell, Flirty and Dirty Book Blog: "I'm not sure what I expected when I started Dear Emily by Trudy Stiles but one thing is for sure, I had no idea how emotional of a read it would be. Not your fluffy and mushy love story, Dear Emily was so much more."

Becca Manuel, Becca the Bibliophile: "It's a love story that is so profound and yet it is hardly ever spoken of. It's the story of two women, torn apart by life that had left them scarred and a bond that they will forever share in a little girl neither have met yet – Emily."

Rebecca Shea, USA Today Bestselling Author: "When a book leaves you thinking about it days later – that's a good thing. This was a 4.5 star before because it was good, really good...as in amazing. It's now a 5 star because it did something to me...it left me wanting more – needing more. That is the sign of a 5-star amazing book."

Jen Skewes, Three Chicks and Their Books: "I am not even sure that I can begin to express just how much I loved this book and how truly amazing and touching it was. Dear Emily is by far one of my favorite books this year. It is one of those books that will stay with you."

Jesey Newman, Scmhexy Girl Book Blog: "Dear Emily is a beautiful story about love, lust, family and the tragedies endured by Carly and Tabitha, our leading ladies. Trudy Stiles has woven the lives of these women both past and present, in such an amazing way."

Amanda Maxlyn, author of "What's Left of Me": "There are books that will pull you along as you read, and then there are books that will literally pull you into the story as you read. Dear Emily is the book that will suck you in with the first sentence and not let you go until the last word. Trudy Stiles has a gift. She created a beautiful, yet pained world of two strangers that become connected in the most stunning way."

JJ Rossum, author of "Thou Shalt Not": "Well, Ms. Stiles, you really knocked this one out of the park. I loved it. Unique story line, characters you could root for and emotions you could really feel."

Kelly, Perusing Princesses Book Blog: "Trudy Stiles has entered the indie writers world with an impressive boo – get ready for the shockwaves to hit, because this is one debut you do not want to miss!"

Kathryn Perez, author of "Therapy": "With so many books out there today, it's hard to find one that isn't just a cookie cutter version of the next. I personally enjoy books that are more than a "surface" read. I like to walk away from it having gained a message. I like to feel the story and characters.

Trudy Stiles does just that with this book. She conveys with her writing a beautiful story that grips you, touches you and stays with you."

Tiffany Marie, Everything Marie Book Blog: "The entire story will leave you in tears and provoke strong emotions from you. It is very touching and so personal, it's hard not to love this book. For a debut novel, this book really hit the mark."

Dee McGee, Booze, Bookz and Bad Boyz: "I absolutely loved Dear Emily. Trudy Stiles debut novel impresses the heck out of me. She took what could have been a straight forward dark, tragic plot and turned it into a beautiful story about coming to terms with adversity."

Virginia, Love N Books: "Trudy's writing is detailed, emotional and beautiful. She tugs at your emotions and makes you feel as if you know these characters. You can't help but feel for these broken women and wish their heartache would end and they would find happiness."

Dear Tabitha Reviews

Natasha Tomic, Natasha is a Book Junkie: "Confession time. I was terrified of this book. Literally, breaking out in a cold sweat the moment I decided to read it. This is truly a book like no other. This story is told with honesty and heart, making the reader feel so many different emotions page after page, but most of all the author's reverence for her own characters. I walked away feeling like every half-empty glass in my life was suddenly full to the rim, thankful for this journey and determined to read every word this author ever decides to write.

Robin Segnitz, Hesperia Loves Books: "Dear Tabitha is a powerful story of healing, love an family. I felt a range of intense emotions while reading including anger, rage, sadness, love and joy. I found Dear Tabitha absolutely satisfying and the best work yet for Trudy Stiles. Five stars for Dear Tabitha!"

The Danish Bookaholic: "Ms. Stiles has a wonderful way with words, and I find it difficult to fully express how uch I love this book. Every single page moved me, sometimes to laughter, sometimes to tears. My heart was hurting so much for both Tabitha and Alex, and my romantic soul could not stop hoping and praying that, despite Tabitha's silence, they would somehow find their way back to each other again.

Annie Gabor, All is Read: "Trudy is an amazing storyteller who easily makes her characters become so realistic. You will feel every emotion they feel, the frustration that boils up and puts you on the edge of your seat, the heartbreak, forgiveness and love."

Beth, The Indie Bookshelf: "This is a great emotional read. Ms. Stiles makes you feel, laugh, cry and hope. Sometimes hope is the most dangerous emotion."

LL Collins, Bestselling Author: "Trudy Stiles is an amazing storyteller, reaching in a gripping your heart right from the get go. She's an author to watch, and I'll be sure to read anything she writes.

Jesey, Shmexy Girls Book Blog: "This is a journey that will tear your heart out. The past, the present, and the future all come together beautifully to bring this story to an end."

Sarah Griffin, Books to Breathe: "I will leave you with this: the emotions displayed between Alex and Tabitha, when they allowed their walls to crumble and their hearts to open, were enough to make the darkest of hearts smile. Just know this, it wrecked me, completely and utterly wrecked me, and I'm a better person for it."

Dee McGee: "Trudy Stiles writing continues to keep me enthralled. Dear Tabitha is a heart-wrenching, deeply emotional story about two people overcoming a turbulent past and trying to find themselves...and love."

Synopsis

This book is not suitable for young readers. It is intended for mature adults only (18+). It contains strong language, adult/sexual situations and some violence.

Dear Juliet is BOOK THREE in the Forever Family series. Dear Emily and Dear Tabitha are BOOKS ONE and TWO.

Reading *Dear Emily* and *Dear Tabitha* first will enhance your reading experience by giving you some insight into the characters that you meet in this book.

The bestselling Forever Family Series concludes with this emotionally gripping story. Follow the lives of two incredible people as they battle their way through many years of heartache, loss and love. This story will take you on an epic journey that spans almost 20 years.

Two best friends connected by childhood, broken by tragedy and healed by trust.

He's known her since the third grade.

He's loved her since their teen years.

But her heart belonged to his best friend.

Everything changes when a tragic accident threatens to destroy both of their lives.

Juliet Oliver was adopted at birth and has always been haunted by the reality that she wasn't wanted. Despite her loving family, she emotionally detaches from everyone in her life, except for one person. He's been a rock and a much needed source of support, love, and encouragement.

Seth Tyson has had his share of tumultuous relationships. He's constantly battling his own demons, led by issues at home. His father is a womanizer. His mother is an alcoholic, battling depression. But he makes a choice to leave his family behind and start a new life across the country.

When Juliet's life spirals out of control, she needs her best friend Seth more than anything. Can he stop her from self-destructing? And will he open his heart to her once more?

Can they each find...

Redemption?

Love?

Family?

Dear Juliet is the third book in the **Forever Family** series.

Foreword

Dear Reader,

I've gone back and forth as to whether or not I needed to write a foreword. Actually, I wasn't sure I wanted to, but then I asked myself this question over and over: *Will people read this book if they haven't yet read Dear Emily or Dear Tabitha?* The answer is still not one hundred percent clear to me. I originally thought I'd be writing this story as a standalone but as I began writing, I realized that would be pretty difficult to do. I've rewritten this story several times and each time I realized that I couldn't be true to Seth and the characters without tying important things back to the first two books in the series. In my opinion, you can't know Seth in his entirety without experiencing those books. I want my readers to experience everything that he did in Dear Emily and Dear Tabitha, even though his 'part' in both books was a supporting role.

Dear Juliet will take you through various times in Seth's life and some will overlap with events that take place during the time that Dear Emily and Dear Tabitha did but Dear Juliet will not mirror or retell those books. I hope that makes sense.

Therefore, I encourage you to read Dear Emily and Dear Tabitha first, because I'd love for you to get to know all of my characters. I understand that some of you may choose not to do that, so I will do my best to give you a glimpse into who Tabitha is to Seth in this book. She does indeed play an important role in how he makes his decisions, and I'd like you to see that unfold rather than me giving you a summary of what has already happened.

Just know this. It's time for Seth to move on, from Tabitha and from the past that continues to haunt him.

Seth Tyson has indeed polarized my readers in both Dear Emily and Dear Tabitha. Some wish for his happily-ever-after and some aren't quite sure he deserves one. But he holds a very special place in my heart, and I hope this story gives those of you in either corner a new perspective and you're able to open your hearts and let him in.

Yours,
Trudy

P.S. I strongly suggest you listen to all of Snow Patrol's albums on repeat while reading this book. It will enhance your experience. □

Dedication

Every single one of my books has a piece of me in it, some pieces larger and more significant than others. This book is no different.

*To my husband,
Olive Juice*

Content Warning

This book is not suitable for young readers. It is intended for mature adults only (18+). It contains strong language, adult/sexual situations and some violence.

To contact Trudy:
Email:authortrudystiles@gmail.com
Facebook: http://www.facebook.com/authortrudystiles
Instagram: https://instagram.com/trudystiles/
Goodreads: http://www.goodreads.com/trudy_stiles
Twitter: @trudystiles
Amazon: http://www.amazon.com/Trudy-Stiles/e/B00H3O0OJ8

prologue

Kelsey Oliver

Past
Philadelphia, Pennsylvania
Age 34

MY HEART IS BEATING wildly in my throat as we walk through the doors of the maternity ward at St. Joseph's Hospital. My husband, Kevin, squeezes my hand as tightly as he can.

"I'm a mess, Kevin," I blurt out. "Is this even real?"

"Yes, babe. This is very real. And we're about to meet our baby," he says, his voice shaking.

Our plane touched down in Philadelphia less than twelve hours after we received a call from our adoption counselor, Jessica, from Forever Home Adoption Agency. We had been on their waiting list for almost two years and had just about given up hope that we would ever be selected to adopt a baby when she called us late last night.

"Kelsey! Hi, it's Jessica. I'm sorry to be calling you so late, but I have the most incredible news."

I immediately reach to my right, shaking Kevin's shoulder to wake him up from a sound sleep. We were both exhausted after the last trick-or-treater left our front porch at around ten o'clock tonight, and were asleep before our heads hit our pillows. I look at the clock. It's only eleven thirty. It feels like we've been asleep for hours.

"Hmm?" he moans before he flips over to see me sitting straight up in bed. "Is everything okay?" he asks hesitantly as his eyes widen and then squint. "What time is it?"

I know exactly what Jessica is about to tell us, and tears pool in my eyes as Kevin focuses on my face. God, I love this man, and we're about to get the news we've been waiting for.

I grab his hand, place the phone on speaker and say, "Jessica, we're both awake. What's going on?" Kevin's eyes glisten as a warm smile spreads across his handsome face.

"A baby girl was born earlier today and the birth mother, Lily, has committed to an adoption plan. She was presented several profiles to choose from, and she immediately chose the both of you. How soon can you be in Philadelphia?"

That phone call took place twelve hours ago, and I'm still in shock and disbelief. Our dream of starting our family is right in front of us, and I never thought this moment would arrive. I clutch Kevin's hand harder as we walk to the nurses' station.

"Excuse me," I say quietly. The nurse behind the desk looks up and nods. "We're here to meet with Jessica Hyde. She's a social worker." I hesitate, unsure of what's going to happen next.

"Oh, you must be the Olivers. Jessica mentioned she was expecting you. She's in the nursery right now." She gets up and comes out from behind the desk. "Come with me."

We follow her down the hall and I realize that she's either walking very fast or we're walking very slowly, because there is a huge distance between us. Kevin speeds up his pace and I follow suit.

We catch up to her and turn the corner together. My heart races as I stand in front of a large glass window with at least ten infants on the other side. All are asleep in their bassinets except one. That baby is wrapped tightly, pink cheeks barely visible. She looks so warm and cozy and is being rocked in the arms of an older woman. She looks up and smiles, and I recognize her face from the adoption agency's website. It's Jessica.

The nurse swipes her key card and unlocks the doors to the nursery.

I'm suddenly frozen in place. I wasn't expecting to meet the baby so soon.

Our baby.

I don't know what I was expecting, but this wasn't it. Aren't we supposed to do more paperwork? Get parenting lessons? My apprehension increases as Kevin places his hand on my back. This is all happening so fast.

Am I ready for this?

Are we ready for this?

I remain frozen in place as I try to picture that little baby at home in our empty nursery that we've had ready for what seems like forever. Yellow walls and neutral safari bedding suddenly don't seem right. Insecurity builds as thoughts of our future swirl in my head.

Will she be happy in our home?

Will she be happy with us?

Kevin eagerly pulls me into the nursery, and Jessica's warm voice fills the room.

"Kelsey, Kevin, say hello to Juliet."

She raises the baby's head so we can see her small face, her pink cheeks so perfect and round. My breath is immediately taken away, and my heart melts along with some of the uncertainties that I felt just moments ago. She's sound asleep and softly sucking on a green rubber pacifier that seems to take up half of her tiny face. Jessica motions to the empty rocking chair next to her, and Kevin leads me over to it so I can sit.

Before I know it, she's placed into my arms. My hold on her is awkward at first, because, well, I've never done this before. My arms are stiff, and Kevin places his hand over the crown of Juliet's head, engulfing it in his palm.

Protective.

Loving.

He's mesmerized by her. In love with her already.

Yes, this feels right.

"Relax, Kelsey. She'll know if you're nervous and you'll wake her up." Jessica softly chuckles and nods again.

I begin to relax my arms and settle more comfortably back into the rocking chair, Juliet softly molding into my chest.

"Isn't she beautiful?" Kevin asks. I look down at the little bundle and she twitches slightly in my arms, settling back into a deep sleep. Her baby scent suddenly hits my nose, and I begin to feel more at ease.

"Yes. She is beautiful. *Perfect*," I say as Kevin's thumb sweeps across her tiny forehead. His eyes lock onto mine and he nods slowly, a smile spreading across his face.

"She looks perfect in your arms, Kels."

We sit there for what seems like hours, but only minutes have passed. Kevin asks the question that's been on my mind for the better part of the last twelve hours.

"Where is her birth mother?"

Jessica takes a deep breath and seems hesitant to tell us.

"Lily doesn't want to meet you. Or see Juliet," she responds with sadness in her voice.

"Oh?" I reply, surprised.

"She's very young. Only sixteen. She just wants to sign the papers and go home. Well, go home as soon as the hospital will discharge her. She's already been moved to another floor." She pauses momentarily, as if she had hoped for another outcome. "We will typically move birth mothers so they don't have to hear other babies crying. It helps them begin to heal. We have to respect her wishes."

This is surprising to me, and Kevin and I exchange worried glances. *What could this mean?* My chest tightens and I realize that I'm holding Juliet closer, more protective.

"Sixteen? Can she even give this baby up? Can her family intervene?" I'm suddenly terrified that the beautiful little girl in my arms is about to be taken away from us.

"No. She can legally sign the adoption paperwork. It's her choice. Her family cannot intervene, nor do they need to be present during her revocation of rights. They are actually completely unaware of the birth of Juliet since Lily has been living with a family member for some time," Jessica states matter-of-factly. I have to trust that our social worker is speaking the truth, but her words don't comfort me at all. "I'm sorry, but I'm unable to discuss anything more with you about Lily."

"But she's only sixteen," I push, suddenly feeling very sad for the child who just gave birth to this beautiful little girl. "And her family doesn't know?"

How can this be?

"She's sixteen and scared. She absolutely does not want her family to know. But believe me, she is very clear-minded when it comes to the decision to give up this child," Jessica assures us.

Kevin's free hand swipes through the back of my hair and rests on my shoulder. While this all seems like a whirlwind, his gesture comforts me immensely.

"Okay, what's next?" Kevin and I ask at the same time.

Jessica smiles warmly and says, "It's time to become her family."

THE NEXT FEW DAYS are a blur. We spend every single moment we can with our daughter, experiencing all of the wonders and joys of having a newborn. The hospital gives us a room in the maternity ward where we can spend our first precious moments together as a family.

First bottle.

First diaper.

First bath.

The nurses practically have to pry her from our arms both nights we're there so they can take her back to the nursery.

Every single moment feels so right.

So perfect.

But.

It breaks my heart that we don't get the chance to meet Lily. I want to thank her. Tell her that Juliet is going to have a wonderful life.

That her decision to give her up was so selfless and strong, even for a young girl. My heart tugs whenever I think of Lily and how scared she must be. I ache to comfort her. To hold her and tell her everything is going to be okay.

"It's time to go home," Kevin whispers in my ear as his lips brush against my hair. This simple gesture distracts me from my sadness, if only slightly. I tighten the car seat straps and tuck the pink fleece blanket around our daughter.

"Yes, it's time." My cheeks warm as tears prick my eyes.

Jessica enters the room and her expression is stoic. My breath hitches and I'm suddenly nervous.

"Before you go home, I wanted to give you this." She hands me an envelope with Juliet's name scrawled across the front.

"Lily asked that you give this to Juliet when she's old enough to understand all about her adoption. She wanted to explain why she did what she did." Jessica purses her lips and bows her head. "You have to know how incredibly difficult this is for her."

"Of course. I can't imagine," I say softly.

I'm overwhelmed, thinking about how to even explain all of this to a child, much less promise to give her a letter from her sixteen-year-old birth mother.

I touch my lips softly to Juliet's nose, lingering for a moment. Kevin reaches down to take the carrier, kisses my cheek and says, "We'll make sure that our daughter knows her story and how Lily loved her enough to make this heart-wrenching decision. She's given us a gift, and we'll repay her by raising Juliet with more love than she can absorb."

His words should be comforting to me, but my heart is pulling me in another direction.

I'm terrified of what this letter could possibly contain.

My chest clenches and fearful thoughts swirl through my mind.

Dread for what this letter could contain.

Sadness for Lily and what she could be going through right now.

Fear for the future when we have to explain to Juliet about her adoption.

I try to compose myself, but the envelope feels like it's about to ignite in my hand.

I tuck it into my purse and promise myself to hide it away forever.

Lily's words have the potential to destroy Juliet's happiness.

Our happiness.

No.

I vow to myself that Juliet will *never* see this letter.

Part One

The Past

chapter one

Seth
Sausalito, California
Age 10

Dear Juliet,
I picked your name out of a hat that my teacher, Miss Morgan, passed around the class. I thought that I knew all of the kids in our grade, but I don't think we've ever met. Are you new to our school?
Juliet. That's a cool name. I've heard of Romeo and Juliet. Is that where you got your name?
Miss Morgan says that it's sad that we don't write letters anymore. She thinks that we use email too much. So as part of our class writing assignment this spring, we need to write a lot of letters. We have to pick someone from our same grade, but in a different class. So, I guess now you're my pen pal? Or something like that.
My name is Seth Tyson. I like to play baseball, run track and swim. I have a big family—two

younger sisters and an older brother. My sisters are twins and are six years old. Their names are Chloe and Chelsea. My brother is twelve and his name is Sean.

I also have a black lab named Mollie. She's a year and a half old and likes to play a lot. She sleeps in my room and likes me the best out of everyone in my family. It's probably because I give her so many treats and play fetch with her.

Okay. Time is up. Miss Morgan is collecting the letters so she can give them to your teacher.

Write back soon!

Yours truly,

Seth

After I sign my name, I fold the piece of paper and hand it to Miss Morgan.

"Cutting it a little close, Seth," she says as she quickly takes the first letter that I've ever written. I mean, I've written letters to my mom for Mother's Day, but nothing like this.

It's so weird, writing letters. Why can't we be email pen pals? That would make more sense, but Miss Morgan says that we don't appreciate the 'art of communication' anymore. She came up with this project with one of the other teachers, and I now have a pen pal for the rest of the school year. She says it will help us appreciate the anticipation of waiting for a letter, like in the old days.

Juliet Oliver. I hope she's not boring. I mean, I would rather have been paired with someone like me, who plays baseball and stuff. But a girl? I don't know about this.

The bell rings and I shove all of my books into my backpack. Our driver, Bob, should be outside waiting to pick up my brother, sisters and me. There aren't a lot of school buses that come to Chester Academy since most kids get rides from their parents or their family drivers. This is not a normal school, and I kind of hate it.

"Hey! Seth, wait up." I stop and turn to see Jeremy running toward me. "Are you going to baseball tonight?" He catches his breath and tosses his backpack over his shoulder.

"Yeah," I answer. Duh, I always go to baseball.

We walk outside and see both of our cars waiting for us. "Dude, will you hurry up?" Sean yells from the back seat of the limousine. He's always outside before me and is annoyed with me every single day. I chuckle to myself a little bit. I like to make him wait.

"See you later," Jeremy calls over his shoulder, "and don't forget to bring my catcher's mitt!"

"It's already in my bag at home," I shout to him as his car pulls away from the curb. Jeremy Reed is my best friend, and we play practically every sport together.

"God, Seth. Can't you *ever* be on time?" Sean asks, irritated as usual. He has golf lessons every day after school and hates to be late. Our father wanted me to take golf too, but I'd rather play baseball. It's so much more fun and I can see all of my friends. Golf is boring.

Our next stop is the building at the other end of the parking lot, where Chloe and Chelsea's classrooms are. They're in first grade.

I see the twins running toward the car as we pull up to the curb. Chloe is wearing pink ribbons in her pigtails today while Chelsea wears purple. It's their color code so their teachers and friends can tell them apart. Chloe is *always* pink and Chelsea is *always* purple. Their bedrooms are color coordinated the same exact way. I shake my head and smile at my little sisters. They are such girls.

"Hi, Seanie and Sethie!" they say in unison as they slide into the seat across from me. Sean doesn't even acknowledge their presence in the car, but I grin. They can be a pain in the butt most times, but I like that they look up to me as one of their big brothers.

The girls giggle and whisper during the drive. It's a short trip home, and we pull up to our big house. It's *really* big. Our family has a lot of money because our father does something with real estate. He buys and sells a lot of buildings in the Northern California area. He says that someday my brother and I are going to run his company. It seems boring and I hope that I can just play baseball instead.

Bob stops the car in front of the stairs and I jump out. I have to get myself ready for baseball and I've got to sit with my tutor, Mrs. Johnson, to do my homework before any after-school activities. It's my mother's rule. I bet Mrs. J. is already in the house, waiting for me.

I open the door and hear my mother's voice coming from the kitchen. It sounds strained. *Is she upset?* Glass shatters as she cries and yells. I swallow hard and get the chills. Sean drops his bag and reaches out to stop my sisters from running through the foyer as he looks at me with worried eyes. I've never heard my mother yell before, much less cry.

"Why do you keep doing this to me, Ted? *To us?*" I hear her weep. "I don't deserve this!"

I can only hear her voice. My father isn't replying to her questions, or if he is, I can't hear him. Sean starts to usher the girls upstairs and I follow. I try to peek around the large, winding staircase, but I can't see anything.

"Goddamn you, Ted! We can't continue to live like this. You're making me look like a fool." Her voice becomes weak and trails off as we all go upstairs. Sean brings us all into his room and closes the door.

"Why is Mommy yelling?" Chloe asks quietly.

"I don't know, but we should give them their privacy," Sean replies and turns on his television. He puts on Nickelodeon for the girls.

Oh man, it must be serious if he's allowing Chloe and Chelsea's favorite channel to play in his room. His room is usually off limits to everyone, but especially the girls. I look over to him. When our eyes meet, he just shakes his head. He seems just as worried as I feel right now.

I flop down into the beanbag chair next to the twins as I strain to listen to the muffled argument that is still taking place downstairs. A knot forms in my stomach and I'm suddenly sad for my mother. I've never heard her this upset. What did my father do to her? Is she angry about something one of us did?

The girls are huddled together watching their favorite show, Rugrats. They're quickly absorbed in the cartoon and I look back at Sean. He's on his bed with headphones on, listening to his MP3 player.

The front door slams and I grip the fabric of the beanbag chair. I hear my mother rush past Sean's room. She's still crying as she closes her bedroom door. I clench my teeth together, afraid of what's happening.

"Is Mommy going to be okay?" Chelsea asks. She has tears in her eyes and cuddles into Chloe.

"I don't know, Chelsea. I don't know what's going on," I answer, and I look over to Sean, hoping that he'll say something to me. To the girls. But he's just lying there, staring up at his ceiling. The music piping into his ears is so loud I can actually hear it.

"I don't want her to be sad, Seth. We need to do something to make her happy again," Chelsea states as Chloe nods in agreement.

I'm afraid to get up and leave the room. I don't want my mother to know that we heard her.

I look over at the clock on Sean's nightstand. It just changed to four o'clock.

Crap. I'm going to miss baseball tonight.

I immediately feel guilty for thinking this, but I don't want to be here right now.

I slouch lower in the beanbag chair and fix my eyes on the television, attempting to lose myself in the cartoon on the screen and drown out my mother's sobs coming from the other room.

chapter two

Juliet
Sausalito, California
Age 8

"SAY CHEESE!" MOM SAYS from behind her camera.

"Cheese!" I sing with a huge smile on my face. Dad is standing next to me and squeezes me close to his body. We're standing in my favorite park, near the Golden Gate Bridge.

"Happy Adoption Day, Sweetheart," Dad whispers in my ear while he kisses my cheek.

We celebrate my Adoption Day every year on April sixteenth. Today is the anniversary of the day that my parents signed all kinds of legal documents that say that I'm theirs forever. It's kind of like having another birthday. Even though I've been with my parents since the day I was born, Mom says someone from the state needed to visit us for six months after I came home. She was a social worker and Mom said she was so nice. She helped make my Adoption Day official.

My real birthday is on Halloween, which is really cool. All of my birthdays have been costume parties, and my parents find special ways to make it fun every year. Like last Halloween, when I turned seven, they planned a trick-or-treating party where each of my neighbors had a special game set up for me and my friends. We all got candy and prizes at each stop along our street, in addition to special clues to my birthday surprise. When we got back to our house, a puppy was jumping around in my backyard. He's a yellow lab named Buster, and he's my very best friend. That was the best birthday ever!

My parents also make *this day* very special for me every year. Today, we're taking a road trip up north. They took me out of school early so that we can get out of the area before all of the traffic starts.

We're heading to Portland, Oregon. I'm excited to see the pretty mountains and waterfalls up there.

Dad says that we can go to a place called Mount Tabor and play in a park there. It's a real volcano! He says there are a lot of fun things to do in Portland, including visiting a zoo, Timberline Lodge and tons of waterfalls, and I can't wait. I'm so excited. I feel like I'm going to burst.

"That was a gorgeous picture, Juliet," Mom says while tucking her camera into her purse. She takes a lot of pictures. Like, *a lot*. She makes beautiful photo albums and sends them to my birth mother, Lily. I've never met her, but she gets letters and pictures from us a few times a year. I write letters to her, too, and make pictures for her in art class. Dad says that she made them the happiest people on earth when she chose them to adopt me.

I wonder what she thinks when she sees my family and me.

"Okay, let's get in the car, Jules," Dad says. "We have a long ride ahead of us."

I hop into our big SUV, buckle myself and reach for the remote control for the DVD player. "Give that to me, please," Mom says, reaching to take the remote from my hand. "You have homework to do, remember? Why don't you get that done first? *Then* you can watch a movie. Deal?" She smiles and I reluctantly hand her the remote.

"Okay, Mom," I say, reaching for my backpack. I take out my homework assignments for the week and find the letter from Seth Tyson. Mrs. McCaskey gave us a writing assignment for the remainder of the school year; we have each been assigned a pen pal from Miss Morgan's class, and Seth is mine.

"What's that in your hand?" Dad asks, peering into the rearview mirror.

"My pen pal letter from Seth Tyson. He's in Miss Morgan's class."

My mother quickly looks at my father and he nods at her. She turns around and says, "Your father works with Seth's dad. Did you know that?"

"No. That's cool."

We moved to Sausalito a few months ago when my father's company was bought and he was relocated. When I came here, I tested at the fourth grade level, even though I was in third grade at my old school. My parents tell me that I'm practically two grades ahead, because at my old school, the age cutoff was different than at this school. My mom warns me that I'm going to be much younger than everyone else in my class by at least a year or two, but they know I'm smart and mature enough to handle it. I'm tall, so I fit in with the other girls. My mom says I'm not only as smart as them, but also more mature. I don't know what that means, but I think it's good.

My mom turns to look out the front of the car and we start to drive. I reread the letter that Seth wrote to me. He seems nice.

Mrs. McCaskey told us that our first letter should consist of things that are unique about us. That should be easy, so I start this assignment first.

Dear Seth,

Hi! My name is Juliet Oliver and I'm your pen pal for the rest of the school year. To answer your question, no, I'm not named after the Juliet from that play. I actually don't know how I got my name, since my birth mother, Lily, named me.

That leads me to the first part of my assignment. Here are five things that I think are interesting facts about me:

1) I'm adopted
2) I was born on Halloween
3) I love waterfalls (and I'm driving on a trip to see a TON of them)

4) I can hold my breath under water for a really long time

5) I have a Labrador puppy named Buster (our dogs can be puppy pal(s)

I'm excited to have a pen pal, and I think this assignment will be fun. Since I just moved here, this will be a nice way to get to know new people. I hope you write back soon.

Have a good day.

Sincerely,

Juliet

P.S. My Dad says that he works with your Dad. That's pretty cool!

Well, that was easy! I tear the note out of my composition book, fold it and place it into my homework folder. Next up is my reading assignment, and I'm excited about this. I take the book, *The Indian in the Cupboard*, from my bag and flip to the chapter where I left off. Next to exploring waterfalls, reading is my most favorite thing to do. I settle into my seat and get ready to read.

"Jules, wake up," I hear my mother's soft voice in my ear. I take a deep breath and stretch, realizing I'm still strapped into the back seat of the car. My shoulders and neck ache from being hunched over. She takes the book from my hand and places it into my backpack. "We're here, sweetheart," Dad says from the front seat.

I perk up, realizing we're about to start our fun weekend away. My mom's camera is out again, and I throw my hands in the air to cover my face. "Mom! Can you wait until I wake up, please?" Sheesh, this woman will take pictures of me clipping my fingernails, she's so camera happy.

"Of course, Jules." She backs up so I can get out of the car. There are guys taking our luggage from the back, and she nudges me to stand in front of the hotel with my dad.

"It's about time you get into a picture or two, Kelsey," Dad says to Mom. He walks over to her and kisses her, removing the camera from her hand.

"Yeah, Mom, you're never in any pictures." I giggle as she pulls me close. She bends down so our cheeks are touching. Her cheek is so warm and soft. "Cheese!"

Dad snaps the photo and says quietly, "My two beautiful princesses." His eyes linger on my mom and she blushes.

"You guys! Gross! Save the googly eyes for your alone time," I complain. Although I'm secretly happy to see my parents act like this. So many of my friends' parents are divorced or hate each other. My parents are always happy, or at least it seems that way. They almost never fight and seem really grateful for everything that they have. My parents are honestly two of the happiest people that I know, and I'm thankful that they're mine.

We get settled into our hotel and head down to dinner. The restaurant is quiet since there's barely anyone here. It feels cool to practically have the place all to ourselves.

Mom and Dad raise their wine glasses in the air and my mom speaks, "A toast." I quickly grab my lemonade and raise it next to their drinks. "To Juliet, our beautiful daughter. Our gift. We're thankful each and every day that you're here with us. Happy Adoption Day. We love you so much." Her voice quivers a little and her eyes are teary. Then she sniffles as she clinks her glass with mine and Dad's.

"Jules, I couldn't ask for a better daughter. Every single time I hear you call me Dad, my heart grows. We're so lucky to have you in our lives. Truly blessed. We love you." He clinks our glasses together again, and then I take a quick sip of my drink, making a wish. You know, because it's bad luck if you don't take a sip after a toast, and I know that I want my wish to come true. I want my family to always stay together. So I sip and sip until I'm nearly slurping my drink.

My dad kisses my mom and wipes away the tear that trickles down her cheek. "I love you, Kels," he whispers into her ear.

My mom and dad make me so happy.

Dad turns to face me as Mom sniffles a little bit more. "Tell me about your pen pal. What else has he told you about himself?" he asks.

I put down my lemonade and smile. "Well, you already know that his name is Seth Tyson. He likes to run track and play baseball," I state. "It's cool that you work with his dad."

"Yes, I do work with his father, Ted. Although I've never met Seth, I'm sure he's a nice boy." My dad looks strained as he says that, and my mom shakes her head a little bit. Judging by the expression on my mom's face, I would guess that she doesn't like Seth's father. *Oh well.*

Once we're finished with dinner, we head up to our suite in the hotel. After I get my pajamas on, I go into the living room area to say goodnight to my parents.

"Are you ready for some fun tomorrow, Jules?" my dad asks me while pulling me tight against him, hugging me.

"Yes! I can't wait."

"Tomorrow is our waterfall day, so we'll be visiting a few after we go see the Bonneville Lock and Dam," my dad tells me.

"Locks?" I'm confused. Why on earth would I want to go see a lock?

"Sweetheart, it's a historic landmark. It was built by the U.S. Army Corps of Engineers a long time ago to help generate power and provide a passage for ships up the Columbia River. There's also a pretty cool fish ladder." He smiles at me.

"A fish ladder. Dad, c'mon. Fish can't climb ladders!" I giggle uncontrollably. Now he's just being ridiculous.

He laughs heartily. "Jules, it's a way for the salmon to feel like they're swimming upstream and get them through the dam so they can mate."

Gross.

"Okayyy... sounds pretty cool," I lie. "What about the waterfalls?" That's what I really want to see.

"There will be plenty to see on our trip tomorrow. I promise. Off to bed now, sweetheart," Mom says as she kisses me on my forehead.

"Goodnight!" I rush off to my room and jump onto the soft bed. I wish Buster were here to sleep on my feet like he does every night. *I miss him.*

When I'm settled under the soft comforter, I hear my mom's voice from the living room. "I don't know when the right time is, Kevin." She sounds upset, worried.

"The time is never going to be right, Kels, but she's getting old enough to begin to understand her full story," I hear my dad say. What are they talking about? Is it about me? He doesn't sound too happy either.

"I know. I know," my mom says quietly. I feel bad eavesdropping on their conversation, but they sound like they're right outside my door. It would be impossible not to hear what they're saying.

"It's almost time to share Lily's letter with her. I think she's ready to read her birth mother's words," my dad says, and I cover my mouth with my hand, almost letting out a yelp.

Lily. My birth mother.

I've only ever heard stories about her. My parents tell me how much she sacrificed so that I can be a part of their family. *Our* family.

But they have a letter? From her? *Whoa.* Through all of the years that my parents have been sending her photo albums and letters, I didn't think we ever got anything back from her.

I want to know about Lily. I really do. But I'm also scared.

Mom is nervous. Dad is upset. *Why would they keep Lily's letter from me?* My heart pounds in my chest and I pull the covers up to my chin.

What if Lily hated me? What if she gave me up because she thought there was something wrong with me?

Oh my God.

"No, Kevin. She will never be ready to read that letter," I hear my mother say outside my door. "*I've* read that letter. So have you. How can you even suggest that?"

The room feels like it's spinning and I begin breathing very fast. I can't hear my parents' voices anymore because my ears are ringing.

I think I'm drifting off to sleep, but my heart is beating like crazy against my chest.

My feet and my fingers are tingling and I somehow don't care anymore.

I give in to the darkness.

chapter three

Seth
Sausalito, California
Age 11

One Year Later

"TRICK OR TREAT!" WE YELL at the top of our lungs, and shove our bags into the foyer of the house at the end of Juliet's street. It's her birthday, and Jeremy and I are part of the entourage in her neighborhood.

This year, I'm in the same class as her, and she invited our whole class to go trick-or-treating and to a costume party afterwards. I'm dressed in my well-worn J.T. Snow jersey and my uniform pants from baseball. Not much of a costume, but I've been J.T Snow for the past three years for Halloween and I won't stop now.

I have to admit, for a girl's party, this is a lot of fun. The driveway is filled with all of our classmates, and it seems like everyone is having a great time. I look into my bag and grab one of the full-sized Milky Way bars, tearing at the wrapper with my teeth.

"What are you, a caveman?" Jeremy asks. His voice is muffled by the hockey mask that he's wearing. I'm not quite sure if he's trying to be a real hockey player or a serial killer since there's fake blood all over his jersey.

The caramel from the candy bar practically glues my teeth together. I nod vigorously, and he clocks me on the back of my head with his hockey stick. I laugh, practically drooling chocolate out of my mouth.

"You guys are so gross!" Juliet says, disgusted, and begins to walk away from us. She's dressed as a cheerleader and it's the perfect costume for her. She's at almost every single one of our baseball games and track meets; she should be on the squad.

"Hey, he's the one spewing chocolate!" Jeremy quickly replies. If I were to guess, I would say that Jeremy likes Juliet *almost* as much as he likes baseball. She giggles and reaches into Jeremy's bag to steal some candy. "Hey!" he laughs, grabbing her wrist before she can get any of his haul. They walk ahead of me as I wipe the chocolate that's dripped down my chin and onto my jersey.

Less than an hour later, I'm watching as Juliet bobs for apples in a giant tin bucket. Her entire head is underwater, and she's grasping the sides of the bucket with purpose. Man, she can hold her breath! She emerges with her teeth sunk into a giant apple that she quickly discards, and dives in again. The timer buzzes and she throws her arms into the air when she sees that she got eight apples. Her curly hair is soaked and matted to the sides of her face.

"Close, Juliet, but Jeremy's the winner with nine apples," her father says.

"What? Doesn't that big one count for two?" she asks, gasping for breath. She has a huge smile on her face, so I know she doesn't have any hard feelings. Some of our classmates are still here and are cheering on this makeshift competition.

Her father hands Jeremy a gift bag that contains the prize for this contest. He reluctantly takes it and passes it to Jules. "Happy Birthday, Juliet," he says, blushing.

"No, I can't take this, Jeremy. You totally earned it. But I'm going to kick your butt in the clothespin game!"

And before I know it, we're at the next game station that her father set up. There's an empty glass gallon jug with a small opening at the top, and her father is demonstrating how to play this game. His toes are touching a chalk line, and he's leaning over the jug with an old-fashioned wooden clothespin lined up under his chin. He releases it and it smoothly falls into the jug. "The person who can get the most clothespins into the jug will win this!" He holds up a gift card to Best Buy, and suddenly all of the guys in the class push their way into line. I'll sit this one out to let Jeremy kick everyone's butt.

I watch as everyone misses their clothespin drops. Juliet is able to get six into the gallon jar. Jeremy steps up and systematically drops the first five in, but then misses the next seven. As the last one misses, he turns his head to the side and winks at Juliet. She blushes again and clasps her hands in front of her. "Jeremy! You missed on purpose. Dad, please give him the gift card." Her dad doesn't hesitate and drops the card into the gift bag from the last contest. Jeremy tries to pull the bag away, but Mr. Oliver is too fast. I have a feeling that Jeremy is going to leave that somewhere for Juliet.

"Mr. Oliver, can I use your bathroom?" I ask.

"Sure, son. You know where it is, right?"

"Yeah." I trot inside, through the back door and take care of business. As I'm washing my hands, I hear voices in the hallway outside the door.

"Kels, are you okay?" Mr. Oliver's voice sounds concerned. I don't open the door, because I don't want to walk in on their conversation.

She takes a deep breath and responds, "I don't know. This is such a happy day for our family, but I can't help but feel that Juliet could one day wish that she wasn't part of it. That she may wish that she was never given up for adoption." She pauses and I hear Mr. Oliver walking closer to her.

"You have to stop feeling like this," he says, trying to soothe her.

"You don't feel this way, ever?" she asks.

"No. She belongs with us. End of story."

"But there's Lily. She didn't know what she was doing. She was only sixteen. Why would she give her up? Juliet's perfect. How do you think she feels every Halloween? Hell, what do you think she feels every single day of her life?"

More silence.

"I feel Lily's pain every day that I watch our daughter grow into a beautiful young girl. I can't help it. I feel her loss. Her grief. Her *regret*." She sniffles, and I hear Mr. Oliver move closer to her.

"Honey, I know her birthday triggers these feelings, and I'm sorry. But Juliet's happy, and we've given her a life that Lily could have never given her. Let's not dwell on what her life could have been like if Lily had never given her up, okay? Let's think about all of the positives and how happy she is."

I'm frozen in place as I listen to this very private conversation. In the year that I've known Juliet, she's been very open about her adoption and all that her family does to remind her of the gift that she is to them. Hearing her mother so upset makes me wonder what it's really like to know that you were given up, not wanted.

What would it be like if my family had given me up? How would I feel? Would I even have known any better? The way my parents have been fighting so much lately makes me wonder if I'd be better off someplace else. My thoughts immediately go to my sisters, and I know that they'd be lost without me. Would Sean care? As messed up as my family is right now, I can't imagine being anywhere else.

"Hey, Kels." He pauses, and it sounds like he's pulled her into a hug. "It's a day to celebrate, not to worry, okay? I love you and I love our perfect family."

She sniffles and says, "Okay. I'll try. I know I need to stop feeling this fear that she's going to realize she doesn't belong with us. That she should be someplace else."

"She belongs with us. Stop making me repeat myself."

"But... Lily's letter. It's—"

"Shhh. Let's not talk about her letter. You know—" he pauses and then sighs "—I don't think it's that bad. Soon enough, Juliet will read that letter and know why she was given up. Why she's a part of our family."

"No. She won't read it. Ever." Mrs. Oliver's voice trails off, and I feel weird that I've just heard this very personal discussion.

I wait by the bathroom door, and when I don't hear anything for a few minutes, I decide it's safe to open it. I walk out and turn the corner, and I'm surprised to see Juliet in the dark hallway.

"Hey, I didn't see you there," I say. I wonder if she heard anything her parents were talking about and realize she must have when I see fresh tears on her cheeks.

"Oh, hey. It's about time you're out of there. I really need to go." Her voice is shaky as she awkwardly pushes past me, slamming the door behind her.

Should I stay to make sure she's okay? I stand in the hallway outside the bathroom door for about five minutes, listening to her soft sobs. I can't imagine overhearing the conversation that her parents just had. Her *perfect* parents. Doesn't she realize that her family is awesome? I would kill to have two parents who clearly loved me more than life. Lately, my mother has been so distracted. She definitely hasn't been herself since she and my father had that blowout argument last year. And my dad never seems to be around anymore.

Mr. and Mrs. Oliver have so much more love to give than my parents. They actually show affection and care. Touch. Hug.

I'm jealous.

I can tell Mrs. Oliver is upset and scared, but Mr. Oliver is there to support her. I never see my own father display this kind of affection and love with my mom.

"Juliet?" I say quietly. I want her to know that someone is here for her.

She doesn't respond, and her sobs silence. I walk up to the door and speak quietly. "If you're okay, can you just knock once? To let me know?"

There's silence, and I hope I didn't just embarrass her. "Knock twice if you're not okay," I say, and then quickly follow it up with, "Three times if it's your birthday."

Her sobs turn to quiet giggles, and the tense feeling in my chest starts to loosen up. She knocks once, then three times. I take a deep breath and say, "I think your parents are getting your birthday cake ready. It's Happy Birthday time," I lie. I don't know what they're doing, but I don't want to walk away without trying to get her out of the bathroom. I just don't want her to be sad anymore.

"I'll be out in five minutes, okay? See you outside."

I place my hand against the door and hope she's okay. It's hard to see her sad like this. "Okay, see you in a few minutes." My heart hurts for her. Ever since the day we exchanged pen pal letters for the first time, we have become close and tell each other practically everything. I feel the need to protect her right now, so others don't know what she's going through.

I walk outside as Jeremy is on his way in. "Hey, have you seen Jules?"

"Uh, yeah. She's in the bathroom." I see her father on the patio and quickly change the subject.

"Mr. Oliver, are we having cake soon? I'm starving."

"Yes, Seth. Juliet's mom is getting it ready now. Why don't you tell everyone to join us on the patio in five minutes."

Good. At least I won't look like a liar when Juliet finally comes out of the bathroom. I see Tiffany Green and let her know that cake is coming and watch her quickly alert the rest of the party guests. Job done.

"I wonder what's taking Juliet so long?" Jeremy asks.

"There was a line for the bathroom, so she's been inside for a while," I lie. I'm not sure Jules would want anyone knowing about what just happened.

"They have like seven bathrooms! How could there be a line?"

"I don't know."

"Hey! Did you miss me?" Juliet's voice puts me at ease. I turn and see her next to Jeremy. Her face is a little puffy, but maybe I see it because I know that she's been crying. Hopefully nobody else will notice.

Jeremy softly bumps into her shoulder. "I always miss you when you're not here." I see her reach out and touch her fingers to his briefly, and then Mr. Oliver's voice booms through the crowd.

"Are we ready to sing a song to the birthday girl?" Cheers from the crowd follow him as he and Mrs. Oliver push the cart that her cake is on. Candles blaze, and he uses his arm to protect them from blowing out.

DEAR JULIET

The "Happy Birthday" song is sung loudly, and I watch Juliet's eyes glaze over. She seems to forget that there are thirty people singing around her as she closes her eyes to blow out the candles, as if the earth hangs in the balance over the wish she's about to make. She doesn't open her eyes until all of the candles are blown out. Everyone cheers, and her father rolls the cart away. She remains in place while her mother pulls her into a tight embrace. Her eyes seem unfocused and she barely acknowledges her mother's presence. I can only imagine what's going through her mind right now, after hearing the conversation that we both just heard.

"Thank you," she says, looking at me quietly. Am I the only one who's meant to hear that?

"Happy birthday!" Jeremy's voice bellows and I watch her eyes brighten.

"Thank you," she says again, this time more loudly, and I can tell she's saying it to me.

"Who wants cake?" her father asks. The group of kids surrounding us moves toward his voice, leaving me, Jeremy and Juliet on the patio together.

"This is the best Halloween ever!" Jeremy exclaims as he wraps his arms around Juliet, lifting her off of the ground. They both have surprised expressions on their faces that quickly turn to laughter.

"Put me down, silly!" Juliet pushes on his shoulders and he awkwardly eases her onto the patio.

"Sorry," he says.

My cell phone vibrates in my pocket and I quickly pull it out. "Hey, Bob."

"Are you ready for me to pick you up?" he asks.

"Yeah, I guess." I see that it's ten thirty. *Would my parents care if I stayed longer? Would they even know?* It's definitely past curfew for many of my friends, and I know that Jeremy is already a half hour late. I nudge him and say, "Bob will be here in a few minutes to take us home."

He looks at Juliet and says, "Crap! My parents are going to kill me. It's late."

"Chill out," I say. "They aren't going to kill you."

I turn to Juliet. "I hope your birthday was great." Her hollow eyes tell me all that I need to know. I wish she hadn't heard her parents talking. She didn't deserve to hear any of that on her birthday. Does she even realize what a gift she is to them? To us?

"Thanks, Seth."

"Thanks, Jeremy." Her voice hitches and she instantly throws her arms around his neck. I smile as I watch them awkwardly hug.

"I'll see you on Monday," I say as I walk through the gate and out toward my waiting car.

"I'll be out in a minute. I need to get my hockey stick." Jeremy runs toward the house.

I'm about to open the car door when I hear Juliet's voice. "Hey, Seth."

I turn to see her standing on the sidewalk, looking down at her feet.

"Jules, what are you doing out here? Your party is still raging back there." I smile as she makes eye contact with me.

"Listen. About before. Umm..." Her eyes dart around and she doesn't make eye contact with me. "I'm sorry you had to hear—see me like that. Please don't tell anyone, okay?" Her voice is desperate as her eyes finally lock on my own.

"Never."

She doesn't say another word; she just stares into my eyes.

"Jules, I don't know what I heard, really. Your mom seemed upset. She probably didn't mean for you to hear what she was saying."

"I've heard it before. Too many times. And I'm afraid."

"Afraid of what?"

"What she meant by everything. What's my birth mother like? Why didn't she want me?"

I don't have any time to answer her as Jeremy runs up to us, flailing his hockey stick in the air. "Found it!"

"Thanks for coming, guys. My party wouldn't have been the same without you." She touches Jeremy on his arm. "And congratulations for winning almost every challenge. Fair and square."

He shrugs and smiles back at her. "You let me win. You're the real star of this party."

Her arm drops back down to her side and she smiles from ear to ear. "You just made my day, Jeremy Reed."

We both slide into the back of the car as Bob says, "Ready, boys?"

"Yup," we both say in unison.

When her eyes light up, my heart smiles.

chapter four

Juliet
Sausalito, California
Age 9

THERE ARE THREE BIRDS dancing outside the window: a cardinal and two sparrows. They don't seem to be fighting, just fluttering about, looking for food. It's nice to see them getting along, possibly working together to achieve the same goal. A gust of wind blows them about a bit, but they recover easily.

"Miss Oliver? Hello? Are you with us?" Mrs. Alexander asks, jarring me back to reality.

Math. That's where I am. I glance out the window and the birds are gone.

"Sorry," I say feebly.

"Did you finish the equation already? You seem to be all done. Would you care to share your solution?"

"No. I—I didn't start yet. I'm sorry," I stammer.

A few giggles and sneers come from behind me, and I know that Ashley and Rachel are having a field day with this one. They just can't help themselves.

"Nice, Juliet. Way to pay attention," I hear one of them snicker.

I've tried to be nice to them, but they are always like this with me. Ashley told me one day that I just don't 'fit in.' *What does that mean? Is that why most of the girls in my grade don't pay attention to me?* I'm so much younger than everyone else in my grade; maybe that's the reason.

"Well, you know what to do, Juliet," Mrs. Alexander says sternly. More snickers from the girls behind me.

I press my pencil into the paper and the tip breaks off immediately. Ugh! I brush the broken lead from my desk and grab a new pencil from the book bag at my feet. I solve the problem quickly and finish before the bell rings.

"Sorry, Mrs. Alexander. I was a little distracted," I say as I place my math work on her desk and turn to leave the room.

"Is everything okay?" she asks, concerned.

"Yes, I'm good," I lie. Overhearing my parents the other night, disagreeing about Lily's letter again, is really bothering me. I don't understand what could possibly be in that letter that my mom is so upset about and doesn't want me to see. It must be really bad.

Did Lily hate me that much to write something so awful?

"Great party the other night, Jules." Jeremy is standing outside the classroom, waiting for me.

"Yeah, it was."

"Sorry that Mrs. Alexander caught you daydreaming." He laughs and nudges me with his shoulder. "I hope you didn't get in too much trouble."

"No, she was cool." Thank goodness. A tongue lashing from her would have riled up Ashley and Rachel even more, and I certainly don't need that.

"The 'Mean Girls' were running their mouths again. I hope they didn't get to you."

"Nope," I lie. I'm constantly wondering what I've done to them to deserve the treatment that I get.

"You know, they're just jealous because they weren't invited to your birthday party. And *everyone* is talking about it today."

"I honestly don't care." I laugh nervously and swing my bag over my shoulder. I need to change the subject. "Do you have practice today?"

"Yeah. I'm meeting Seth near the gym."

"I'll walk with you. My mom won't be here for another ten minutes or so."

"That's cool."

We reach the gym and Seth is waiting there, smiling huge.

"Hey! What are you doing here today, Jules?" He punches Jeremy on his arm.

"Just killing time before I go home."

Jeremy smiles as he rubs the place that was just punched. "Ouch, dude. You better hope this doesn't hurt while we're practicing today."

"Wuss," Seth says, laughing as Jeremy walks past him into the locker room. Before he disappears, he turns toward me. "Hope you have a great night, Jules."

"Thanks," I say, and I can feel myself blushing. He acted a little weird with me at my birthday party and he almost held my hand. *Does he like me?*

"Hey, is everything okay after the other night?" Seth asks, his voice low, almost whispering. He looks concerned.

"What?"

"Never mind." He grabs his bag and begins to walk into the locker room.

I don't want to talk about the other night. Seth is the only person who knows what I overheard. He saw me cry. *I'm so embarrassed.*

"Have fun," I say weakly and head toward the exit.

"Jules." I turn back around and see Seth right next to me. "Listen, if you ever want to talk about it, I'm here. Okay?" He softly touches my shoulder and drops his hand back down to his side.

"Okay." I smile and walk out of the door to the parking lot. It feels good to know that I have someone I can talk to, but would he really understand? I see my mom's car at the curb.

"Hi, Mom." I smile as I slide into the back seat.

"How was school today?" she asks.

"The usual." I shrug. "Good, I guess."

"Oh good. I'm glad to hear that." I take my iPod out of my pocket and plug in my earbuds. I don't want to have an awkward conversation with my mother when all I can think about is what I overheard her saying the other night.

She shifts her eyes back to the road and we drive in silence the rest of the way home.

We pull up to the house and I quickly jump out of the car. "Dinner's at six thirty, Jules," she calls after me.

Once inside my room, I pull out my computer and start typing an email to Seth. We've been emailing each other since last year's exercise, and it feels good to 'talk' to someone.

Dear Seth,

I'm sorry things were weird the other night at my party. I'm sorry you overheard what my parents said. It got me upset, like always, but I wish you didn't see and hear it. I'm nervous about a lot of things and what could have my parents upset. I've heard them whispering about Lily and her letter for years. It can only mean bad things and I'm scared.

Sorry if it made you uncomfortable.

Your friend,

Juliet

I send the email and suddenly feel like my heart is on my sleeve. I have never been able to talk about my feelings about my adoption and how much I worry over what my parents are going through with that letter. But more importantly, I'm worried about the fact that I'm adopted and how others may view me if they knew that someone else didn't want me. The 'Mean Girls' would surely have enough ammunition to make the whole school think the way that they do. I just don't fit in.

Throughout dinner, my parents make small talk, but their awkward glances across the table make me feel like they want to bring up something important. I get up as soon as I finish my last piece of broccoli and head toward the stairs. "No dessert tonight?" my mom calls after me.

"No, I have homework to finish," I lie.

Once I'm upstairs, I open my computer to see if Seth has responded to my message. I'm nervous about what I told him and curious to see his response, if any.

> Dear Juliet,
> Hi! I'm sorry it took me so long to get back to you, but practice ran late tonight and I had to make my own dinner.
> I'm not upset or uncomfortable AT ALL. I can't imagine what you're going through and can't imagine what could be in that letter that your parents don't want you to see. Maybe they're right? Maybe you shouldn't see it?
> You're very lucky to have two parents who love you as much as they do. They wouldn't try to hide things from you if they didn't, right? I'm sure they just want to see you happy.
> Try forgetting about the letter for a while and focus on other things. Like coming to cheer for me and Jeremy at our baseball game this weekend. Just kidding. Although it would be great to see you there. My family barely comes to see me. It makes me feel weird. Jeremy's family is always there, especially his older brother. He's been coming to Jeremy's baseball games since the very first day. Anyway, you can do whatever you want, no pressure.
> I'm always here if you want to talk.
> Your friend,
> Seth

DEAR JULIET

I stare at the computer screen and keep reading the part about forgetting about the letter for a little while. Maybe that's a good idea. If I can focus on other things and not think about it, maybe I'll be happier?

I guess I can try. This weekend I'm going to their baseball game. That's a start.

chapter five

Seth
Sausalito, California
Age 13

Two Years Later

"TYSON! YOU'RE ON DECK," Coach says, pulling me from my concentration. I was visualizing smacking the ball over the fence.

"Right," I respond, nodding to him while grabbing my bat. The clouds move quickly overhead and the wind picks up. I get a chill as I make my way out of the dugout.

Jeremy smacks my shoulder as I walk past him. "Go get 'em," he says encouragingly.

I watch as our short stop, Mikey, swings hard at the ball and strikes out. He curses under his breath and throws his bat toward the dugout, nearly hitting me in my knees. He's had a tough game and can't seem to get a read on this pitcher from the other team. "Good luck, Tyson," he mutters as he trudges past me and into the dugout, continuing to sling curses before chucking his batting helmet into the wall.

I walk toward the batter's box and narrow my focus on the pitcher, their ace. He's been trouble all season for us and for the other teams in the league. He averages fifteen strikeouts a game, and he's been scouted by several prep schools in our area. We know that he's in line for a serious high school scholarship and more.

He's not going to strike me out. No way.

I take my time, and I know he's getting agitated. He kicks his foot into the pitcher's mound and glares at me. He won't get set until I do. I stay outside the batter's box, taking a few swings and showing no interest in his discomfort. I'm in no rush. I feel a few raindrops on the tip of my nose and cheeks and look up toward the sky. It's ominous.

My eyes then scan the bleachers. My family isn't here to see me. They never are. I glance over to where Jeremy's older brother, Jason, is sitting, and he nods toward me. He's at every single one of our games and is one half of my biggest cheering squad.

Juliet is also here. Of course.

She's been coming to all of our baseball games for a while now, and I'm certain that she and Jeremy have a thing for each other. A twinge of jealousy grabs my chest. She and I have shared so much more together, but she has a crush on Jeremy? My best friend? I push aside my feelings and just focus on what's important. She's here to see both of us, even if my family couldn't give a crap about me.

I see her quietly clap her hands together and smile at me. The sun seems to reflect off of her shiny metal braces on her teeth. Jason waves his hand to get my attention and gives me the thumbs up. I scan the field and see that the opposing team has brought their infield in. Those idiots. I'll show them. I laugh to myself and the catcher shifts slightly.

I finally step into the batter's box and plant my left foot behind me, glaring into the eyes of the pitcher. He winds up quickly and throws a wild pitch, bouncing it off of home plate and over the shoulder of the catcher.

I clench my teeth together and smirk. He's nervous. *Good.*

The catcher runs out to the mound and they cover their mouths with their gloves. This always cracks me up. I already know what the catcher is saying to him. What all of the catchers say. Pitch around me. Try to jam me inside.

The catcher runs back, and it's hard to read his face through the mask that he's wearing, but I hear him breathing uneasily.

I get myself set for the ace's next pitch, which I know is going to be high and inside. It's his signature pitch to lefties.

As soon as the baseball leaves his fingertips, I step back and get myself ready.

High and inside.

I swing and feel the vibration from the bat in my palms. I make solid contact, and the ball flies into shallow right field, and I sail easily into first base.

The pitcher kicks the mound again and the first baseman chuckles sarcastically next to me. "You nailed it, slugger. Although we made it easy for you by shifting the infield."

I ignore him and stretch toward second base. Jeremy jogs to the batter's box, and I already know what he's going to hit. The infield is back to where they should have been when I hit, so I know that I'm making it to second base regardless.

The pitcher throws another wild pitch and I steal easily. Now Jeremy doesn't need to bunt.

The next pitch is a huge mistake, and as soon as I hear Jeremy make contact, I know that we just won the game. I look over to where Jason and Juliet are sitting and they're already on their feet, arms waving wildly in the air.

I'm jealous that he has his own cheering squad.

I bite my lip as I jog around the bases and see my team waiting at home plate, jumping up and down. I join the celebration as Jeremy rounds third base and speeds up to jump into the huddle waiting for him.

We've won the District Championship.

After our celebration at home plate, we quickly run to the dugout so Coach can congratulate us on our victory. I go through the motions, listening to his victory speech, barely paying attention. I grab my gear and stroll past the team, toward Jason and Juliet.

"Seth! That was awesome!" she says, jumping up and down.

Jason pats me on my shoulder and smiles, looking past me. "There he is," he says, addressing Jeremy. "That home run cleared the fence and then some. Great game, guys." His pride shines through and lights up Jeremy's eyes.

Juliet hugs Jeremy and smiles at me over his shoulder. "I'm so proud of you *both*," she cries.

"J," Jason says to his brother, "we need to get home. Remember, we have Gram's birthday dinner tonight?"

"Right! I gotta go, guys," he turns to Juliet and blushes a little bit. "Thanks for coming, Jules." He grabs his bag and says to me, "Thanks for getting on base, Seth. We wouldn't have won if you hadn't." We bump fists and he leaves with his brother.

I shake my head and start walking toward my driver. He's been our family chauffeur for as long as I can remember and is always ready to take us anywhere.

"So, that was a great game, Seth," Juliet snorts as she quickly jogs to keep up with me.

"Thanks," I respond.

"Did you read my last note?" she asks, out of breath.

"Not yet, Jules. I've been busy with a few things," I say vaguely. I don't tell her that my mother spilled a bottle of vodka on my laptop the other night, and I hope Bob has my new one waiting for me in the back of the car. "I'll try to read it tonight," I shrug and open the back door of the car.

"Oh. Okay," she says softly and walks toward the rack where her bike is.

A large clap of thunder shakes the ground, followed by the sky lighting up brightly with lightning. Torrential rain begins to fall, and I watch Jules try to take cover under the tree near the bike rack.

Bob gets out of the car and takes her bike from her hands. She doesn't waste a second and runs toward the car, sliding into the backseat next to me. He jams her bike into the trunk and slams it closed.

I turn to look at Jules and she's soaked, running her hands through her long wavy brown hair, trying to ring out the water. She's out of breath and laughing uncontrollably. "That was a bad idea!" she sputters.

"What?" I ask her.

"Riding my bike here, silly!" she responds, still giggling.

"Oh, yeah. That was a bad idea," I say, laughing as I look out at the sheets of rain falling outside the window.

I notice the signature Apple box sitting on the far end of the seat at the same time Juliet does.

She slides along the seat and grabs the box that contains my new Macintosh laptop. "Oh my God! This is the same *exact* laptop that I got last week. This is *so* awesome, Seth. You're going to love it." She pauses for a second, furrowing her brow, almost looking worried. "Did I miss your birthday or something?" she asks.

"No. No. My old laptop got... broken," I say and look out the window.

"Really? What happened?" she asks innocently.

I really don't want to tell her. What would I say? I certainly can't tell her that my mother drinks a lot and gets clumsy. I just can't. It's embarrassing.

"I knocked over a cup of water onto the keyboard of my old laptop and it fried," I lie as I shrug and look out the window.

"Bummer," she says. "Hopefully you'll get to read my note tonight." She seems anxious, but I don't want to talk about it right now. It's so much easier when we're on opposite ends of a keyboard, in different rooms and parts of our town.

I know that she constantly struggles with her adoption, and it's just weird to talk about it in person. We *never* talk about real things in person; we hide behind our keyboards.

"I'll try to read it tonight," I respond and shift in my seat. "I still need to get my new laptop set up."

"Oh. Yeah. Don't worry about it. Really." She stammers through her words as she rubs her hands on the top of her jeans. She looks out the window and I think I see her eyes glistening a little bit, like she's going to cry.

Damn! What did I say?

I suddenly stress out, trying to remember what my last letter was about. I know I emailed it a week or so ago. Did I tell her about the fight that my parents had last week? The last time I told her about my parents arguing, she emailed me practically every twelve hours, making sure that I was okay. She didn't push me to talk about it, but I know that her extra attention toward me at school was because she felt sorry for me. I remind myself that I should stop telling her about their constant fighting. Especially if I don't understand what their arguments are even about.

"Hey," I say to her. "I promise I'll read your note tonight." I pause and she turns to face me. "Pinky swear," I say, reaching my pinky across the space between us. She slowly raises her pinky up to mine and grasps onto it weakly. I squeeze our fingers together tightly and say again, "Pinky. Swear."

"Thanks, Seth. Whenever you can. It doesn't matter." She pulls away as the car slows down in the circular driveway in front of her house. The rain finally stopped, thankfully.

Bob takes her bike from the trunk. Then he opens the door and extends his hand into the cab, toward Juliet. She grabs hold and looks back at me. "Seriously, whenever you can read my note. No rush." Then she hops out of the car and squeals.

"Look, Seth! A rainbow!" She points over the roof of her large house. A huge bright rainbow spans the entire sky and seems to end miles away. I look at Jules and her smile is beaming.

"Wow. That's pretty cool," I say, leaning out of the back of my car. I haven't seen a rainbow in a really long time. Probably not since I was five or six years old and my mother and I were on the patio out behind our house after a pretty huge thunderstorm. She and I were snuggled together on one of the lounges by the pool and she was running her fingers through my hair, massaging my scalp. It was the last time she showed me affection that I can remember.

This rainbow means more to me than Juliet can even imagine, and I suddenly feel sick. It's been almost a long time since I've felt like that. *Loved.*

"Let's go, Bob," I say as Juliet backs away from the car. "See you around, Jules."

She looks disappointed, as if she doesn't want me to leave.

She watches my car as we slowly pull away, down her long driveway. I watch out the back window and she never leaves the spot she's standing in.

"Bob, can you go any faster?" I state. I feel so vulnerable, and I suddenly want to get home quickly so I can configure my new laptop and read her latest letter.

I feel like crap that I don't know what's going on with someone who I consider one of my best friends.

I'm a jerk.

We get home ten minutes later and I don't wait for Bob to even hit the brakes. I grab all of my things, including my new laptop, and run into the house.

I hear my sisters cackling from the kitchen. This is unusual, to say the least. I walk through the foyer, and as I get closer to their voices, I also hear my mother's. This is even more unusual.

As soon as the twins see me, they yell in unison, "Sethie!"

My mother turns to me and her smile fades, almost as if it had been fake to begin with.

"How was your game?" she slurs slightly. I can't believe she's been drinking *again*.

"We won," I say tersely and feel bad for how short I'm being with her. This isn't her fault, it's *his*.

"Jeremy hit a two-run homerun. We won Districts," I clarify and watch her smile fade. She feels bad that she wasn't there. That none of them were there.

"That's great, honey," she says, taking a long sip from her coffee mug. I know she's not drinking coffee.

She notices the new laptop box under my arm. "Oh! I'm glad that you got your new laptop today. I'm so sorry for spilling water all over your old one last week." *Water?* She and I both know that it was Grey Goose.

Chloe and Chelsea jump down from their stools and run toward the stairs. "Yay, Sethie!" Chelsea exclaims as Chloe giggles. "He's a baseball superstar!" They dart out of the room toward their playroom.

When they're gone, I pick up my laptop and start to walk toward the stairs.

"Seth, wait." I hear my mother's weak voice behind me. I stop in place, but don't turn around to face her. "I'm sorry we missed another game."

I look down at my feet and keep walking. "Yeah, Mom. Whatever," I say under my breath and trot up the stairs. I hear the cabinet open and the clamor of glass from the kitchen. I know it's my mother topping off her drink with the bottle of vodka hidden in the place she thinks is so secret.

Once inside my room, I lock the door behind me and flop onto my bed. Why do I have to constantly pretend that I have a normal family? My father is always gone, and when he's here, my mother screams at him about one thing or another. It's always about something that he did wrong. I wonder what he keeps doing.

Maybe we should just leave. Or he should. I don't know. But I hate what happens here when both of my parents are under the same roof. It's ugly and embarrassing.

I open my new laptop and go through the setup process. Within a few minutes, I have Yahoo! mail open and am searching for Juliet's latest email. It's easy to find, since it's sitting at the top of my inbox.

I remember when we used to send letters back and forth through the mail. I'd eagerly wait for her next letter, and it usually took a week or two between them. These days, it's instantaneous. Juliet's parents restrict her Internet use quite a bit, but we will usually email with each other every other day. I click on her message titled 'News.'

Dear Seth,

I feel like a broken record. Delete this message if you don't want to hear about it again.

But.

I want to read the letter. And I don't. But I really do...

I'm scared. Like really scared.

What if Lily tells me how she really felt? What if she tells me that she hated me the moment she laid eyes on me? That she didn't want me because I was going to be a huge burden on her?

What would you do, Seth? Would you want to read it?

Maybe you can be here with me if I read it?

No, forget it. That's ridiculous. My mother will never give me that letter.

Okay, talk to you later.

Jules

Whoa.

I feel like such a jerk. I should have read this sooner. She must have thought that I'd left her hanging and didn't care about her dilemma.

I quickly hit reply and type my response.

> Dear Juliet,
> I should just call you Jules, right? It seems silly to address a letter to Juliet when I really only ever call you Jules.
> Anyway, thank you for coming to my game today. Our game. I know Jeremy is also happy that you're always there to support us. It means a lot. More than you can imagine.
> It sucks that you got rained on a little bit today. I don't know why you always ride your bike to our games, considering how far you live from school. I hope you rethink your means of travel in the future.
> Well, I just read your note and I'm so sorry that I didn't respond sooner. If you're allowed to read the letter, don't worry about her words, Jules. I think you're going to learn a lot and

it will help you understand more about your adoption.

She's been seeing pictures of you for many years now, right? So it only makes sense to me that you should hear what she has to say. There is no way that she's going to tell you that she hated you, so stop thinking like that, okay?

I'm here if you need to talk about it. Let me know if your parents let you finally read it. Good luck!

Seth

I hit send and immediately regret it. *Good luck?* I sound like a jerk. She wanted me to be with her when she's able to read it, and I just said 'good luck'?

Regretting the 'good luck' sentiment, I open the email that I just sent and start to send another reply when I hear a loud crash coming from downstairs. My heart jumps in my chest and I jump up to open my door. I hear Chloe screaming incoherently while Chelsea yells, "Help! Help! Someone help!"

I run down the stairs three at a time, and I hear Sean behind me. "Out of the way, Seth!" he yells as he pushes me down the remaining stairs. Chloe's screams are getting louder, and Chelsea's voice hitches and sounds more panicked. I brace myself as I round the hall into the kitchen, not knowing what I'm going to see.

Sean screams, "Seth! Call 9-1-1!"

Chelsea joins in Chloe's screams.

I grab the phone off of the counter and begin to dial when I notice the pool of blood on the floor. My mother is lying on the kitchen floor with a broken bottle of Grey Goose in one hand and a giant shard of glass sticking out of her wrist, just above her other hand. Her eyes are fluttering and her breathing is shallow.

A voice on the other end of the phone jolts me. "9-1-1. What is your emergency?"

"My mother. She's... hurt. We need help. Quickly." I don't know how I get the shaky words out.

The voice responds, "Okay. Is she breathing?"

"Yes—I think so." I can barely get the words out as my panic sets in.

Sean has his hand wrapped around her wrist where the blood is coming from and it's now seeping down his arms. He looks up at me and says calmly, "Tell them where we live. They need to get here quickly." I don't know how he can be so calm while I'm literally shaking.

Somehow, I'm able to give them our address and the voice says, "You're doing very well. Who else is there with you?" Her voice is also calm, and I can't believe people around me are acting so calm. Well, except for my sisters, who now look like they're going into shock at the sight of so much blood. They're huddled on the floor together, staring at Sean and my mother.

I answer, "My two sisters and brother, Sean. He's trying to stop the blood. There's so much." I feel like I'm going to puke. I see Mom's chest rising and falling, so I know she's still breathing. Her eyes are closed though.

"Is anyone else hurt?" she asks me.

"No. Just my mother." I'm numb. This is all too surreal. I hear sirens in the distance. "That was fast," I say quietly into the phone. "Please stay on the line with us until the paramedics are in your home." I stare out the door as an ambulance pulls up. "They're here now." I disconnect the call without thinking and watch as they rush toward the house.

Everything that happens from that moment on is a complete blur. It seems like a dozen people rush into my house to work on my mother. One of the paramedics is talking quietly to Sean while he tries to explain what he found when he rushed into the kitchen. Three other emergency workers are loading my mom onto a stretcher while wrapping thick bandages around her bleeding wrist. They are yelling

DEAR JULIET

back and forth to each other as they roll her out of the house to the waiting ambulance.

Sean kneels down in front of the twins and wraps his arms around them. I can't hear what he's saying, but they seem to calm down almost immediately after hearing his voice.

"Son, are you okay?" I hear a deep voice behind me and turn to stare at a police officer.

"Yeah," I cough, trying to get my voice back. Was I screaming too? My throat feels dry and scratched. "Yes, sir, I'm okay."

He nods toward me, and then Sean, and turns to leave. I hear the ambulance pull away from the house.

"Seth, can you come sit with the twins? I need to call Dad," Sean asks as he pulls the girls up and leads them into the den.

"We'll be just outside until your father comes home," the police officer says, closing the door.

I sit between Chloe and Chelsea as they whimper and put their heads on my shoulders. "Shhhh," I whisper as I try to calm them. My heart is still beating wildly in my chest, and I hope that they don't feel how scared and worried I am.

I can hear Sean's voice rise in the next room, and it doesn't sound good.

"When you get this message, *Dad*, call me right away. Your wife just tried to kill herself. I thought you'd want to know." I hear the phone slam down as Sean yells, "Fuck!"

She tried to kill herself?

I pull Chloe and Chelsea closer and wonder what on earth happened to make Mom do something like this. Is it my fault? Did I make her upset about missing my game?

I realize how much I'm shaking when the twins pull away from me, both of their faces streaked in tears.

"Is she going to be okay, Sethie?" Chloe asks in a hoarse voice.

"I don't know," I answer truthfully.

I keep repeating, whispering the words.

"I don't know. I don't know."

chapter six

Juliet
Sausalito, California
Age 11

I SLAM MY LAPTOP shut after reading Seth's email to me. I'm so freaking angry right now!

"Good luck?" I yell into my empty room, clenching my fists at my side. "Good luck?" I repeat.

I bite my bottom lip in anger and taste blood in my mouth. My braces constantly dig and tear into my lip, and that just made it worse.

Why would he say that?

I asked him to be here with me when I read the letter, for moral support. And all he has to say is 'good luck'? He's the only person who knows what I've been going through the past few years. I really wanted him to be here.

Does he even care?

I'm absolutely terrified to read the letter that's sitting on my desk in front of me. The letter that my mother thought I would never be ready for. My mom brought it in about an hour ago and it's sat there, unmoved. I reach for it and run my shaking thumb along the top. The envelope is neatly torn open, reminding me that my Mom has already read it. I drop the letter back onto my desk and walk over to my dresser. I need to see how badly I cut my lip.

I peer closely into the mirror and pull my bottom lip away from my teeth. There's a big bump already, and blood is dripping out of my mouth. I quickly grab a tissue to blot the bright red drops of blood.

These darn braces! They make me look even dorkier than I already am. I'm too tall for my age and skinnier than almost everyone in my class. No wonder Jeremy and Seth treat me the way that they do, like one of the guys. I look at my chest and see that my sternum sticks out further than the pimples that I call boobs. I *am* one of the freaking guys, and the girls in my class don't let me forget it.

"Honey, are you okay?" I hear Mom's voice from the hallway outside my door.

"Yes," I huff, and I turn as she opens the door and walks into my room.

"Do you want to talk about it?" she asks, sitting down on the bench at the foot of my full-sized bed.

I sit on the edge of the bed, wringing my hands together. "No," I state quickly.

I see her look over to my desk where Lily's letter is sitting, unread.

"Did you read it yet?" she asks, reaching out to place her hand over mine.

"Nope," I mumble, sucking on the bumpy sore inside my lip.

"Jules..." She takes a deep breath, squeezing my hand and I look up into her eyes. They're glassy, and it almost looks like she's about to cry.

"I don't think I want to read it." I squeeze her hand back.

She hesitates. "Oh..." She looks relieved and scared at the same time and continues to nod through her weak smile.

She gets up, kisses me on my forehead, and is about to leave my room.

"Wait!" I yell and she stops in the doorway.

"Take it. Take it away. I'm definitely not ready."

I remember all of the muted conversations between her and my father. Her terrified voice. His soothing words.

No. I'm not ready. If I read it, everything will change. The way I look at my family, myself. It will all change.

She doesn't hesitate and swipes the letter from my desk, tucking it into the pocket of her cardigan. "Okay, Juliet. I'll keep this in a safe place until you're ready."

She leaves my room quickly. Too quickly. *She never wanted me to read that letter anyway.* My heart pulls as I hear my mother walk down the stairs. *Did I make a mistake?*

I don't know how long I sit on my bed, but I eventually grab my laptop and open up my email when I hear my parents' voices coming from the bottom of the stairs. I move closer to my door so I can hear them better.

"She didn't read it?" my father asks.

"No. And I'm glad. I know you said she's ready, but she's not, Kevin. She'll never be ready to read how selfish Lily really was. These words are not soothing, nor will they give her the answers she's looking for. It was a mistake giving this letter to Juliet today."

A sob escapes my throat and my chest clenches.

"Kelsey, I don't agree. She has to know what happened. She's old enough to understand, and she has *us* to help comfort her and answer whatever questions we can."

My mother doesn't answer him, and I hear her move away from the stairs.

"Where are you going?" my father asks, his voice agitated.

"To put this somewhere safe."

"Kelsey... " My father's voice trails off, and I can no longer hear either of them.

I'm glad I made this decision. For now.

chapter seven

Seth
Sausalito, California
Age 18

Five Years Later

"HEY," I SAY, answering Jeremy's call.

"Where are you? I thought you were coming tonight." He sounds annoyed and I realize that I forgot to tell him I was going to be late. I had to help out with the girls tonight since Mom went to bed early and Dad was nowhere to be found.

"Sorry, dude. I am. Just running late. I had to bring the girls to a sleepover. I'm outside now." I end the call and jump out of my car. I look up the long driveway and see dozens of cars already here. I'm not in the mood for a party tonight, but with graduation a week away, this may be the last time I get to see some of our friends before we all go our separate ways this summer.

The music is loud and pumping through speakers from behind the house. As I walk toward the gate leading to the backyard, the front door opens and Jason emerges. "Hey, Seth, coming to join the mayhem?"

I laugh, knowing that a party at the Reed house is usually pretty tame. "Mayhem? Is it really crazy back there?"

"It's a bit more lively than some of Jeremy's other parties." He gestures to the dozens of cars littering their driveway. "It looks like most of your graduating class is here. Good thing our parents are away for the weekend, because they wouldn't be too happy about this one. There's a bunch of half-naked girls in the pool right now. You may want to go check that out. They all conveniently forgot their bathing suits."

"Whoa, really?" I laugh nervously. The party seems to be on its way to rager status, and it's not even nine o'clock.

"Yeah. I'm heading back to my place, where I'm sure the cops won't be paying a visit any minute." He tosses his keys up in the air and catches them in a swiping motion. "Oh, and can you help Jeremy keep an eye on Jules? She's so drunk she's not feeling any pain right now, and I don't think you guys would want to see her get into any trouble."

"Of course." I would never let anything happen to her. "Don't you want to stick around?" I ask Jason as he slides into his car.

"Nope. Underage drinking and naked teenagers aren't my thing. Besides, I have a manuscript to get to my editor by Monday that isn't going to finish itself." Jeremy mentioned to me that a couple of Jason's stories were purchased by a big publishing house, and their family was thrilled. That's pretty cool.

"Good luck with that."

"See you tomorrow. I'll be by to help put the house back together before my parents come home." He drives off, and I push open the gate and head into the back yard.

"Seth!" Juliet calls to me from the hammock at the corner of the patio. I watch as she clumsily tries to sit up and spills her drink down the front of her pink tank top. The hammock swings wildly back and forth, and her giggles turn into hiccups.

Jeremy and I reach her at the same time, and it's apparent that he's just as drunk as she is. "Duuude!" Juliet is still trying to balance on the hammock while swiping at her drenched chest.

Looks like I'll be babysitting both of them tonight. I need to remedy that. Sober is not what I want to be. As if he's reading my mind, Jeremy hands me a bottle of bourbon, and I bring it to my lips and swig. Warm liquid glides down my throat and I tilt my head a second and third time in an attempt to catch up to these two drunk bozos.

"That's what I'm talkin' about!" Jeremy slurs, and I chug some more before I hand him back the almost empty bottle. Warmth spreads through my chest, and I immediately feel more relaxed.

"Guys, a little help?" We both look toward Juliet and see that she's sunken into the hammock with little hope of getting out on her own. We each grab hold of one of her arms.

"One, two, three!" Jeremy yells as we pull her onto her feet.

She falls into me, and the dampness from her tank top spreads onto the front of my tee shirt. "Oops." She laughs and places her hands on my chest, lingering for a moment then pushing away. I suddenly miss her touch. I shake my head and back further away. *She's Jeremy's girl.* "Jeremy, I think I need to change. Did you put my bag in your room?" She's blushing. *She's spending the night with him?*

"Yes," he answers. "Hurry back, babe." Their relationship became official at the beginning of senior year, when Jeremy finally got the courage to ask her out. He went back and forth a hundred times about what he should do. He didn't want to ruin the friendship that we've all had since we were younger, but his feelings for her had grown so much, and he wanted to make it official. I encouraged him, of course, as any best friend would do. But Jules and I have something even more special, and we've been doing it since we were kids. We share things with each other. Our hopes, fears, sadness. Does she have that with Jeremy?

We both watch her walk through the doorway, into the house. She's walking slowly. Purposefully. She's hammered.

"How much has she had to drink?" I ask accusingly.

"Relax, she's only done a few shots. She's a lightweight. She just needs to eat something." I frown, concerned about Jules.

"This is a hell of a party, J." I look around, acknowledging the swarms of people in and around his pool. My ears feel warm, and I know that the bourbon is doing its job, but I need more.

"I don't know how it happened. I only mentioned it to like twenty people or so. Then this." He swipes his hand in the air, gesturing toward all of the drunk idiots. I grab the bottle of bourbon from his hands and swig the last few shots from the bottle.

"Hey. What the hell?"

"You don't need any more of this, J. Thanks for letting me catch up to your buzz." I chuckle and toss the empty bottle into the recycling bin next to the patio.

"Let's go eat." We walk past the snack table that looks like it was cleared off to become a makeshift DJ booth. Travis Stonington is behind the table with headphones on and a laptop in front of him. He nods toward us as we walk through the back door. Trays of food are covering the countertops. "Tell me again how you only told twenty people?" I raise my eyebrow and smirk. There's enough food here to feed at least five times that.

"I guess I got carried away?" Jeremy responds, shoving a pizza roll into his mouth.

"You think?"

He laughs and opens a cabinet, pulling out a full bottle of bourbon. "Secret stash," he says, and is clearly very proud of himself.

"I'm pretty sure you don't need any more of that stuff, and I know Jules doesn't either." He takes a quick swig and puts it back in the cabinet. "Don't worry, she won't have any more. Where is she anyway?"

Before I have a chance to answer, Ben Taylor practically trips into the kitchen.

"Jeremy! C'mon, I've been waiting forever, man. Pool game. Remember?"

"Oh! Yeah." Jeremy turns to leave with Ben. "I'll see you in a few. Do you want to play winner?"

"Nah." I suck at pool.

They leave and I grab a napkin, filling it with as many pizza rolls as I can and shoving it into the front pocket of my hoodie, along with a can of Sprite. Then I swipe Jeremy's secret stash and slip up the back stairs. I reach his room at the end of the hallway and hear retching coming from his bathroom.

Juliet.

I rush through his room and knock on the bathroom door. "Jules? Are you okay?"

"No. Please don't come in. I'm a mess." The toilet flushes and she becomes quiet. I ignore her request to stay out and push the door open. She's curled up on the floor with her face pressed against the tiles. She grunts when I slide down onto the floor next to her.

"Feeling better?"

She grunts again.

I reach into my pocket, open the Sprite, and slide it on the tile next to her. "Take a small sip; it'll help you feel better."

"Seth," she whines, curling into a tighter ball on the floor. Seeing her like this makes me not want to drink anymore, so I push the bottle of bourbon away from me. I'm already pretty drunk myself. *That was fast.*

I push her hair away from her face, resting my hand on her cheek. "You're warm."

"I know, I feel like I'm burning up. Drinking tonight was a bad idea." She closes her eyes and exhales softly.

I stand up and grab a washcloth from the shelf next to the sink. I run it under cool water, squeezing out the excess. "How's this?" I ask, placing the cool compress onto her forehead. She shivers and nods. Her hand covers mine as she drifts off to sleep.

"Jules, you can't sleep here."

She doesn't respond and begins to snore softly.

"Jules?"

I look around the bathroom for something to cover her up with. There's a towel balled up in the corner next to the shower, and that's it. I can't leave her in here. I stand up too quickly and the room begins to spin a little. *Damn, I'm drunk.*

She moans and rolls onto her other side. I bend down and scoop her into my arms, trying to remain upright myself. As I carry her into Jeremy's room, I trip on something on the floor, causing me to catapult her onto his bed. She lands with a bounce and moans again.

Shit!

"Jules, are you okay?" I ask hesitantly and start laughing. Seeing her fly through the air was terrifying and hysterical at the same time.

"Mmm hmm."

I pull the comforter up over her shoulders. "Are you going to be alright now?" I ask, my hand lingering. The urge to climb into bed and pull her against me is strong. *Too strong.*

Her clammy hand covers mine and she nods, her eyes still closed.

I swipe her hair from her forehead with my free hand when I hear her slur, "Olive juice."

What?

"You want olive juice?" *Gross.*

"What?" She opens her heavy eyes, looking confused.

"You asked for olive juice."

"I did?" She shakes her head and then adds, "No, silly, I said I love you."

I laugh nervously and let go of her hand. "What?"

She closes her eyes and smiles. "I love you." She's snoring again, and I'm slightly stunned by her admission. *She loves me? What about Jeremy?* I slide down onto the floor next to the bed and rest the back of my head against the mattress. I exhale deeply, closing my eyes. *I love her too.*

As I curl up on the hard floor next to the bed, I try to convince myself that she didn't mean what she said. How could she love me when she has Jeremy? This is wrong.

But I want it to be right.

"Olive juice too," I whisper as I drift off to sleep.

chapter eight

Juliet
Sausalito, California
Age 16

THUMP-THUMP.

Thump-thump.

I feel warm. So warm.

Thump-thump.

Thump-thump.

My head feels like it's in a vise. *What the hell?*

I open my eyes, and the first thing I see is Jeremy's window. The sun is streaming onto his bed, causing me to squint. An arm tightens around my waist, and I'm pulled closer into a chest. "Hey, sleepyhead, how are you feeling?"

Jeremy's chest.

I hear his heart pounding again and he stretches. "How did I get here?" I ask.

A hand shoots up from the floor, blocking the sun from my eyes momentarily. "I can fill you in." Seth's groggy voice comes from below.

Shit. Did I make a fool of myself last night?

The last thing I remember is doing shots of tequila—or something. Maybe bourbon? I feel nauseated thinking about all of the alcohol I consumed last night. "Ugh," I groan into Jeremy's shirt.

He laughs. "When I came up here at around two in the morning, Seth was passed out on the floor and you were tucked neatly into my bed." He squeezes me close and kisses the top of my head.

"That was after she puked her guts up," Seth comments and then adds, "several times."

Jeremy laughs, "I had no idea. I'm sorry, babe." I snuggle closer into his side and close my eyes.

Seth's face comes into blurry view. "Don't worry, nobody knew. You came upstairs quietly without anyone noticing." He smiles at me and stands, walking to Jeremy's bathroom. I wince, thinking about what he may find in there.

"Did I puke everywhere?" I call after him, embarrassed.

He peers out through the half-open door. "Nope, you were very precise."

"I'm sorry, Jeremy. I hope I didn't screw up your party." I close my eyes and hold onto him tight.

"You didn't mess anything up, Jules. You had a good time last night, and then I guess the bourbon caught up to you. I'm sorry for letting you drink so much. Thank God Seth showed up when he did, because I was in no state to take care of you myself."

He pulls me into his chest so our noses are practically touching. "Hey," he says softly.

"Hey," I say back, turning my head so he can't smell my breath. It must be awful.

"You're in my bed."

"Yeah." I've never been in his bed before. Not like this.

"I wish we were alone right now. Completely alone." He pulls me against him, and I can feel how much he wants to be alone with me.

"Jeremy," I whisper as the bathroom door flies open.

"Don't let me interrupt you two lovebirds," Seth says awkwardly. His eyes are darting around the room and his discomfort is beginning to make me squirm a little.

A buzzing sound comes from my cell phone on Jeremy's dresser, and Seth immediately picks it up. "It's your mom." He tosses the phone onto the bed and Jeremy catches it for me.

Shit.

Did I call her last night to let her know that I was planning to stay here?

"Hi, Mom," I answer, trying to sound awake and coherent.

"Juliet. Where are you?" Her voice is strained, and I feel bad that she's worried.

"I'm at Jeremy's."

"I tried calling you several times last night and you didn't answer. I'm so upset right now, and your father is beside himself."

"Mom, I'm sorry. I thought you knew I was planning to stay here. I'm really sorry. I'm okay."

She breathes heavily and I can tell she's relaxing a little. She loves Jeremy and knows that I'm okay over here.

I continue my explanation to try to calm her down more. "I didn't want to bother you late last night. I figured you knew I was staying since we talked about it over dinner. Remember? I told you that I probably would stay here since the party would be over late?" My explanation is lame, and I know I should have at least texted her.

"We'll talk about it later. When are you coming home?"

"Um... I don't know. Jeremy and I planned to go to lunch today." He looks down at me and frowns. He knows I'm making it up on the fly and using him as an excuse to avoid my parents.

"Okay, we'll see you for dinner, then. Juliet, I really wish you would have called us back last night. You know I'm not comfortable not knowing if you're okay."

"Don't worry, Mom, and I slept in the guest room," I lie again. "We have a lot of cleaning up to do here, so I'll see you later, okay?" I say, biting my lip.

"Okay. Goodbye, Juliet." My mom hangs up abruptly and I immediately feel terrible.

"Ugh," I say into Jeremy's side.

"Why didn't you tell her your plans for last night?" he asks.

"They knew I was coming to a party at your house. I assumed they knew I wouldn't be coming home," I whine.

"Jules, you know how protective they are. You should have called them. They must have thought you were in a ditch somewhere."

I huff. "That's ridiculous."

"Now I feel weird that your mom knows that you slept here." He tenses up underneath my cheek and exhales.

"On that note..." Seth heads toward the bedroom door. I had completely forgotten that he was still here, and now I'm even more embarrassed.

"Seth, thanks for helping me last night," I say. His eyes meet mine momentarily and then drop to the floor.

"It's what best friends do. We take care of each other." He leaves the room, closing the door behind him. I get the feeling that Seth would do anything for me, and I like it.

"Truer words have never been spoken." I can hear Jeremy smile through those words. He slowly rolls us so I'm pinned beneath his body. He buries his head into my hair and breathes deeply. "You smell so good." He kisses me softly beneath my ear and nuzzles into me.

"Jeremy, I smell like puke." I laugh and gently press his shoulders away from me. His lips trail along my collarbone and stop right above my breast. My breath hitches, and I stiffen underneath him. "I need to brush my teeth. And shower."

He rolls off me onto his side while caressing the side of my face. "You're beautiful, no matter how messy your hair is." My hair feels like it's knotted and plastered to the top of my head. I feel hideous right now.

I sit up too quickly and the room begins to spin. "Shit," I say, placing my hand against my forehead.

"Take it easy, babe. Here, take a sip of this." He hands me a glass and I slowly sip the lukewarm water. The room begins to stabilize a bit, and I hand the glass back to him. I stand up and walk toward the bathroom.

"Are there clean towels in there? And do you have a toothbrush I can borrow?" He jumps up and walks past me and into the bathroom. He pulls open a drawer and takes out a brand new toothbrush. Then he nods toward the linen closet in the corner. "Clean towels and washcloths are in there."

"Okay, thanks." He backs out of the room, shutting the door. I turn the water on in the shower and walk back to the sink. The girl who stares back at me in the mirror is a mess. Hair disheveled. Face pale and eyes sunken. I open the toothbrush and begin brushing my teeth. As I continue to stare at myself, I can't help but wonder...

Do I look like *her*? Do I look like *him*? Do *they* think of me as much as I do them? Graduation is right around the corner, and I wonder how different my life would have been if Lily hadn't given me up for adoption.

I finish brushing my teeth as the bathroom begins to fill with steam. The girl in the mirror is blurry and distorted. I take off my clothes and step into the shower. I just stand there, letting the steam rise around me as warm water pounds into my skull. My mind wanders to last night and this morning. I'm so embarrassed that Seth saw me completely wasted and puking last night. It was nice of him to take care of me and make sure I was okay, but I'm mortified. He's such an awesome friend, always there to help me out. I remember the time at my ninth birthday party when he witnessed my sadness and worry over hearing my parents talk about Lily's letter. He just understood me and wanted to help.

Waking up in Jeremy's arms was a first. I know we didn't do anything last night, but it was weird waking up in his bed. And then he pulled me against him and I *felt* him. Felt his body's reaction to me. I'm not sure what Jeremy was hoping to happen out there, but I'm not ready. He knows it too, but to press into me so I could *feel* him. *Whoa*.

I grab the shampoo and begin washing my hair. I feel my fingertips burn into every inch of my scalp, and I rinse the suds quickly. *I need Advil.*

After I finish washing up, I towel-dry myself off in the shower and realize I have no clean clothes with me. My bag is out in his bedroom. *Shit.*

I wrap the towel around myself and call out from the bathroom, "Jeremy?"

The door opens quickly. "Are you okay?" He peers through the steam and slowly walks toward me.

"Um... yeah. My bag, it's near your closet," I say as his eyes remain locked on mine.

"Oh." He reaches me and pulls me against his body. His lips brush mine and linger. "You brushed your teeth." He smiles as he pulls me into an embrace. He kisses me hard and parts my lips with his tongue. "And you taste amazing." He deepens our kiss and I let him. Our tongues entwine and his arms wrap around my waist. As I tighten my arms around his neck, my towel falls, exposing my breasts. Startled, I pull away and cover myself.

"Sorry." He backs away a little. "I didn't mean to…" he stammers and is clearly uncomfortable. He knows I'm not ready for more.

"It's okay. It's just, we've talked about this. I want to. I really do, but…"

He walks out of the bathroom and he returns quickly, carrying my overnight bag. "Here," he says, handing it to me. "Let's talk when you're dressed."

"Okay, be right out." He leaves, and I scramble to get clothes on as quickly as I can. I look at myself in the hazy mirror and finger-comb my wet hair. I'm disheveled, but not as bad as before my shower. The dark circles are still underneath my eyes, and I scrunch my brows. *What does Jeremy see in me that he loves so much?*

I open the door and see him sitting on his bed. He pats the mattress next to him and I sit down. He pulls me against his side and kisses the tip of my nose. "Juliet, I love you so much. You know that, right?"

"Yes." I relax into his chest and drape my leg over his.

"I want to be with you. I want us to be *together*." His voice wavers, unsure of my response. I know exactly what he means, but I'm not ready for sex.

"I want the same, Jeremy. I really do." I don't know how to convince him if I can't convince myself. It's a big step. Huge. I'm only sixteen. I'm afraid.

"So let's not rush. We can wait as long as you need to. We can wait until you're ready." He bends down and places a chaste kiss on my lips. I can't explain it, but there's a force holding me back from giving in to him. From giving in to the urges that scare the shit out of me.

I'm thankful for his restraint, because I'm not sure what would happen if he were more persistent with me. I might do something that I know we're both not ready for. *It just needs to feel right, and right now it doesn't.*

"I have something for you. Something I was planning on giving you after graduation, but I can't wait." He reaches into his nightstand and pulls out an envelope with a ribbon wrapped around it.

"What's this?" I ask after he places the gift into my hands.

"Open it." His grin is huge, and I can't imagine what could be in this envelope. I pull the pink ribbon and it glides to the floor. He holds his breath while I open it.

I tug at the thin piece of paper inside the envelope and pull out a plane ticket. He smiles even bigger and says, "Surprise!"

"Where are we going?" I ask, holding the ticket in front of me.

"Not we, you. Look at the ticket, Jules. It's from Philly to San Francisco. I'm flying you home for your birthday. I know it's months away, but I wanted to be with you when you turn seventeen. I want to be with you for all of your birthdays."

Wow. This is just... so thoughtful.

"Thank you, Jeremy. This is amazing." The thought of spending my birthday alone was troubling, and the fact that Jeremy planned this incredible gift so I could come home is wonderful.

"Sorry I couldn't wait to give it to you."

"This is great. Thank you." I kiss him softly.

I'm already thinking ahead to October. My birthday. Maybe then I'll be ready to make love to Jeremy. I want to be ready.

"I love you," I whisper against his lips and deepen our kiss.

"I love you more."

chapter nine

Seth
Sausalito, California
Age 18

I LOOK OUT AT THE CROWD in front of me from my seat on the stage. I see a sea of royal blue gowns and white caps with gold tassels hanging and blowing in the light breeze. Chester Academy Graduation. The future is at our fingertips and I feel numb.

I want to freeze time right now. *Am I ready to begin the next chapter in my life?* I'll be leaving for Stanford in a few short months to follow in my father's footsteps. To become the asshole that he's been preparing me to be my entire life.

I find *him* in the audience, sitting next to my sisters and brother. My mother should be here too, and my blood runs cold. It's his fault that she's not.

After her suicide attempt six years ago, she spent almost ninety days in rehab and came out a new woman. She was sober and appeared happy. My father spent more time at home, and they seemed to become the parents that I remembered from my early childhood.

But it was all a façade. My mother slowly became a shell of herself, heavily medicated to cope with her debilitating depression. My father was putting on a show for everyone's benefit, including hers. She bought it hook, line and sinker.

She relapsed and binged on vodka and pills two weeks ago, after a violent argument with my father erupted during a cocktail party at our house.

She's back in rehab.

The 'spa.' That's what her socialite friends think.

I glare at my father, who's looking down at his cell phone. *I fucking hate him.*

Chloe catches my gaze and tries to get me to smile. I nod at her and look over to Chelsea, who also smiles huge at me. Sean is looking off into the distance and doesn't seem to want to be here. I know he's worried about my mother and is having a difficult time with the constant battles in our home.

"Hey, aren't you excited?" I hear Jules's voice as she leans her shoulder into mine. I immediately think about her admission of love to me last week. She was so drunk, I wonder if she even remembers. *I know I can't forget.*

"Not really," I huff in response. She's rubbing her palms on the front of her gown, trying to calm her own nerves. She's valedictorian and is terrified to get up to give a speech in front of the entire school.

As head of the National Honor Society students at our school, I have the pleasure of sharing the stage with my fellow honorees.

"Calm down, babe." Jeremy places his hand over hers and kisses her cheek. She turns to him and leans her forehead against his. He just sat down after delivering his commencement speech. He commandeered the crowd, as usual, and told all of us that we have bright futures ahead. His speech was riddled with sports analogies and motivational blurbs. They loved it.

"I'll be okay." She grabs both of our hands and says, "My two favorite guys are here to support me. What more could a girl want?" Her voice wavers, and I know she's hiding her pain.

She's been struggling privately for the past few years over her adoption. She confided in me that her parents still have the letter from Lily. She almost read it when she was eleven years old, but she changed her mind. Her mother took it away and she hasn't seen it since. She's been lying to herself and her parents about how the existence of that letter makes her feel. Hell, she's even lying to Jeremy.

I'm the only person who knows how much she hates herself. She thinks she was a 'mistake' and that's the reason why Lily had to give her up. She doesn't know the reason for sure, since she never read the letter, but she can only guess why her parents never gave it back to her.

She doesn't tell this to me directly. No. We email each other. The pen pal correspondence that we established back in grade school. She doesn't feel comfortable speaking the words that she writes so eloquently. She's so uncomfortable in her own skin. She dislikes herself, and I wish I could help her through it. But I don't have the skills to. I'm dealing with my own self-hate every single day for not being able to bring any normalcy to my own family. So I get it. I get her self-loathing. It's a burden.

She has incredible parents. The perfect family, even. Her mom and dad love her undeniably. Unquestionably. They've given her everything a girl could ever want. The almost perfect existence.

If they only knew the power that Lily's unread words have over her.

Jules puts on a good show. She pretends to be so happy, but beyond her smile is a profoundly sad girl.

I wish I knew how to help her. I can't even help my own mother through her depression. Mom is a broken woman, barely keeping it together by the meds that she takes everyday. I recognize some of the same behavior in Juliet that I do in my mother. Not as pronounced, but it's still there. It worries me.

I'm useless in helping the people who matter to me the most. Maybe it's good that I'm leaving for Stanford soon.

Principal Thomas's voice drones on in the background since he's been talking this entire time. I haven't heard a word that he's said. I'm sure it's along the lines of 'the best and the brightest.' Blah blah blah.

He raises his voice and says, "Ladies and Gentlemen of the graduating class, I give you, Chester Academy's valedictorian, Juliet Oliver!" Applause ripples through the crowd as Jules squeezes Jeremy's hand and mine. Her palm is warm and clammy as I squeeze it back before releasing her to the podium.

"You got this," I say encouragingly, loud enough for her to hear me.

She looks back at me, then over to Jeremy. He winks at her and mouths, "I love you."

A false look of confidence replaces the worried look on her face. She grips either side of the podium and looks out at our peers. The very people who made fun of her during freshman year because she was super smart and a little dorky. The same classmates who shunned her from the popular cliques because she didn't look as glamorous as the rest of them. She's sixteen years old and one of the youngest graduates ever from our school. It's incredible to see her stand at that podium while struggling with demons that her peers couldn't even comprehend.

Our classmates look back at her, excited. *Hypocrites.* Suddenly, Jules is the most popular girl in school. Not only is she our valedictorian, she's also *their* prom Queen. She and Jeremy were voted into the highest social status a few weeks ago.

She clears her throat and looks over to her parents, who are sitting in the front row. Her mother is clutching a white handkerchief and her father's arm is wrapped tightly around her mom's shoulders. They are both so incredibly proud of Juliet. You can see it in their beaming smiles. They are wearing their hearts on their sleeves.

"You may all wonder..." Jules speaks into the microphone and her voice trails off. *Oh no, her nerves are back.* She rustles the papers in front of her and tries to regain her composure.

She begins again. "You may all wonder how I got here. How I'm standing in front of all of you as your valedictorian." She pauses and looks out to our graduating class.

"I was nobody, really. None of you knew who I was for years. Most of you didn't care who I was until a few weeks ago." She chuckles nervously, gripping the podium so tightly that her knuckles turn white.

"I was a scared, dorky freshman four years ago. Someone who didn't fit in, yet still managed to survive. I was a newbie and still feel like one today. I bet you didn't know that besides being prom queen..."

She's interrupted by applause from the *popular* girls, along with a few whistles from some others.

She waits for the clapping to stop and nods. "Aside from being *your* prom queen, I'm a lot of other things." She turns the paper in front of her over, and I notice there are no words on it. Is she reciting her speech from memory? Where are her notes? Cue cards? The pages are completely blank.

"So let me introduce myself to those of you who don't know me. I'm Juliet Oliver. I'm your cross country champion three times over, and I currently hold the fastest time in the history of the school. I'm also the captain of the debate team, and the lead singer in the ensemble for every production since freshman year. *These* are the things that have defined me in this school, without many of you ever noticing until I became your *queen*."

I see her glance over to her parents, whose faces are unmoved. They are so proud of her, even as she subtly insults ninety-five percent of the audience. A smile forms on my lips, and I look over to Jeremy, whose grin is huge.

"But there is something else that has defined me throughout my entire life. Something that *none* of you know," she pauses, and this time I'm certain it's for dramatic effect.

"I'm adopted."

I watch as the graduates' heads are turning to the left and the right.

"But it doesn't matter." She raises her voice. "It doesn't matter, because *that* doesn't define me. Not in your eyes. Nor should it. I have the family that I was always meant to have. The family that has loved me unconditionally since the moment they first held me in their arms. Where I come from doesn't matter. Who I came from doesn't matter."

I suddenly feel that she isn't speaking to three hundred people, but just her parents. Begging them to believe the words that she's saying, even though I know she doesn't believe them herself. Her mom raises the white hanky to her nose, and her shoulders shake slightly.

"I'm the exact person that I was always meant to be. The person you didn't really even know until prom."

She quickly looks over her shoulder at Jeremy and me and says, "And, in addition to my perfect family, I have the two best friends that a girl could ask for."

She squares her shoulders and stands up straight, releasing her firm grip on the podium.

"These are the people I have to thank. These are the people who supported me throughout the past four years and will continue to do so for the next four years and beyond. My fellow graduates, look to your right and to your left. Recognize what you have that is right in front of you, and never let it go. In a few months, *you too* will be that awkward, maybe even dorky, freshman. Maybe, for a brief second, you'll feel like I did four years ago. And maybe *you too* won't let it define you. I hope that you too will form lifelong friendships and relationships like I have. Maybe this will get you through the rough times. Maybe you'll be accepted into that sorority or fraternity that you so desperately want to become a part of. You'll want to *belong*."

The silence is almost deafening. They are hanging on her every word, and some of them even look a little worried about what lies in their future.

"Remember that person to your right and to your left. Because they will be feeling the same thing as you. Keep their phone number on speed dial, just so you can hear a friendly voice. Send them an email every few days to let them know that you're thinking about them. For some, the next steps in our lives are going to be terrifying. Be there for each other, even when you don't think they need the support. Trust me. It goes a long way."

She looks down at the blank sheet of paper in front of her, then looks back up, scanning the audience.

"I know that I wouldn't be standing in front of you today, as one of the most accomplished students of this senior class, if I didn't have the love and support from the people who matter most in my life. And I wouldn't be standing here if one woman had made a different decision sixteen years ago. Thank you for allowing me to stand here as I try to share whatever wisdom I can with all of you, my peers. Maybe my experiences over the past four years will give you a new perspective on what it means to be a little different. Thank you, Mom and Dad. You've given me everything and more. I love you both so much." Her voice shakes a little bit as she says, "I hope that you're proud of me." I'm not sure if she says that to her parents or to the audience. Maybe both?

She turns and walks back toward us and quickly wipes a tear from her cheek. What happens next is astounding, considering the speech she just gave. The entire crowd is on their feet, clapping and shouting their praise for Jules. The roar of the crowd drowns out her laughter, but I feel her shoulders shaking against mine. She's laughing hysterically, and I realize how truly hypocritical our entire senior class is. This is just so ironic. She basically insulted everyone in our class, and they're giving her a standing ovation.

I shake my head and join her and Jeremy in laughter.

Principal Thomas begins the presentation of diplomas and the rest of our graduation ceremony flies by.

My sisters and brother are waiting for me after the final declaration of our freedom from high school. Sean grabs and squeezes my shoulder. "I'm proud of you, Seth." His words grip me, and I couldn't be more shocked by the words that just left his mouth. Don't get me wrong, he isn't a total douchebag, but I'd never expect him to utter those words.

"Sethie!" Chloe and Chelsea practically tackle me as they both fly into my arms. Their nickname for me is only slightly irritating, and I think I'm going to miss hearing it every day, actually.

I look around, but my father is nowhere in sight. "He left. Apparently something important came up and he had to get to the office," Sean says as he makes finger quotes when he says the word 'office.' I know what that means. He's been called by one of his mistresses.

What a motherfucker.

I truly hope that the twins have no idea what a royal asshole our father is. But somehow I doubt that. They will learn, just like Sean and I have.

Bob walks up and pulls me into a tight hug. "Congrats, Seth. I'm really proud of you, and sad that I won't be driving you around in September." He's been a constant presence in my life, and I am going to miss him this fall when I leave for school. He's been more of a father to me than my own. "Let's go, kids," he says. "You have someplace that you need to be, remember?"

Mom wants us to visit her at 'the spa' so she can celebrate my graduation. She's planned a little party for us in her private residence at rehab, and I'm actually looking forward to it.

"Give me a minute," I say as I jog over to where Jeremy and Juliet are standing. Their families are discussing where they're going to go for dinner.

"Dude! Are you joining us? I think we're going to go to the club for dinner, then hit a few parties after," Jeremy says.

"Please come," Jules begs. I really want to say yes, but I do have someplace important to be.

"I can't. We're going to see my mom."

They both nod in understanding and Jules grabs Jeremy's hand. "We'll miss you," she says.

She then turns to her boyfriend. "Really, Jeremy? Parties? After I basically insulted every single one of these people, you want to spend more time partying with them tonight?" She laughs.

I chuckle and punch Jeremy softly in the shoulder. "Take care of our girl, okay?" She's been 'our girl' for years, and while this phrase may piss other guys off, he isn't fazed by it in the least.

"You bet I will," he says, grabbing Jules around the waist and burying his face in her neck. She squeals and waves goodbye as I stand there, hiding my own jealousy.

I turn and jog back over to the limousine waiting to take us to celebrate with my mom.

And for once, I don't give a shit about what I'll be missing out on tonight.

I look around at my siblings and smile. I'm looking forward to spending some time with them.

And I hope my dad is getting a fucking STD as he bangs his latest whore.

chapter ten

Juliet
Sausalito, California
Age 16

I HEAR RANDOM, MUFFLED SOUNDS in my head and I feel funny. My head is killing me. I have pins and needles in my arms and legs, but I can't move. I can't see anything.

Why can't I open my eyes?

My pulse quickens as I try to take a breath. There's something in my mouth and down my throat, and I start to gag uncontrollably. The pressure in my chest is intense and I still can't breathe.

What is happening?

I'm now in full panic mode, and I try to lift my arms to my face. They're strapped down to the cold mattress that I'm lying on. I try to scream, and my head is spinning as I continue to gag.

"Juliet, we need you to relax," a soft voice says into my ear. A voice that I don't recognize. "We're going to be taking the tube out of your throat so you can breathe on your own. Please try to relax." I feel her hand on my shoulder as she continues to whisper instructions into my left ear. Or is it my right?

Tube? *What is going on?*

I gag one last time as I feel a slow tug from my lungs and up into my throat. My gags turn into gasps, and I begin to cough and suck much needed air into my lungs. My chest is burning and feels so heavy. I still can't see anything, and the tingling in my arms and legs is getting worse.

And the pain! Oh my God, the pain!

I begin to scream and wail, not knowing where the pain is coming from. It's all over my body. Crushing pain in my chest and abdomen. I'm gasping for air and screaming at the same time.

I hear the soft voice speak with firmness. "She can't handle the pain. I'm pushing five milliliters of morphine right now." Before her words resonate in my head, blackness takes me.

"JULIET? CAN YOU HEAR ME?" Finally, a voice that I recognize. My father's voice. He sounds desperate and scared, and it sounds like he's crying. "Jules? Please..."

I feel him squeeze my hand, and I try to squeeze it back.

"Dad?" I whisper. My throat burns, and I'm not sure if he can even hear me.

"Shhhh. Don't strain yourself, Jules. I just need to know that you can hear me," he says desperately.

"Yes. I—I can hear you," I stammer as I try to open my eyes. I can barely focus, but my father's blurry figure slowly comes into view.

"Thank God. Thank God," he murmurs as he kisses my forehead. "We were so worried about you." He sobs loudly and kisses me again.

Why is he crying? What's going on?

Where the hell am I?

"What happened?" I ask, confused. He doesn't answer me right away, and I think he's trying to compose himself.

"Let's not talk about that right now," he says softly. "Let's focus on getting you better, okay?"

Better? I'm confused. What happened to me?

"Where am I, Dad?" I croak as tears fall from the corners of my eyes. I know I'm hurt. Really badly. I'm throbbing with pain everywhere. I feel his soft hand on my cheeks as he wipes away my cold tears.

"You're at San Francisco General Hospital," he says, squeezing my hand again.

Well, I guess I could have figured that out. Of course I'm in a hospital, but for the life of me I can't figure out how I got here. *Where is my mom? Jeremy?*

"Please tell me what happened. How did I get here?" I beg him. My voice is barely registering a sound and I hope he hears me.

"Jules, we were in an accident. A very bad one," his voice trails off, and suddenly I remember where I was last. Sitting next to Jeremy and across from my mom and dad in the back of our limousine. We were on our way home from the club after we celebrated our graduation dinner. Jeremy's family went home, and we were going back to our house for a quiet dessert.

My heart begins to beat wildly in my chest and my breathing speeds up. Machines start to beep behind me, and a nurse comes rushing into the room.

"Mr. Oliver, please step aside." She begins to fiddle with the wires that are connected to my chest and pushes buttons on the machine above my head.

"Juliet, can you take a couple of slow, deep breaths?" she instructs as she places her hand on my shoulder to try to calm me down. I try to listen to her and slow my breathing down.

I blink away the tears in my eyes as I hear the machine start beeping at a more normal rate. "There you go." She smiles at me warmly and turns to my dad. "Let's try to keep things calm for now, Mr. Oliver."

He nods at her as she leaves the room.

I'm calmer, but still terrified by what my dad needs to tell me.

"Dad?" I beg him, "Please tell me what happened. Where's Mom? Where's Jeremy?" I sob softly, knowing he's going to tell me something terrible. I'm not ready to hear anything he has to say, but I desperately need to hear it too.

He walks back over to me and sits down, grabbing my hand.

"Jules," he repeats what he said earlier, "we were in a terrible accident."

He takes a deep breath and I hear him choke on another sob. "Honey, your mom and Jeremy were hurt really badly."

I realize that I already know this. I close my eyes and the accident begins to replay in slow motion behind my eyelids. I see the left side of the car collapse toward us as a large vehicle rams into us from the side. The look on my mother's face is terrifying as she's thrown into my father but can't take her eyes from me. She's scared for me. For my safety. She reaches out across the aisle in front of her seat, and her arms are thrown widely around as her eyes roll back into her head. I see my father try to pull her into him, but he bounces up and down in his seat as my mother's body goes limp and is torn from her seatbelt.

I don't see Jeremy, because he's sitting to my left. I don't even feel him next to me, which is odd. I feel a breeze on the back of my neck, and my eyes spring open and I'm gasping for air again.

"It's okay, honey. Please calm down. Take a deep breath and calm down," he whispers into my forehead. "It's going to be okay," he says, and I'm not sure if he's convinced of that himself.

"Are they dead?" I ask quietly and hear him suck in a labored breath.

But I already know the answer.

chapter eleven

Seth
Sausalito, California
Age 18

"CONGRATULATIONS SETH. You know I'm really proud of you right?" As the words leave my brother's lips, I expect the car to come to a screeching halt. It always surprises me when I hear any words of encouragement from him. We left my graduation ceremony about twenty minutes ago, and I've been appreciative of the silence in the car. We're on our way to see Mom at 'the spa' to celebrate my graduation.

"Thanks," I say as Chloe and Chelsea both chime in with their praise.

"Seth, you're going to college! Are you excited?" Chloe asks, barely able to contain herself.

I'm definitely excited. Jeremy and I are going to be roommates at Stanford and we leave at the end of the summer. What's not to be excited about? It's going to be epic. Jeremy and I will also both be playing baseball in addition to running track. Even though I'm not going too far for school, getting out of our house and away from all of the daily reminders of what a prick my father is seems to be high on my list of priorities.

The only thing that I'm bummed about is the fact that Jules will be on the East Coast, thousands of miles away.

My cell phone rings and I jump. Chelsea grabs for it and quickly swipes across the phone to answer it. "Hi, Daddy!" she screeches.

Why is that fucker calling me right now?

Doesn't he know where we're heading?

Chelsea continues her exuberant chatter and then I hear her say, "Sure, he's right here." She shoves the phone up to my ear and quickly lets go, so I have to scoop it up to keep it near my head.

"Seth? Are you there?" I hear his gruff voice say through the speaker.

"Yes," I answer very tersely. I don't want to talk to him right now, and I certainly don't want to hear his well wishes. He'll just pat *himself* on the back for *my* successes.

"I just wanted to let you know that I had an emergency at work and I'm sorry that I couldn't stay for your graduation and after party." There is no emotion in his voice as he delivers this truly un-heartfelt comment. What kind of real estate emergency could there possibly be?

"Whatever," I respond. As I'm about to hang up on him, I hear him say, "Tell your mother that I'm thinking about her."

I disconnect the call without responding and turn my phone onto silent. What a fucking asshole. I will absolutely not say a word to my mother about him. He's the reason why she's a complete and utter mess. He's a lousy bastard.

A cheating fucker.

I look up angrily and make eye contact with Sean. He just nods and looks out the window. I'm glad to know that he gets it. Sean hates our father even more than I do, if that's possible.

Bob turns into the long driveway leading up to the tall wrought-iron gates that we've become used to seeing too frequently. Our mother's home away from home. This is at least the sixth or seventh time she's come here. She frequently states that she needs a 'reset,' whatever the hell that means. Bob lowers his window as he responds to the voice coming from the speaker. "The Tyson family is here to see Celeste." The gates open automatically, and we drive silently as Bob pulls up to the entrance.

We don't wait for him to put the car into park as Chloe throws open the door and jumps from the car. "C'mon, guys! I know Mom has been waiting all day to see us," she says as Chelsea follows close behind. Sean and I exit the car right behind them and I take a deep breath as I stretch my legs.

This is not how my graduation day was supposed to be. Dammit. These past few years have gone completely wrong. Mom doesn't deserve to be here. This place was created to shroud her problems. To hide her away from the public and from us while she tries to fix herself after crashing and burning yet again. This is all *his* fault.

As we walk through the facility, it doesn't escape me that this place is made to look and feel like a spa. The lights are dim, and the scent of vanilla wafts through the air as zen music plays through the speakers. The staff is dressed in comfortable white uniforms, and several are even barefoot.

We reach Mom's suite at the end of a long hallway. Her door is already open slightly and I hear her laughter coming from inside. Chloe pushes through into the room and Mom is sitting at her salon-like chair while one girl is painting her fingernails and another seems to be putting the finishing touches on her hair.

"Oh!" she exclaims through a bright smile on her face. "You made it." The girl fixing Mom's hair backs away and quickly leaves the room, while the one doing her nails takes a fan to start drying them.

"Sally, this is my family." She gestures toward us with her free hand as Sally turns to greet us.

"Hello," she says very timidly. "Congratulations—Seth?" She looks between me and my brother as she tries to figure out which one of us just graduated high school.

"Thank you," I quickly respond, letting her off the hook.

"These should be dry soon, Mrs. Tyson," she says as she pushes away and walks out of the room. "Please let us know if you need anything," she says before she closes the door, leaving our fucked-up family to ourselves.

"Mom, you certainly are getting pampered during your stay," Chloe observes.

"Come here, my graduate. Let me see you and squeeze you." She opens her arms wide, carefully holding her hands out. She's trying not to damage her nail polish, but I lean in and let her close her arms around me. "I'm so proud of you, Seth. So incredibly proud." She kisses my cheek and releases me so she can fall back into her chair.

"So, tell me everything! How was the ceremony? Was the weather as nice as it is here? How was Jeremy's speech? Juliet's? I want to hear everything!" She seems almost manic as she fires out these questions rapidly. Her eyes are wide and her smile seems forced, bittersweet. Not because she isn't happy for me, but because she couldn't be there to celebrate with me.

Chelsea jumps in to answer her questions before I can even get the chance. "Mom, it was amazing! You would have loved it! Chloe and I cheered the loudest when they introduced the President of the National Honor Society!" She looks over at me while Mom smiles warmly.

"Oh, and you should have heard Jeremy's speech. It was so motivating. He had everyone on their feet after he was finished," Chloe adds. "It was like a pep rally!"

As soon as I'm able to get a word in, I say, "Juliet's speech was really good too, Mom. She really got the crowd's atten—"

Chelsea once again interrupts with, "Yeah! Mom, she told everyone that she was adopted. I couldn't believe it. I mean we all know this, but she never—and I mean NEVER—talks about being adopted. Right, Seth?"

"It was a very nice speech. It was great to see her open up and see the positive effects that her adoption has had on her life," I answer.

"Well, you must all be so happy to have high school behind you so you can move on and pave through mountains. The rest of your lives are ahead of you and the possibilities are limitless." Mom's eyes are now shining and glistening with happy tears.

She picks up the phone in front of her and presses one button. "We'll be ready for our dinner shortly. Is the dining room set up?" she asks the person on the other line. "Splendid," she says and hangs up.

"Let's go, shall we?" She gestures toward the door. Chloe and Chelsea lead the way, and Mom loops her arms through both mine and Sean's. "You boys make me so proud. Thank you for coming here tonight." She quickly kisses us each on the cheek, and we walk to the grand dining room. It's empty except for one table lit with candles in the center of the room. I know that there are at least thirty other 'residents' here, and I can't believe that she arranged for us to have this entire dining room just for us.

"Mom, this is gorgeous!" Chloe exclaims and rushes to the table to find a seat. We all sit around the table as we would at home. Mom at one end and Sean at the other.

Where my asshole father should be sitting.

Chloe and Chelsea sit next to each other as I sit on the other side of the table by myself. The seat next to me is empty and would typically be Sean's, but he has so frequently filled in at the head of the table for Dad that it seems natural to see him in that place now.

Salad and appetizers are quickly served to us and our main course of filet mignon follows soon after. The food is fantastic, just like at a five-star restaurant. I can't help but wonder how much money it costs to recover in a place like this, and I know that as many times as Mom has been here, a small fortune has been spent by my father. *Hell, for all I know, we own the place at this point.*

We don't speak much during our main courses. Small talk, mostly.

When tiramisu is brought out, Mom leans over to me and says, "Seth, I promise that I will get out of here soon so I can be home with your sisters. I want to be present for them. I want to be their mother." She says this quietly, as if she's reading my mind. It's been weighing heavily on me recently, since I'll be leaving for school soon. My brother goes back to school as well, and then he'll be traveling abroad as he prepares for an internship in the family business. Dad is prepping him for big things in the future. He says we're both going to run Tyson Industries someday, but I don't feel like I have it in me to follow in his footsteps. Sean is a bit more ambitious than I am.

"I'm glad you'll be home for the girls, Mom." I wonder how long she'll be able to last before she relapses again. When her depression takes hold, it drags her into a downward spiral that's hard for her to climb out of. She starts to drink and abuse her prescription medication, and then the cycle begins all over again.

Knowing all of this, I try a new tactic. I pull one from Juliet's arsenal. I extend my pinky and wrap it around my mother's.

"Mom, do you promise?" I ask her.

"Promise what, Seth?" she asks curiously.

"Promise me that you'll do your best. Do your best to be yourself. For the girls," I plead.

"Of course, Seth. I promise," she says as she smiles warmly, her eyes filling with tears.

"Pinky swear?" I ask her.

"Pinky swear?" she asks and laughs a little bit.

"Pinky swear," I state, determined to get her to solidify this promise.

Her pinky squeezes mine. "I promise," she says.

I don't know why this encourages me, but it does. I feel something that I haven't in a very long time. I feel as if Mom just made a true commitment to her mental health and sobriety. Even if it was a silly pinky swear.

We spend the next few hours looking at the pictures that Chloe and Chelsea took on their respective phones, reminiscing. We laugh about Sean's graduation and how he tripped onto the stage, knocking our principal over. We laugh about many happy times. I watch as my mother's face seems calm, enjoying this rare, lucid time with all of us.

"Seth, your phone is lighting up. Should I answer it?" Chelsea asks as she begins to reach for the phone. "It's Jason Reed," she states, looking at the caller ID.

"Give it to me," I respond, not wanting one of them to intercept another call from my phone.

I swipe my hand across the screen and place the phone against my ear. "Hey, Jason. What's up?"

He quickly cuts me off with two words, "I'm sorry—" His voice trails off and it sounds like he's crying. What the hell? I get up from the table and walk away so I can hear him better. My heart is pounding.

"Jason, what's going on? You're scaring me, man."

I hear him take a deep breath on the other end of the line, and I'm not prepared for what he says.

"There's been an accident, Seth. It's bad. Really bad." He's now crying into the phone, and I believe him that it's bad.

As he tells me the details of what happened, I stand up and begin to run toward the nearest exit.

"Seth?" Mom calls after me as Sean's phone rings. I hear him say, "It's Kevin Oliver, Juliet's father."

My mother gasps and practically begs, "Somebody please tell me what is happening!"

Somehow I'm able hear the address that Jason gave me and give it to Bob. We quickly drive away, leaving my sisters and Sean at the rehab facility. He calls one of the other chauffeurs who regularly drive my father and directs him to pick up the rest of my family.

Jason's voice is no longer on the other end of the line. My hand is shaking, and I look down and immediately press the speed dial to Jeremy's phone. It rings and rings and eventually goes to voicemail. I hang up and dial it again.

And again.

And again.

I know he won't answer. That he can't answer.

I do the same with Juliet's number and the same thing happens. No answer.

I drop my head into my hands and yell their names over and over as tears stream down my cheeks.

chapter twelve

Juliet
Sausalito, California
Age 16

"WHEN SOMEONE YOU LOVE... dies... there is a strong desire to remember them in a different way. You may forget all of their faults and forgive them for small wrongdoings. You may remember fondly some of the most seemingly insignificant things. Only the most brilliant features of our loved ones make it into the version of them that we keep with us when they depart..."

I close my eyes as the voice coming from the speakers in the church begins to fade. My ears are filled with a soft hum, and soon I'm in another place. Another time.

A time when I was happy, when I was younger. A time when it wasn't hard to exist in my world. A time when Lily's choice didn't haunt me. A time when her letter didn't even *exist*. I was—I AM—a gift to my family. Something they could never achieve on their own.

But I still can't believe that *I'm* a gift.

And unwanted at the same time.

I tense as pain shoots through my body. My broken ribs throb while I take small and painful shallow breaths.

I feel like a curse.

I've doomed so many lives through my own existence. If I hadn't come into the world and lived the life that I have, Jeremy and my mother would still be here.

This is the second time in two days that I've heard similar words in this same church.

We buried my mother yesterday, and today we're here to say goodbye to Jeremy.

We. Buried. My. Mother.

These words seem unreal and implausible. Yet they are so very real.

All of this is very real.

Just a few days ago, she was squeezing me tight as we took our last family picture together. She and my dad were kissing each of my cheeks as Jeremy took the picture. My graduation cap slipped from my head and my mother caught it behind my back.

"Thanks, Mom," I whispered to her when she placed it back on my head.

"I'll *always* be here for you, Jules." She smiled and then said, "I'm so proud of you. You make my heart swell."

I hear that word as I close my eyes again.

Always.

At dinner, my Dad raised his glass to toast our graduation. Jeremy's family raised their glasses next to ours, and although I don't remember his exact words, it ended with, "Don't forget to make a wish, Jules."

My Dad knows me so well. I make a wish every single time we toast.

Every.

Single.

Time.

As Jeremy squeezed my hand under the table, I remember closing my eyes and wishing that I would always feel as happy as I did right at that moment. Something changed during my commencement speech. I felt confident. Confident that I could take control of my emotions and finally put my worry and grief over wondering why Lily gave me up behind me. I had been worrying for years about that damn letter and all of the reasons why it even exists. But at that moment, I was ready to forget that it even existed. Because it didn't matter. What *did* matter were the family and friends who had surrounded me and loved me for as long as I could remember.

But that fucking letter *does* exist. The letter that I hadn't seen again until a few days ago, when my father found it hidden in my mother's closet. He was searching for my mother's final outfit to wear. He gave me the letter without saying a word. I would burn it just to have my mother back. I would do anything to have her back with us.

Alive.

I pull myself out of my memories from a few days ago and realize that I'm here to say goodbye to Jeremy. My best friend. My boyfriend. My first love.

His mother is sobbing uncontrollably in the pew in front of me, and I can't bear to watch her. I hear Jason's soothing voice over her sobs. "It's going to be okay, Mom. Hush."

His father is staring straight ahead at the casket in front of the church. There are flowers draped over it. The arrangements say things like 'Our Son,' and 'Brother' and 'My Love.' I realize that I don't remember ordering anything for Jeremy. Jason must have taken care of everything. He's such a strong person. I don't know how he's coping with all of this grief and sadness. He and Jeremy are—*were*—so close. Although Jason is ten years older than us, he has always been a supportive and a wonderful brother to Jeremy. I don't know how he's going to go on. His baby brother is gone.

Jeremy is gone.

Mom is gone.

Who's next?

The pressure in my chest is unbearable, and I open my mouth to gasp for air. I start to cough and heave, and I suddenly feel like I'm going to throw up. A strong arm wraps around my shoulder and I hear Seth's voice. "I'm sorry, Jules. I'm so sorry…"

My cries drown out his voice and seem to trigger louder wails from Jeremy's mother. I can't catch my breath, and I now feel my father's hand patting my back and rubbing firmly. It hurts everywhere, and his touch makes it worse, but I welcome the pain. I feel myself being slid along the pew, and I suddenly feel a cold towel over the back of my neck. The jolt of coldness snaps me out of my crying jags for the moment, and I hear Chelsea's soft voice say, "Jules, try to drink some water." She takes my hand and guides a cold plastic cup into my hand. "Drink."

I open my eyes and see Seth's sweet sister crouching down on the floor in front of me, squeezed into the pew. She smiles slightly and blinks back tears. "This will make you feel better. It always works when I get upset."

Water drips down my neck, into my dress and down my back, from the cold paper towel she placed there a few moments ago. I nod and take a small sip of water. I feel the water as it paves a cold trail down my throat and into my stomach. I hiccup as my sobs begin to subside.

As I try to calm myself down, I hear rustling coming from the pew in front of me. Jason is standing up and gathering some papers next to him. He kisses his mother and father both on their cheeks and walks to the front of the church.

He pauses briefly, touches his brother's casket and genuflects before approaching the podium. He places his papers in front of him and slowly looks out to the congregation.

Before he begins, he turns to our priest and says quietly, "Thank you, Father Romero, for your kind words about my brother. You've been wonderful these past few days." The priest nods his head and closes his eyes in prayer.

Turning back to us, he says, "God, what are we even doing here?" His calm expression changes to disbelief as he gestures toward Jeremy's casket. Silence seems to take over as we all stare forward. His mother's shoulders start to shake as his father pulls her tight against him.

"We don't belong here today. And neither does—neither does my brother. Two beautiful lives were taken from us, and for the first time ever, I'm at a loss for words." He chuckles nervously and bows his head. I find myself chuckling nervously along with him.

His voice wavers as he speaks.

"Jeremy brought light into our house every single day." He pauses and then folds up the pile of papers in front of him.

"I can't read this; it just doesn't feel right. So let me try to tell you a story. That's what I'm good at." He smiles and looks over to his parents and then to me. Fresh tears roll down my cheeks.

"Our family is one of those that supports you entirely. You can do what you want—be *whom* you want—and my parents would be proud of you no matter what. Jeremy set his sights on sports, and he excelled at every single one. He held more records in baseball than our high school has ever seen. The only sport he ever came in as a close second was track. Seth has him beat by a few seconds." The audience looks toward our pew and Seth shifts uncomfortably in his seat.

"He was a natural athlete, and we're all so proud of how well he could balance that with school, his friends and Jules. As competitive as he was with his sports, he was so curious about the world around him and what made people tick. I remember the day that I told my family that I wanted to be a writer. And then I remember Jeremy's excitement when my first story was published in the San Francisco Times. He was about ten years old, and he was so excited and proud that I was an author. He told everyone about my story, and it was by far his favorite work that I've written." Jason wipes tears from his cheeks and sniffles back more tears.

"What I never told him—" He loses his composure and bows his head while his shoulders shake through tears. "What I never told him was that the story was about him. His light and energy inspired me to write *Soaring*. For those of you who haven't ever read it, it's a short story about a young boy's journey across the country in a hot air balloon. This boy was curious and bright and a risk taker. He found an abandoned hot air balloon on his family's farm and climbed into it, unafraid. The story follows his journey from city to city across the country. We get to experience his joy, fears and escapades as he has a unique adventure in every city. After the story was published, Jeremy read it over and over, trying to picture himself in all of the places in my story. He told me that someday, when he played professional baseball, we would be able to do a cross country trek and visit all of these magical places I'd written about." Jason laughs a little bit and looks up at the crowd. "Then he said that he would take his family on this journey someday. Maybe even take his future wife in a hot air balloon for their honeymoon."

"What ten-year-old is thinking so far into the future that he's imagining his honeymoon with the girl of his dreams?" Seth squeezes my hand and Jason makes eye contact with me.

"My brother was a free spirit and a dreamer." He turns to Jeremy's casket and says quietly, "Goodbye, Jeremy Douglas Reed. You're in the clouds now, buddy. I hope your dreams come true."

Jason slowly steps down from the podium and slides into the pew next to his mother while the congregation stays silent.

Seth chokes back sobs, and I sit there as I stare ahead. I'm calm now. Silent.

I hope your dreams come true.

Jason's words resonate and play back over and over again.

I hope your dreams come true.

What are my dreams? What are my wishes?

I suddenly wish that I were in the clouds, floating away so I can't feel this pain any longer.

chapter thirteen

Seth
Palo Alto, California
Age 18

Dear Juliet,
I hope you've settled into your new place. How's Penn treating you? Do you like Philadelphia?

I slam my finger on the keyboard and delete everything I just typed. This is so unnatural and I'm just lost. Jeremy was supposed to be here with me. He was supposed to be my roommate. I wonder what she must be going through.

I'm terrified to ask her. Petrified to hear the details of the accident that killed him and Juliet's mother. Afraid to ask her to live through the most traumatic moment of her existence that sucked away two people she loved in an instant. *Literally.*

She and I haven't spoken since the funeral. She retreated into what I can only assume is her own Hell. I tried several times to contact her, but she hasn't responded. I miss her. Tons. I miss her words and wish like hell I could help her through her grief. I miss her needing me. Needing my shoulder to cry on. Someone to talk to about Lily.

I miss my best friends. *I miss her.*

Jason told me what he could about the accident, but I couldn't put him through the gory details.

So I Googled it. It made all of the local papers and some of the larger news broadcasts in our area.

It was horrendous. After Jeremy's family left their graduation dinner, Juliet, her parents and Jeremy got into their limousine, and about two miles from her house, a tractor-trailer's brakes failed and broadsided their car at an intersection.

Jeremy was thrown from the car, apparently through the rear window. The reports stated that he died instantly. Mrs. Oliver was seated next to her husband and torn from her seat belt, dying from 'extensive bodily trauma.' How Mr. Oliver was able to walk out of the car is a miracle. Juliet suffered serious, but not life-threatening, injuries and was released from the hospital in time for her mother's and Jeremy's funerals.

I stare at my laptop and minimize the story that I've read at least two dozen times. I can't look at the wrecked vehicle again, but I feel like I *need* to. I need to feel what they went through and try to understand some of their loss and devastation.

I feel lost without them. I need them. I need her.

The door to my dorm room flies open and my roommate, Andy, barrels in. "Hey, Seth..." he slurs and falls onto his bed, laughing. "You missed another great party tonight, duuuuude."

I've been at Stanford for almost two months, and the only times I leave my room is to go to class or track. I can't bring myself to socialize, and watching Andy get hammered at least four nights a week isn't very appealing.

"That's great," I respond to him, and I hear him snoring heavily already.

My computer dings, alerting me that I have a new message. I hesitate as I open my inbox.

It's a note from Juliet, with 'Hey' in the subject line. My heart speeds up as I open it. There is no salutation, just three words.

I miss them.

I blink and the words just seem out of place.

Another ding from my inbox and a new message awaits. This one with nothing in the subject line.

I'm empty.

I quickly respond to the last message.

Me too.

I hit send and wait for her reply.

Nothing.

I stare at the screen and refresh my inbox every two or three minutes until hours have passed.

Still nothing.

※

LOUD RINGING IN MY EARS brings me out of a deep sleep. My alarm clock is buzzing relentlessly, and I turn my head to look at the time. I'm in the same exact position I was in when I last hit refresh on my laptop. I'm sitting up, propped against my headboard with my laptop on my stomach, hand still on the keyboard. It's six in the morning, and I have to get at least a five-mile run in before my sociology class.

I hit refresh another time before I get out of bed, and I see that there is still no response from Jules. I close my laptop and stow it away in my knapsack.

I quickly brush my teeth, swish some Listerine in my mouth and throw on my running clothes and sneakers.

Running will clear my mind. At least that's what I tell myself as I jog outside to the quiet campus. I start my run with a steady trot, Marilyn Manson's "The Beautiful People" blasting in my ears as I pick up my pace and begin sprinting through the streets. I'm used to this pace. I've been kicking up the intensity of my runs all summer. But today, for some reason, I need to run harder. Faster.

I pump my arms higher and lengthen my stride. The burn starts in my quads and my abs tense from the motion of my arms. I'm running faster than I have before, or so it seems. The passing cars are blurred in my peripheral vision as sweat pours down my face.

Something catches my eye ahead, and I stop in my tracks. It's a tractor-trailer, and I begin gasping for breath. It's parked in a lot, not moving, but for some reason I panic as I picture that same truck barreling through Jeremy's car. I bend forward and place my hands on my thighs, trying to stay upright. Behind my closed eyes, I see the mangled car and two bodies lying in the wreckage.

My heart is pounding in my chest, and I lean back onto the building behind me to steady myself. How did Juliet survive that crash? How did her father survive? All I can see is metal bent around more metal, and I realize that their survival was a miracle. Why couldn't Jeremy have survived too? And Jules's mother? *Why weren't they saved?*

I lift my head up and watch the truck slowly pull out of its parking space and into traffic. My panic fades as it safely drives away. I have a sudden urge to call her, just to hear her voice. To be sure she's okay.

I look down at the GPS on my phone and see that I've run a little over seven miles. Shit, I went too far, and now I have to get back. Sociology starts in twenty minutes. I hail the first cab I see and pat my pocket to make sure I grabbed cash before I left. There are a couple of folded bills in the tiny pocket inside my shorts.

I jump in the cab and say, "Wilbur Hall, please."

The driver quickly pulls out into traffic and takes me back to my dorm. I pay him and rush inside to grab my gear for class. I'm a sweaty mess, but I don't have time to shower. Oh well, at least I have practice later, so I'm ready for that.

I open my laptop quickly and hit refresh on my inbox.
Nothing.
Dammit!
Juliet and I need to talk. We need to feel.
I need to feel what she's going through. Something. Anything.

I don't want to be alone with my grief anymore, and I want to absorb all of hers.

chapter fourteen

Juliet
Philadelphia, Pennsylvania
Age 17

Dear Juliet,
Happy Birthday.
Seth

It's been weeks since we last spoke. Our last chat was depressing, and I haven't been able to bring myself to respond to his last message.

How can he know what I'm going through? 'Me too'? That's what he said. Of course he's sad. His best friend died. Well so did mine. And so did my mother.

'Me too' was what he typed.

Is he really empty? He can't possibly feel as empty and alone as I do right now.

My fingernails dig into my palms, and I realize that I'm letting my anger and emotions get the best of me. It's not Seth's fault. My therapist tells me that I'm planted firmly in both the anger and denial stages of grief and loss. She's right. I'm angry about everything. All of the time. She also says that I'm too closed off. I don't let anyone in. She asked me how many friends I've made since I came to Penn. I lied and told her dozens, when it's really only three or four, if I count her. *Why am I like this? Can I get better?*

Seth doesn't deserve my anger. It's not fair.

I hit reply to his birthday message and respond.

Hey Seth,

Thanks. It really means a lot.

Be well,

Juliet

I hit send just as my phone rings. It's my dad. My heart pulls in my chest as I answer, "Hi, Dad."

"Hi, Jules. Happy Birthday, sweetheart," he says, and I know he's trying to make himself sound as cheerful as possible.

"Thanks," I respond quietly and wonder where our conversation is going next. I hesitate and then say, "It's only six in the morning at home. Why are you calling me this early when you could be sleeping?" I sometimes wonder if he remembers that I'm three hours ahead of him in the Eastern time zone.

"I didn't sleep last night. I just couldn't. It's the first birthday of yours that Mom isn't with us." His words tear through my heart without warning. God, I can't do this today.

"Dad, I don't know what to say."

"Make a wish," he answers.

"What?"

"Make a wish while we virtually clink our coffee mugs," he answers.

"But I don't have a coffee mug." And I don't want to make a wish. Ever. Again.

He sighs on the other end of the line, and I know that I'm making this so much worse for him.

"I wish that from now on my birthdays get happier and happier," I say with mild sarcasm, knowing this is never going to be true again.

"You weren't supposed to say your wish out loud, Jules. Now it won't come true," he says with sadness in his voice.

Shit. This is the most depressing birthday conversation ever. He's desperate to pull me through this grief that I can't shake. And maybe he can't either.

"I'm sorry. I just don't know what to do or say today, Dad. I'm lost without them."

He chokes on a sob and says, "I know, honey. So am I."

We're silent for a while and strangely comfortable in that silence.

"Thanks for the birthday wishes," I say. "I promise that I'll try to end the day with a smile." That's a lie, but I don't know what else to say to him to make him feel better.

"Have a good day, Jules. Oh, and Buster says happy birthday too."

I love that crazy old Labrador. "Scratch him behind the ears for me, will you?"

"Of course. Goodbye," Dad says, and we hang up.

My computer dings and there's another message from Seth.

> Jules,
> I'm sure it's going to be a difficult day, but I'm here if you need to talk or anything. I really wish we could celebrate your birthday together, and it's weird that we're on opposite coasts. I don't know about you, but I'm sick of going through my grief alone. Do you ever feel like you need to talk to someone who just understands how you feel? I don't know, maybe it's just me. All of this loss consumes my thoughts, and I don't know what to do or say anymore.
> Well, I'm here. You just need to call.
> Seth

Oh my God. Before I have a chance to respond, my computer dings again.

Shit. I accidentally hit send when I tried to delete all of that depressing stuff. I'm sorry. I don't want to get you even more upset on your birthday.

> So have a happy birthday, okay?
> Seth

I don't know why, but this makes me laugh out loud. Even though he's spewing sadness through the Internet, the fact that he didn't actually mean to send it but accidentally did is very comical to me at the moment.

I quickly hit reply and type a new message.

> Hey,
> No worries. I'll have a happy birthday. Or at least I promise to try.
> Jules

His reply is almost immediate.

> Pinky swear?

These two words warm my heart a little bit. I reply.

> Pinky swear.

The dings from my inbox have stopped, and I decide it's time to get out of bed and face the day. Thankfully, my dorm room is a single, so I don't have to worry about a noisy or nosey roommate. I was supposed to have one, but she backed out at the last minute because she decided to travel Europe this year. I'm happy to be alone, at least for now.

I slip into comfy clothes, pull up my hair into a ponytail and head out to class. As I'm walking through campus, I hear many students talking about trick-or-treating tonight. I can only imagine what that entails on a college campus in downtown Philadelphia.

THE BUSINESS SCHOOL at Penn is anything but easy. My father says that as a Wharton graduate, I'll have the best opportunities ahead of me. I'm studying marketing, but so far my freshman undergraduate classes have nothing to do with my major. Today was a day of electives: biology, sociology and behavioral sciences. I'm exhausted, and all I want to do is sleep.

As I enter Gregory House, I quickly bolt to my room before I'm distracted by the Halloween escapades. My door is littered with notices and invitations to attend at least a dozen parties on campus. A few birthday messages are scrawled on the white board, and one in particular stands out to me. I don't recognize the handwriting.

> Juliet
> Hey - It's your birthday! Cool ;)
> Romeo

Romeo? How original.

I erase the board, along with all of the reminders of what today is.

I walk in and slam the door behind me, tossing my backpack into the corner. My laptop is open on my desk, and I see that my inbox is lit up with messages. I walk past the desk, ignoring all of the happy wishes that await me, and flop onto my bed. I try to feel myself sink into the bed, trying to imagine that I'm floating in the clouds.

With Jeremy.

We had planned so many things to celebrate my seventeenth birthday. I stare at the plane ticket tacked onto the corkboard next to my desk. Jeremy bought it for me the week before graduation as a promise that living on two coasts wouldn't hurt our relationship. I was supposed to be in Palo Alto this weekend. *With him.*

I roll over and reach for my scrapbook, placing it on the bed next to me. I run my hands over the fabric cover, remembering when my mom helped me place each picture in the perfect spot. Photography was practically her job since she spent so much time taking pictures of us and arranging them in collages or albums. I know that she spent countless hours pouring over a year's worth of photos at a time in order to make albums for Lily. Mom stopped sending the albums to her a few years back when the adoption agency said that they were being returned undelivered. I wonder why? Did Lily move, or decide she didn't want to hear about my life anymore? Was she fed up with seeing all of my happy family memories? *Was she jealous?*

Fresh tears threaten to spill out of my eyes, and I'm about to give in to the familiar grief and self-pity when there is a loud bang on my door. As I walk to the door, I hear giggling and realize that trick-or-treating must have begun.

Make that *drunk* trick-or-treating. Outside my door are three girls, reeking of booze and dressed as Hooters waitresses. *Classy.*

"Trick-or-treat!" they yell in unison, shoving shot glasses under my nose. From the smell of it, tequila was their last treat.

"I'm sorry," I say, "but I'm all out." I shrug my shoulders and start to close my door when one of the Hooters girls says, "Don't rain on our parade, birthday girl." The other two giggle and hiccup simultaneously, and I firmly shut my door as one of their shot glasses falls to the floor.

Their voices trail off down the hallway and I hear them leave. I welcome the silence and hope it lasts. Maybe if I go to sleep and pull the covers over my head, I'll be able to drown out all of the students getting drunk and disturbing my peace.

The smell of tequila is still fresh in my nose, and it brings back memories of the first time I got drunk. I was sixteen years old, and the only thing I remember about that night is taking my first shot of tequila behind the Tysons' pool house bar and waking up the next day in the same exact spot. Jeremy and Seth said that after three shots, I starting giggling uncontrollably and quietly curled up on the floor with my head on Jeremy's lap. They kept drinking, got sick and passed out by the pool. I remember waking up with a fluffy pillow under my head, and my body wrapped in a soft fleece blanket.

It's strange how the smell of stale booze can trigger a memory.

I reach for my laptop and begin to filter through dozens of unopened messages. I scroll by some of the spam and see that there are three from my Dad, one each from Chloe and Chelsea and one from Seth. I'm about to open my Dad's first message when there is another knock on my door.

I hold my breath and try to be as quiet as possible, because I refuse to open my door to another drunk co-ed. After a few minutes, I hear nothing, so I turn my attention back to my inbox and open the message from Chloe.

> Jules,
> Happy birthday to you. Happy birthday to you. Happy birthday dear Juliet. Happy birthday to you.
> Hugs,
> Chloe

This message should make me happy, but I can't bring myself to feel any joy from Chloe's well wishes.

It's hard for me to be happy about anything today. *Maybe it's the perfect time to finally read Lily's letter?*

Before I know it, I'm on my feet in front of a small chest on my dresser. It was my mother's, and this is where she hid Lily's letter from me for all those years. My father gave it to me after she died. She never wanted me to read it, but right now I'm drawn to it more than I ever have been.

I walk across the room and bring the letter back to my bed with me, holding it against my chest. My heart beats wildly into the paper, and I can feel it against my sweaty palm.

Another one of my wonderful traits. I wonder if I get it from *her*. My palms sweat profusely when I'm nervous. I lie back on my bed and the envelope rests on my chest. I rub my palms against my pants to dry them off and take a deep breath. While my eyes are closed, I try to picture an older version of myself, what I think Lily might look like. In my pretend vision, she's tall and thin with long dark, wavy hair and dark eyes. Sad eyes.

My breathing begins to slow down along with my heartbeat.

I push myself up on my elbows as I slide to a sitting position, leaning against the cold cinderblock wall behind my bed.

Am I ready to do this? Why should I read this? What do I have to gain? What do I have to lose?

Will it help ease my worries?

I slowly open the top of the envelope and pull out the handwritten letter. I wish Seth were here with me. I just know that he would be able to help me make sense of this. I just want him to be here in case I fall apart.

I raise my knees up, unfold the letter and smooth it out against my thighs. The date on the letter is from years ago, the day that I was born.

I take a deep breath and begin to read.

Dear Juliet,

Hello.

I'm your birth mother, Lily.

I can't believe I'm writing this letter to you. I don't even know what to say.

I hope your new parents wait until you're old enough to give this to you. It's going to be difficult to understand. It's even hard for me to understand.

Let me start off by saying I'm sorry. I'm so very sorry. This could possibly be the worst decision I will ever make, but it's all I can do. There's no other option for me. I'm sixteen years old. Too young to be a mother. I have no

> support from my family, because they don't know about you. My family can't know about you. They wouldn't be able to deal with this. I know that I can't. My parents haven't even been home for the past few months. They've been traveling the world and at the same time they've been grieving.
>
> My twin sister, Layla, killed herself on our sixteenth birthday. We still don't know why. She didn't leave a note, only an empty bottle of my mother's pills. She left a huge hole in our family that a baby certainly can't fill.
>
> And your father, Mason. He's gone and it's all my fault. I can't bring myself to tell you about him. Maybe someday I will, but right now I can't.
>
> If my family knew about you, I don't know what they would think. Would they hate me for my actions? Would they disown me? They wouldn't accept you into our family. Too many questions and doubts for me to consider trying to be a mother at sixteen.
>
> I'm not sure I can survive everything that I've lost. Or if I can heal all of the holes in my own heart. You don't belong with me, and I need you to be someone else's child. Someone another family can love, because I have none to give. To see you every day would remind me of all that I've lost, and I can't handle that.
>
> I hope you understand someday and forgive me.
> Love,
> Lily Todd

My lungs burn for air. I gasp and take a deep breath. Was I holding my breath this whole time while reading her letter?

My heart is once again beating wildly in my chest. What did I just read?

She gave me up because she didn't want her family to hate her? *My grandparents?* She made the choice so she wouldn't be disowned?

Selfish.

That's all I can think.

She couldn't bear to look at me, to be reminded of her life and all that she's lost? Oh my God. My mother was right to not want me to read this letter. I should have *never* read it. And to find out this way that suicide and depression run through my genes is awful.

I let Lily's letter slide from my lap and onto the floor as I pull my knees into my chest. Warm tears slide down my cheeks as anger envelops my body. I wish I'd never seen this fucking letter. I would be better off not knowing any of this.

I close my eyes and try to picture what my father, Mason, would have looked like. Was he tall like me? A faceless teenaged boy comes to life behind my eyelids, walking toward me with his arms stretched out. I shudder and quickly open my eyes.

She didn't say anything but his name. Who is Mason?

As I wonder about my birth father, my anger builds toward the woman who made this decision. She took my past away from me. As irrational as this seems, I want to scream at her and push her away, just like she did to me.

Who are these people? My *other* family? Would they want me if they knew I existed? What about Mason's family? Do I have aunts, uncles, cousins, siblings?

And Lily?

I wonder how much she still hates herself and me. Is she still grieving over the loss of her sister, her boyfriend, her family? Me? Fuck, I don't even care. I hope she's miserable. *Who tells their child these things?*

I look up to the ceiling and say, "Mom, I'm so sorry. You were right, this isn't something I should have ever seen. I'm so sorry I didn't believe you." Tears fall down my cheeks and I fold up the letter.

Without thinking, I open my laptop, type I read the letter and hit send.

Shit.

I wish I could recall this message, because I don't even want Seth to respond to me.

I just needed to tell someone that I finally read it.

And I wish I never had.

chapter fifteen

Seth

Past
Philadelphia, Pennsylvania
Age 19

I READ THE LETTER.

Her words jump off the screen and I'm frozen. I know how long she's been preparing herself to read this letter, and now I'm not there to help her.

Are you okay? I respond afraid of what she'll say.

An immediate response is in my inbox.

No! She was sixteen! Fucking sixteen, and she didn't want me because I would be a reminder of my birth father. She didn't want anyone to know about me. Especially her family. She gave me up because she couldn't look at my face every day and realize what I took away from her. FUCK! Why did I read this letter?

Shit. My heart is breaking for her right now and all I want to do is hold her.

Can you talk?

I need to hear her voice. Maybe hearing mine will calm her down.

We are talking.

Dammit. She's avoiding actual words. Feelings.

What can I do, Jules?

I want to do everything to take away her hurt. Her anger. I hold my breath as I hit send.

Nothing. I'm over it.

I pick up my cell and hit Juliet's speed dial. It rings and rings. Why won't she talk to me? Really talk?

I send another message.

I'm here for you.

I wish she would pick up her phone. I sit and wait for a response, but another email doesn't come. Frustrated, I slam my laptop closed and grab my keys. I've got to get out of here.

Before Andy left tonight, he mentioned he was going to a party at some frat house. He scribbled it down on a piece of paper and left it on my desk, mumbling, "Not that you'll come, but I thought I'd try again. Maybe get out for a change?"

I swipe the paper with the address scrawled on it and leave our room.

THE PARTY IS IN FULL SWING by the time I get there. Students are everywhere and music is blasting out of the windows. "Duuuuude! You came." Andy doesn't hide his shock and shoves a beer into my hands.

"Yeah, I needed to get out tonight. Blow off some steam."

"There's plenty to enjoy here if you want to blow off steam." He laughs and hands me a second beer. Double fisting. Nice. I chug one beer, crushing the cup when I'm finished.

"That's what I'm talking about!" Andy howls. "Beer pong?"

"What the hell. Why not?" I smirk and follow him through the narrow halls and into a room in the back of the house.

"We're up!" Andy says, grabbing a ping pong ball from the floor. Realizing that dirty ping pong ball could soon be in my drink, I down another beer to get myself ready.

We play several rounds of beer pong and I find that I get better the more I drink. Andy is wasted and flirting with every girl who walks in to watch our winning streak.

The opposing team sinks a ball into my cup and I chug another one. "I can't do this anymore, Andy. We've played six straight games and I can barely stand." I laugh as I watch beer come out of his nose.

"Look! Sneer!" He laughs uncontrollably. "Get it? Snot and beer. Sneer."

"That's nasty, man." I grab my cup and walk away from the table. I'm really buzzed. No, I'm really drunk.

I hate to admit it, but I'm having fun for the first time since before graduation. It's been too long. I follow the sound of pounding music into a den turned dance floor. I'm swallowed by the crowd and I start jumping with them. I don't even know what song we're dancing to but I don't care. I close my eyes and feel my heart pump in time with the bass from the song.

I crash into someone and we both almost fall to the ground. I open my eyes and realize that I'm holding a girl close to my chest. "Don't let me go," she yells over the music, "some dude just practically knocked me over and my heel snapped."

I'm pretty sure that dude is me, but I do as she says. I don't let her go. In fact, her wild, curly brown hair pulls me in, and I breathe in her fresh scent. We continue to jump, her on one leg, with the crowd, until we're pushed into the corner.

"Hey," I say, practically shouting. "What's your name?"

Her blue eyes pierce mine as she cranes her neck to look up at me. "Meredith." She smiles and tightens her hold on my arms. "Help me balance for a second." She reaches down and pulls off her shoe, a bright red spiked pump with at least a four-inch heel. She's now standing at about five feet tall and seems tiny compared to me at over six feet.

"I loved these shoes," she pouts, taking the other one off of her foot. "Really loved them."

I smile into her eyes ,and I think I love those shoes too. "Sorry you broke one of them out there. It's a dangerous crowd." I do feel bad that I caused this, but not bad enough to stop holding her.

"You can let me go now," she says.

"What if I don't want to?" I flirt, pulling her against my chest. I slide my hands down to her waist and begin to sway our hips together. She bites her lip, pulling it into her mouth.

"Then don't." She looks up at me and smiles. We're moving together slowly, our bodies pressing against each other, completely out of time with the music that has others dancing wildly. She wraps her arms around my back and I feel her chest pressing into me.

"Let's go someplace more... quiet," I say, brushing my lips over her ear. She shivers in my arms and nods against my chest.

I let go of her and grab her hand, pulling her through the crowd of dancing bodies. Once we're outside, she squeals. "I'm not wearing any shoes and the ground is freezing!"

I turn my back to her and bend down. "Hop on," I suggest. She jumps onto my back, wrapping her legs around my waist and her arms around my neck. I feel her warm breath tickle the side of my neck as she rests her chin on my shoulder.

"Where are we going... Wait, I don't even know your name," she says, not sounding concerned one bit.

"Seth Tyson. Nice to meet you, Meredith."

"It's Meredith Newman. And the pleasure is all mine." I feel her lips softly brush the side of my neck and I pick up speed.

"If you keep doing that, *Meredith*, we won't get anywhere." I can't believe I have a chick on my back, ready to go anywhere with me.

"You mean this." Her voice lowers, and she nibbles my neck before softly taking my earlobe between her teeth. She's being aggressive, but I like it. I need to get her alone.

I look for someplace to put her down, and I see a picnic table. I slide her around so she's in front of me, her legs still wrapped around me. I place my hand in her mess of wild hair and pull her lips to mine, devouring them. I'm still walking with her hanging from me. I bring her toward the table and place her on top, kneeling down on the bench. Our lips are still connected and her tongue plunges into my mouth. *Damn. This girl is so freaking hot.*

Her breathing picks up and she moans into my mouth. She removes her hands from behind my head, and they fall to my waist. She pulls me forward, pulling me by my belt loops, and I'm pressed between her legs. I'm holding her with one arm and the other hand slides down her neck to her breast. I kiss her harder as I run my fingers over her nipple, teasing her through her clothes.

She throws her head back breaking our kiss. "Seth, can we go to your room?" she begs, pulling my face to hers and kissing me again. I'm rock hard right now, and I'll say yes to anything just to get relief from what's building inside of me. But I know Andy could come back at any time.

"Shit, Meredith. My roommate will be home soon. We won't have any privacy." My mind scrambles to think where I can take her for us to be fully alone. I thrust against her, seeking relief, and she squeezes her legs around my waist. My lips take hers again, and we frantically make out like two desperate kids. Her hands move under my shirt as her fingernails scrape against my abs. She reaches into my jeans and I groan into her mouth. As her fingers graze the base of my cock, I almost lose it. "Slow down. We can't do this here." *How can I be the voice of reason? I'm about to explode.*

"I want you," she says, nibbling a trail down my neck.

"God," I say, almost incoherently, as she wraps her hand around my length and begins to pump up and down inside my jeans. "You need to stop," I barely get out through breaths. "Stop before I finish," I beg her, but she doesn't stop. She leans back and pulls her bottom lip into her mouth again while her eyes light up with passion. *She's enjoying this torture.*

"Then finish," she says as she pumps faster and faster until I explode all over her hand and wrist inside my pants. I slump forward pressing my hands on either side of her hips on the table.

That was... sudden... unexpected. Incredible. I can't believe I just got a hand job in the middle of campus.

"Wow." I gasp and claim her mouth again. I realize she needs to clean up and my pants must be a mess. "Let's go clean up, and then I can focus on you," I suggest. "Can we go to your place?" I'm worried about running into Andy.

"No, I don't live on campus. It would take forever to get there." She pouts a little and I frown.

"I'm patient, but clearly you're not," I tease, and she pushes my chest playfully. "I want you to feel... good." I smile at her and she nods.

"I'm a little sticky. Can we go back to the frat house so I can wash up?"

I guess that's the best solution for the moment. Not the nicest bathrooms, but I don't care. "Yeah, let's hurry though. I want to get you alone." She's still barefoot and demands a ride on my back.

"Your chariot awaits." I smile and turn to let her hop onto my back again. I practically sprint across the lawn, back to the party. It's been a while since I've wanted something—someone—this much. This isn't my first hookup since I came here, but it certainly is the best so far.

She jumps down when we get to the door, stands on her tip toes and kisses me softly. "I'll be right out." Her smile is huge, and I notice how the light shines on her skin. She's gorgeous. Full, plump lips, olive complexion that's red from my stubble, bright, electric-blue eyes that seem mischievous and innocent at the same time. I need to get her alone. Alone and naked.

"Hurry," I say as she turns and rushes into the house. I watch as she's swallowed up by the crowd through the doorway. Once I lose sight of her, I turn to look out toward campus and see the picnic table off in the distance. What the hell just happened out there? *Holy shit.* I laugh out loud and immediately wonder what Jeremy would think of this. Would he high-five me? Pat me on the back? Fist bump? *Yeah, probably.* I laugh again and pull out my cell phone. She's been in there for at least ten minutes. What's taking her so long?

I walk toward the door and realize if I go inside, I'll get lost in the crowd and we may miss each other. So I sit on the porch steps. And wait.

And wait.

And wait.

Fifteen minutes turns into thirty. *This is ridiculous.* I stand up and go through the door. The party has cleared out considerably. I can see the bathroom at the far end of the main hallway and I walk up to the door. It's open slightly. I push it open and don't find anyone in there. *Where is she?*

I back out of the bathroom and scan the room, trying to locate her. She's nowhere in sight. I walk through the main room, into the back where we played beer pong earlier. *Not here either.*

Shit. Did she take off?

I clench my fists at my side in anger. She took off. Ditched me.

The walk across campus back to my dorm is long. When I pass the picnic table where we hooked up, I pick up speed.

What the hell was I thinking?

She wanted a quick hookup and she's done with me. But she gave me all of the signals. I thought for sure she wanted me. We weren't finished.

I break into a run toward Wilbur Hall, and I'm panting once I get there. The beer that I chugged for hours tonight churns in my stomach as it fights its way up. I lean over and start to wretch. Dry heave. Nothing is coming up, but I desperately want it to. "Ah," I moan, placing my hands onto my legs, bracing for what should be coming any second. I dry heave some more and feel like ass.

Once the nausea passes, I slide my key card over the door and enter the dorm. It's dark and quiet in the hallway, and I take the stairs to the fourth floor, grabbing my stomach when I reach the top. *Crap.*

I drank way too much tonight. I have someplace to be tomorrow, and it's going to hurt to get up early. Someplace that I've been dreading going to, but I finally agreed it's what's best.

I kick off my jeans and drop onto my bed, feeling sleep come quickly.

૭౿

MY HEAD IS POUNDING. The gallon of water that I drank and the three Advils aren't working yet. And it's very bright outside. I slide my sunglasses on to help ease the pain from the sun as it tries to burn holes through my skull.

I'm hungover. Big time.

I walk through campus toward downtown. My mind is racing, thinking about what I'm about to face for the first time. It's something my brother has been begging me to do for years, and I'm finally doing it. I stop when I reach the community center. I take my shades off and enter the building, looking for signs pointing to my destination.

Al-Anon.

Sean swears that these meetings will help me deal with my mother's depression and addiction. He even says that our father has an addiction as well, to other women. Al-Anon helped Sean cope with the ailments that plague our family. I don't know why I picked today to start, but I'm committed, even though I'm very hungover.

I walk into the meeting room as dozens of people are assembling. A woman is at the podium in front of the room and says soothingly, "Welcome, friends, old and new." I take a seat in the back, trying not to be seen.

She continues.

"I see many new faces today and that makes me smile. To all of you who are here for the first time, please listen carefully to what I have to say. First, we are here to support each other, not judge. Ever. We all have stories to share and we can share them as equals. I'm not here to judge or give you advice, and neither are your peers. We are all experiencing the same things from one degree to another. So please, ask questions or just feel free to listen. You don't have to share, but we hope you feel comfortable enough to do so. And please keep coming back. I promise you that you'll learn and feel different things each time you do. The most important thing to know is you're safe here. Al-Anon stands by its core belief, we are all anonymous. By being here, you vow to respect our confidentiality pledge." She pauses to look around the room, making eye contact with almost everyone. Her eyes linger on mine briefly and spread warmth through the room.

She steps away from the podium and joins the group. "I don't know why they set these chairs up theatre style, but let's make this more comfortable, shall we?" She grabs one of the chairs and says, "Please move your chairs into a circle. We can make it as large as we want, but it should be a circle." We all grab our chairs and form an oval in the meeting space.

"That's better. Now, would anyone like to share?"

I hear a soft voice from my right. "Yes." I don't want to lean forward and stare, but the voice is so familiar. She's about six people away from me, I think.

"Hi, I'm Meredith N., and my mother is a raging alcoholic. I don't know how to deal with her illness, and I'm worried it's going to take hold of me and not let go."

"Hi, Meredith," everyone responds in unison.

Holy shit.

I sit back so I'm not in her line of vision. She sniffles and continues, "My mother has been drinking for as long as I can remember. I never used to think anything of it, because it seemed so normal for her. For our family. A bottle of wine with dinner. Two after. A bloody Mary for breakfast. I could go on, but you get the idea." I see her hands shaking in her lap, and my heart goes out to her. Even if she did blow me off last night.

"I hate this feeling. I can't describe it. I'm afraid I'm going to go down the same path as her."

"You feel powerless," a man across the room says. "Powerless from the black hole that this disease pulls you and your family into. Hi, I'm Geoffrey. My wife is an alcoholic."

"I don't have anything else to say," Meredith says softly.

The moderator says, "Thank you, Meredith. We hear you and understand exactly how you feel. Thank you for sharing." I hear Meredith exhale and her hands stop shaking.

There are dozens more 'true confessions' from the various members of the group, and I sink into my chair. I don't want to share. I'm not ready to tell these strangers all about my dysfunctional family. It's private, for now. But listening to them makes me realize that I'm not the only one living in Hell with the illness that my mother's been hiding. My heart breaks for each of these people, because I could be any one of them.

At the close of the meeting, the moderator reads the Serenity Prayer while some members recite it along with her.

I hesitate, standing up when it's over. I don't want Meredith to see me.

"Thank you all for sharing, and we'll see you next week." I stand up, grabbing my chair to put it against the wall.

"Oh my God," I hear from behind me. *Meredith.*

I turn to face her.

"Are you following me? How did you find me?" She's accusing and upset.

"What? Following you?" I'm dumbfounded. How could she even think that, considering she ran out on me last night?

"Yes, following me. What the hell, Seth?" I push the chair against the wall and notice there are several members staring at us. I turn and leave the meeting room and hear the clicking of her heels behind me. "Where are you going?"

Once outside, I turn to face her. "What the hell do you care? You ditched me last night, remember? It shouldn't bother you if I walk away from you, should it?" Her face turns bright red and she narrows her eyes.

"Why the fuck did you follow me here? And how did you even know where to find me?"

I laugh. "I came here on my own. My mom's an alcoholic and addicted to pills. There, I said it." I toss my arms out to my sides. Saying that seemed to release a knot in my chest and I say it again, more loudly this time. "I'm the son of a drug addict and alcoholic and a sex addict!" I throw that last part in for good measure.

Her eyes widen and her face softens. "I'm sorry," she stammers. "I thought—"

I cut her off. "You didn't think, Meredith. You just assumed. Just like I assumed you'd be right out last night after going to clean up in the bathroom. But no, you blew me off. Thanks for that. Later."

I turn and walk away. That was a shitty thing to say to her after she bared her soul in the meeting, but I'm pissed.

"You're right!" she calls after me, and I hear the click of her heels again on the sidewalk. I walk faster and the clicking speeds up. "Will you wait a minute?" she yells, panting. I stop and face her.

"What?"

Her face is flushed and she looks down at her feet. "I'm not wearing sensible shoes."

"Not my problem. And I'm not carrying you on my back." I turn and walk toward campus.

"Seth, please?" she begs, causing me to stop and turn back to face her again.

"What do you want from me that you didn't get last night?" Another snipe, but I can't help it.

"Can we get coffee?" she asks.

"I don't drink coffee."

Her eyes start to glisten, and she looks as if she's about to cry. *Dammit.*

"Fine. Starbucks is across the street. Are you coming?" I say to her as I cross the street.

We walk in silence into Starbucks. She orders a grande coffee and I just get a bottle of water.

She sits down at a table in the corner and I sit across from her. "I need to explain."

"I'm all ears. Explain away." I lean back in the chair, crossing my arms over my chest.

"I'm impulsive. Very impulsive. I saw you last night and decided immediately that I wanted you." She blushes and swirls her coffee cup. "As soon as we finished, I regretted what happened and had to get out of there fast."

"Wow, you're making me feel so much better," I say sarcastically.

"No, you don't understand."

"What's there to understand? We hooked up. You ditched me. You blame it on your uncontrollable impulses. Is that all?"

She sinks into her chair, almost cowering. "That's all. But I need you to know that I didn't mean to lead you on or cause any trouble. I just couldn't help myself, and I'm sorry. I shouldn't have run out on you, but I didn't know how to explain it to you. You were drunk, and I didn't know how you'd react."

"You weren't drunk last night? Because it sure seemed..."

"No! I don't drink, Seth. My mom's a raging alcoholic, remember?" she says sternly.

"Oh, so you were trying to take advantage of me?" I smirk and take a sip of my water.

"No. It's not like that. I just needed to feel the thrill of it. Feel the intensity. I never know how far I'm going to take it, and I know someday it's going to get me into serious trouble. If you weren't a nice guy, I don't know what would have happened." Her hands are trembling, and I know she's telling me the truth.

"I don't know what to say." I reach out and place my hands over hers.

She pulls her hands away and places them under the table. Her eyes are darting all over the room, and she looks like she wants to be anywhere but here.

"I would never have done anything last night. You know, if you'd turned me down to my face. I'm not like that, Meredith. But I can't say that about every guy that you're *impulsive* with." Our eyes lock, and the brightness and fire that I saw last night is gone. She nods and grabs her coffee.

"Thanks for letting me explain. I need to go." She gets up and quickly walks out to the sidewalk.

Geez. What is with her? She's opening up, and now I have to chase her?

"Meredith, wait," I call out as I catch up to her. "You can't just drop that on me and walk away. Isn't there a twelve-step thing we need to go through?" I joke and she's not amused.

"Seth, don't poke fun at the disease that my family has. That *our* families have. Don't you get it?" She leans against the side of the building and tosses her coffee cup into the trash can.

"What's there to get? Your issues with your mother's alcoholism are making you overly aggressive. You need to stop before you get hurt."

She pushes my chest angrily.

"What the hell?"

"What about you, Seth? We aren't supposed to judge, and you just did. What about your mother? How is she affecting your life? You were clearly wasted last night. Have you thought about why you were drinking? Do you want to turn into the addict that your mother is?" Her words are angry and harsh.

And honest.

"Well? The gloves are off. Let's do this," she says, and I expect to see her in a boxing stance, but when I look up, her arms are crossed over her chest and she has tears rolling down her cheeks.

"Hey," I say, reaching out to brush them from her face. She flinches and backs away.

"Don't touch me," she demands, and I immediately drop my arms to my sides.

"I'm sorry, Meredith. I don't know what to say. I have no defense, no excuse for why I drank last night. I don't typically binge and haven't since high school. I don't want to be like my mother. I have it under control."

She laughs and says, "Yeah, just like I do. I certainly couldn't control myself last night, and look what happened."

"That was different. It was sex. Well, almost sex," I say, and she glares at me.

"It's my addiction, Seth. My compulsion. I wasn't thinking and I acted irresponsibly. Just like you did by drinking. Don't you see?"

I guess I do see the parallels in what she's trying to tell me.

"I'm sorry," I say again.

Her shoulders fall and she exhales. "Walk me home?" she asks. "We don't need to talk anymore." I fall in stride next to her and we head toward campus.

"I thought you lived far from here."

"I lied," she responds, and I try not to judge. I need to remember what the meeting leader stressed. *No judgment.*

We walk in silence through campus. I'm following her lead, since I have no idea where she lives. I'm surprised to be standing in front of Wilbur Hall.

"This is my stop," I say, and she doesn't move.

"Mine too."

"Is there anything else you want to tell me?" I ask her incredulously.

"I'm on the third floor?" She smiles and the brightness is back in her eyes.

"I'm on the fourth. So, how long have you been in this building?" I ask. I can't believe we haven't run into each other before.

"Since the beginning of the semester."

"Oh." I don't know what else to say.

"Will you come with me to another meeting next week?" she asks hesitantly.

"Why would you want me there? Wasn't today a bit... awkward?"

"I think it will be good for you. And me. Not us together, but separately." She carefully words this so I know that there's no *us*.

"I'll think about it. I don't know if I'm ready to pour out my heart and all of my family secrets to strangers."

"That's what it's all about, Seth. You heard the meeting leader. She said you're free to come and go and not participate if you're not ready. Please think about it." She practically begs me, which I find unusual, considering we were at each other's throats twenty minutes ago.

"Okay, I'll do it. But on one condition."

She smiles and looks relieved. "What?"

"You control your impulses around me. At least try to keep your hands off of me for one or two meetings." I smile jokingly but her face turns sour.

"Not funny, Seth."

"Sorry. Okay, I'll do it." I turn and walk toward the dorm. I hold the door open, waiting for her to walk through. "Taking the stairs?" I ask as I begin to head up to my room.

"Not in these heels. See you next week." She turns and walks toward the elevators.

I watch her walk away, and I shake my head.

As I jog up the stairs, I remember last night and her soft hand wrapped around my... "Stop, Seth," I say to myself.

This can't go anywhere.

We're both too messed up.

chapter sixteen

Juliet

Past
Philadelphia, Pennsylvania
Age 17

"CHEERS!" HOLLY SAYS as we clink our lemonades together. "Happy belated birthday."

"Wait, I have something for that." Summer takes a small bottle from her purse and pours it into our glasses. "You can't drink lemonade without vodka!" she exclaims.

Holly and Summer live on my floor and are roommates. I've been friends with them since freshman week, and they happen to be my very first girlfriends. They knew I didn't want to celebrate my birthday a few weeks ago, so they planned this outing to celebrate after the fact. They convinced themselves that I needed to have fun, and now they're trying to fulfill that wish. They're sweet, and it's nice to have them in my life, but drinking spiked lemonade at Applebee's isn't exactly my idea of a fun time.

I close my eyes and hear my mother's voice in my head. *Make a wish.* Her voice is clear as day, and I open my eyes to see Holly and Summer looking at me funny.

"Are you okay?" Holly asks as she sucks down half of her drink.

"Yeah, I'm okay. Just remembering something." I take a sip of my drink and wince. "Holy shit, how much vodka did you put in this?"

They giggle together and Summer responds, "Oops."

"Can I get you ladies some appetizers?" I look up and see a different server than before. He looks familiar.

"Ryan! Since when do you work here?" Holly asks, acting strange.

"I've been here for a few months, since the beginning of school. Sorry, I asked to take over your table from my friend. She didn't mind swapping." He winks at me, and I can't place where I know him from.

"Ryan?" I ask, trying to remember.

"Yes, but some people call me Romeo." He smiles from ear to ear and asks again, "Appetizers?"

"Way to be subtle, Ryan." Summer sneers at him, and there is definitely something going on that I'm not privy to. Romeo? *Oh, wait.* Someone named Romeo wrote on my white board on my birthday. *Could it be him?*

"Do I know—" I'm interrupted by Summer ordering mozzarella sticks, boneless wings and potato skins.

"I'll get this in for you right away." Ryan turns and leaves the table.

Their giggles are obvious and annoying. "What was that about?" I ask.

"Ryan O'Malley totally likes you. Duh!" Holly retorts.

"What? I don't even *know* him. How can he *like* me?" We sound like high schoolers.

"He knows you. He lives on the second floor in our dorm and is always hanging around in our lounge. I bet it's so he can see you. Oh, and he's also in our lit class."

I never noticed him in lit, maybe because there are tons of people in that class.

"Whatever. I have to pee." I leave the table and go to the bathroom. On the way back, I decide that I need a fresh lemonade—one that isn't polluted with booze. I stop at the bar and try to get the bartender's attention. She's frantically mixing drinks at the other end of the bar, so I sit on a stool to wait.

That's when I notice the group of people next to me, holding their wine glasses in the air. Three girls and a guy.

"Cheers! To Wine Wednesday!" the guy says, and they all take healthy sips of their red wine.

"You guys are the greatest," the blonde girl says. "What a nice surprise. I can't believe that you all came to visit me in Philly while I'm here. Carly, I know it was a hike for you from the Shore, but Manny and Becca, you guys coming from New York is crazy! But I love you."

"Hey, we always need a reason to come to an Applebee's in the city," Manny sneers. I snort at the same time and he turns to me. "Am I right?" he asks. "I mean, we came to see Callie here in Philly, and I was hoping for a nice wine bar. But this is where we meet. Really."

"It's not exactly a wine bar, but they have good lemonade," I respond, feeling a little silly. I raise my hand so the bartender can see me, but she still doesn't.

Manny turns back to his friends and one of the girls responds, "Hey, next time we surprise you in the city, we'll be sure to hit a wine bar. But for now, this was our best choice since the convention hall is right across the street."

"Carly, where's Kyle today?"

The girl with the dark hair looks sad but responds, "Home with the flu. He wanted to come so badly, but he hasn't been able to get out of bed for three days."

Manny responds, "It must be tough to be in bed with *Kyle* for three whole days." Everyone laughs and Carly blushes.

"We're sharing a room tonight; you better not be contagious!" the girl—I think her name is Becca—responds.

"Guys, it's so great to see you. I love you so much," Callie says, choking back tears. "I hope when we're old and gray we still celebrate Wine Wednesday together." They clink their glasses again, and I finally get the bartender's attention.

"Can I help you?" she asks.

"Yes, can I have a lemonade? The one that I have at my table has... a bug in it," I lie.

"Ew. Your meal should be free, then," Manny says, clearly overhearing my lie. "How about a glass of wine?" he asks.

"Oh. No. Thank you though. Enjoy." I grab my fresh glass of lemonade and stop beside the group. "It's nice to see close friends having fun together. Cheers." I raise my drink and they toast again.

As I walk back to the table, I see Ryan. Trying to avoid him, I duck through the back of the bar around the bar tables. "Hey! Juliet."

"Oh, hey."

"Did you need another drink? Because I could have gotten that for you. You didn't have to go to the bar to get it. It makes me look like a bad server."

"Sorry, I just went to the bathroom and then thought I wanted another lemonade. So... yeah." *What the hell am I saying?*

"About before. Sorry, I didn't mean to be overly flirty," he says, looking embarrassed.

"Romeo?" I smile, trying to make him feel better.

"It just seemed appropriate. You know. You're Juliet, and..." He's stammering now and I feel bad.

"Hey, it's no big deal. It happens all the time." The lies are flowing so easily today, I should be alarmed.

"So, when I'm not being completely awkward and dorky, would you want to go out with me? Maybe to dinner or a movie?"

He's asking me out? My heart is racing, and I'm suddenly afraid that I'm doing something wrong by talking to him. I have—*had*—a boyfriend.

"I don't think that's a good idea," I respond and push past him.

I slide back into the booth and Holly and Summer are glaring at me. "Where have you been?"

"I stopped at the bar to get a new lemonade. This one is just disgusting."

Summer swipes it from in front of me and says, "More for me, then."

"Who were you talking to at the bar?" Holly asks.

"Oh." I look over and see the four friends toasting again. "I don't know. They were just celebrating."

"Celebrating what?" Summer asks.

"Their friendship, I guess?" I respond and grab the last mozzarella stick from the plate. I guess I was gone for a while since most of the appetizers have been eaten by the girls.

"That's nice," Holly smiles. "We should be doing the same thing. Celebrating. You haven't even acknowledged your birthday, Jules. Let's celebrate, okay?"

"You guys, my birthday isn't something that's fun for me to celebrate. And it was weeks ago."

Their expressions turn to concern just as Ryan comes back to our table.

"Would you like anything else?" he asks stiffly.

"Jules? Would *you* like something else?" Holly asks.

"Maybe a phone number?" Summer chimes in.

I shake my head.

"Check, then?" Ryan quickly responds.

"Yes, please," I answer.

Ryan quickly walks away and is back with the check within seconds. "Have a nice day." Then he's gone.

"What in the hell was that?" Holly asks. "He was all flirty with you not even twenty minutes ago, and now he looks afraid of you? What happened?"

"He asked me out. I said no. Maybe his feelings are hurt?"

Their heads move from side to side, and I know that they're judging me now. How could I possibly say no to Ryan O'Malley, the perfect specimen of a man, who I didn't even know until today?

"What is it about your birthday that makes you so miserable?" Holly asks.

"Because it reminds me of a girl who decided her life would be better if I didn't exist. I was given up for adoption on my birthday. So it's not an easy day for me, especially when my mom is dead and my dad is on the West Coast." I blurt it all out, and I didn't mean to share any of this with them.

"Oh no. I'm so sorry, Jules. We didn't... We wouldn't have made such a big deal about things if we knew. I mean. Wait. It's not bad that you're adopted. That's great." Summer's mouth seems to be working faster than her brain.

"Forget it. I didn't mean to bum you out. It's just not an easy day for me. I don't like to talk about it." I grab the spiked lemonade back from Summer and start to drink it quickly. They're both silent as I finish the entire glass. "There was a lot of vodka in that," I state matter-of-factly.

"Yeah," Holly says and places her hand over mine. "Are you okay? Can we do anything to help?"

"You know, just being out of my room, away from everything, helps. So thank you." I watch as the four friends get up to leave the bar. They're all hugging and laughing. I'm jealous of what they have and want that for myself. They seem like their friendship will last a lifetime. I wish that Jeremy and Seth were here with me. Now. Seeing these life-long friends makes me realize all that I'm missing. And all that I'll never have again.

I look across the table at Holly and Summer and say, "Thank you both for trying to cheer me up. It means a lot. Really. But let's slow it down on fixing me up with anyone, okay? I'm definitely not ready for that yet."

"Okay, but why? Did something bad happen to you?" Holly asks.

Yes, something very bad. I lost two people this year, and it's still hurts like it happened yesterday.

"My boyfriend died right after graduation. In the same accident that killed my mom. So yeah, it's been a hard year." It feels good to tell someone else, but watching their faces turn to shocked awe isn't fun.

"Oh my God," they say in unison.

"We had no idea," Holly says.

"No, of course you didn't. I don't tell anyone my sad stories. But I'm good. So let's pay this bill and get out of here, okay?"

The rest of the night, Holly and Summer handle me with kid gloves, almost afraid to say anything that would cause me to be sad. The vodka helps clear my mind, if only for a little while.

I press my key into the lock in my door. "Goodnight girls. Thanks for a good time." Their faces change from smiles to frowns, and they both grab me and hug me tight.

"Happy belated birthday, Jules," Holly says as I push my door open.

I fall onto my bed and the plane ticket from Jeremy catches my eye. I never used this ticket to go home. My father wished I was there with him to celebrate my birthday, but instead I stayed here. *Can I continue to feel sorry for myself? Am I being selfish?*

I want them back. I want my mom and Jeremy back right now. If I could do anything to have them back here, alive, I would do it in a heartbeat.

There's a soft knock on my door, and I get up to answer it.

"Juliet." Ryan is standing in the hall and he looks concerned. "You're crying," he says and reaches for my cheek. Startled, I back away as I feel warm tears on my cheeks.

"No. I'm not," I lie.

"But you are," he says and steps into my room.

"Ryan. Or Romeo. Or whatever your name is. I'm not crying. Please go away." I turn to hide my face from him, embarrassed that I'm a mess.

"I'm not leaving until I know that you're okay. And after I apologize."

"What?" I ask.

My door shuts, and he's obviously in my room. *Shit.*

I turn around and wipe my cheeks with my sleeves. "See? I'm not crying." My hands are balled up into fists inside my sleeves.

"Listen, I'm really sorry about tonight. I didn't mean to be pushy or forward or whatever. I thought I'd ask you out and got really bummed when you said no. I promise I won't bother you again. I just had to apologize because you seemed so uncomfortable. And I feel bad that I made you feel that way. Does that make any sense?"

"You came here to apologize because I said no to your date?" I'm confused. But I'm also a little drunk, so that doesn't help the situation.

"Yes... I mean, no. I'm just sorry that I freaked you out at the restaurant." He hangs his head and puts his hands into his pockets.

"It's not a big deal, Ryan. It's just been a shitty couple of... months. I haven't been myself, and I'm sorry I took it out on you. No offense or anything. You seem like a nice guy. I just can't date right now." I'm standing awkwardly across from him as he backs away toward the door.

"Friends?" he asks, and I look up into his eyes.

"Sure," I respond.

He turns and opens the door. "I'm really sorry about tonight. And I promise I won't ask you out again. See you in lit tomorrow."

"Bye," I say as the door closes behind him.

Tears flow again for no reason, and I take the plane ticket to the closet where I keep my mother's chest. I tear it open and throw the ticket in on top of Lily's letter. Having these two pieces of paper touch sends chills down my spine, as if time has morphed and two souls are merging somehow. I shiver and slam the chest closed. I can't keep these things around that cause me to remember all of the pain of losing Jeremy and my mom. I don't want reminders of not being wanted by my birth mother.

I storm over to my bed and grab my laptop.

I want to burn it. I want to burn everything that reminds me of them and all of the pain.

I hit send.

Shit.

I haven't talked to Seth in a few weeks, and this isn't the best way to start up a chat again.

I refresh my inbox a few times, but no response.

I drift off to sleep, hearing my mother's voice.

Make a wish.

chapter seventeen

Seth

Past
Palo Alto, California
Age 21

Two Years Later

"WAKE UP, SETH." Her voice fills my head and I smile.

"No. You come here." I reach out, pulling her against my body.

"It's ten o'clock. We're going to be late."

Shit.

I open my eyes and Meredith is smiling ear to ear. "I can't wait to meet your family today."

I can't believe it's been almost two years, and we haven't brought each other home to meet our respective families. Granted, our relationship started out at a snail's pace. Well, *after* the 'Hand Job Incident' as we both affectionately refer to it. At her suggestion, we started going to Al-Anon together, and then we started going *together*. We haven't attended a meeting in almost six months, because I think we've both gotten out of them what we needed. For now.

And we did have some rough patches during the past few months, as she's been struggling with her impulse issues. But we're better now, I think. I hope.

"I can't wait either." My mom's been home for a long time and hasn't relapsed that I know of. My sisters can't wait to meet Meredith, since I finally told them about her a few months ago. I haven't shared much information with anyone in my family about any relationships that I've had in the past, mostly because they were just hookups. I don't know if my father will be there. My stomach clenches at the thought of it. But I'll deal with that if I need to. Sean is in Europe, working.

"Can we be a little late?" I kiss her neck and nip at her collarbone, knowing exactly what makes her melt.

"No! I don't want to start off on the wrong foot with your family." She slaps my hands away from her waist and reluctantly pulls away from my body.

She gets in the shower and says, "If this goes well and your family falls in love with me, we should think about moving in together. What do you think?"

I don't answer her right away as I power up my laptop. "Hey, did you hear me?" she calls from the bathroom.

"I heard you." I smirk. "Just leaving you hanging. I need to think long and hard about that." I laugh, knowing that I was going to suggest it as soon as our junior year finished. I rent the apartment that I'm in now, but I've been looking for bigger places further off campus to purchase. I would love to start senior year with Meredith in my bed every single night.

"Don't think too long, Seth." I hear her smile through her voice as I open my email.

There's a note from Juliet. "Tell Jules I said hello!" Meredith calls from the shower. She knows that every time I open my laptop, I'm talking to Jules.

Although they've never met, they've spent countless hours chatting about everything from shoes to traveling. At this point, Meredith knows more about Juliet's private life than I do. She knows all about Ryan, Juliet's boyfriend. Jules tells her things she doesn't want to tell me, and that's fine. I still can't picture her with anyone else but Jeremy. According to what she's told Meredith, she and

Ryan started out slow and progressed to the relationship they have now. Jules was fairly guarded, afraid to give her heart so someone else. They've had their ups and downs over the past few years, but according to Meredith, they're in a good spot now.

> *Seth! (and Meredith)*
>
> *I have news. BIG news. I'm going to study abroad for the next two semesters. LONDON! I'm so excited. Ryan and I were both accepted into an intern program with McKinsey. THE McKinsey. It's an exclusive program, and we're almost guaranteed to be offered jobs when the program ends. So my senior year will be in London. OMG! Right?*
>
> *Anyway, hopefully I'll see you before I leave. I'm not sure if I'm coming home this summer, because I have so much to do to get ready. Maybe I'll be back for a weekend. If I am, we need to get together. And I can finally meet Meredith IN PERSON. Ryan is dying to meet you guys, too.*
>
> *Okay, gotta go. I wanted you to be the first to know! I haven't told my father yet. I'm sure he'll be good with it, but... Well, you know how he is. It's hard for him that I'm on the East Coast. London will be a whole different story.*
>
> *Be in touch!*
>
> *XXOO*
>
> *Juliet*

I lean back in my desk chair and wipe my hand over my face. In all of the years that I've known Juliet, I have *never* received a letter like this. Positive. Uplifting. Completely happy. Of course, she does worry about her father a lot and hopes that he can find happiness, but she seems to have finally found it. This is all I've ever wanted for her. Ryan must be a hugely positive influence on her, and while I'm happy for her, I'm also jealous. I wish I could have been able to do this for her.

"Everything okay?" Meredith asks, wrapped in a towel in front of me.

I shake my head in disbelief. "Yes. Everything is great. Jules sounds so happy. She's going to London next year to intern for her dream company."

"She got the McKinsey internship?" she asks excitedly. *How does she know about McKinsey?*

"Yes, and how do you know about that?" I ask, curious.

"She told me about the application process and how tough it was. I thought I told you." She smiles and grabs her clothes from her overnight bag. "I'm just glad that she finally seems happy with everything. And happy with Ryan. She's had a rough few years, as you know."

I guess I'm happy about this, but I'm curious about Meredith's comment about Ryan. *She's finally happy?* Was she not happy with Ryan before?

"I'm glad. I'm really glad," I say quietly, hiding my concern. She leans down and kisses me tenderly. "You've been a really great friend to her, you know. She's grateful and hasn't ever been able to tell you."

"Well, I'm glad she can tell someone," I say, wishing that someone could be me. I get up to take my own shower.

"Hurry up, Seth. We're going to be late!" She giggles and slaps me on the ass.

"Hey, you better watch yourself." I pull her against me and kiss her hard. I wrap my hand around the back of her head and pull her fully into my body. "Are you done?" She laughs against my lips.

I huff and release her. "Tonight. You're all mine tonight." I smile as I get into the shower.

"THEY'RE GOING TO HATE ME," Meredith blurts out as we pull up to my family home. "Oh my god, how long is this driveway?" She's gaping at the grounds and she turns to look at me when she sees the house. "This isn't a house, it's a compound. Jesus, how much money does your family have?"

"Stop, you know what my family does. This can't be that big of a surprise to you." I turn off the car and hop out. She slowly steps onto the paver driveway and looks up at the house.

"Seriously, Seth. This is insane."

I grab her hand and pull her toward the stairs. Her grip is tense, worried. "Get it together, Meredith," I joke and kiss her chastely on the lips.

"Yeah, that's going to be easy," she says sarcastically.

We walk through the door and into the foyer, and her jaw drops even further. We head to the lounge in the back of the house, where I know my sisters will be hanging out, waiting to meet Meredith. It also used to be where the bar was until we had it removed.

"Sethie!" Hearing their childhood name for me warms my heart. Chloe and Chelsea have grown into beautiful teenaged girls, and have all of the drama that goes along with it. Chloe throws herself at me first, hugging me tightly.

"Why don't you ever come home? You're so close and we miss you!" Chelsea chimes in from behind Chloe.

"If I came home too much, you guys would just ignore me and never show me any affection," I joke. "Is Mom here?"

"Yes, she's upstairs getting ready. You know she needs to look and feel her best when we have guests." Chloe turns to Meredith. "Nice to meet you."

Meredith extends her arm to shake Chloe's hand and is instantly pulled into the same hug that I just received.

Meredith looks surprised but quickly reciprocates and hugs Chloe back. "It's so nice to meet you and to be invited into your home," she says humbly. She makes eye contact with me, and her wide eyes tell me that she's still nervous. I place my hand on her lower back and lead her toward the couch.

Chelsea's cell phone rings, causing her to giggle. "I'll be back." She runs out of the room as I hear her say, "Sydney! What happened last night? I'm dying to find out." Her voice trails off and I shake my head, smiling.

"Seth, so good to see you, dear." My mother's voice fills the room, and I stand quickly to hug her.

"Mom, you look great." I kiss her cheek and she pulls me close. She seems so relaxed and at ease. So pulled together.

"And you must be Meredith," she says warmly as she approaches her on the couch. Meredith stands hesitantly and her eyes dart toward me nervously before she reaches out to shake my mother's hand. "Seth has told us so much about you. We're thrilled to finally meet you." She turns to me, still holding Meredith's hand. "And such a beautiful girl, Seth." She smiles and releases her hand.

I don't understand Meredith's stiffness. I know that she never sees her own family, and when she does, it's a disaster. Maybe she doesn't know how to react to a family like mine, who can sweep their issues under the rug and put on a pretty face for guests.

My mother must be at the top of her game, because there isn't a hair out of place and her smile is smooth and even. I hope that Meredith becomes more relaxed, because it worries me to have to manage her anxiety when I don't know if my mother could break any minute or if my father could come home.

I worry about how Meredith's anxiety is going to affect her. I've been trying to manage that issue since we started dating, it seems she's always on the edge of tipping, furthering her bad habits.

I pull her to my side and kiss her cheek. "Calm down, it's going great." She eases into my side and takes a deep breath.

Chloe shows up with a tray of tea and finger foods. I didn't even realize she'd left the room. "Snacks? Tea?" she asks, putting the tray on the table.

"Sure," Meredith says, walking toward Chloe. "What type of tea do you have?"

"Every kind. Here." She opens a wooden box that has a variety of tea bags. Meredith fixes herself a cup and goes back to the couch.

"Meredith, Seth tells us that you're pre-law? How wonderful. A lawyer will certainly keep him in his place." She smiles, and Meredith shifts in her seat.

"Yes, I'm specializing in contract law and hope to some day put my J.D. to use in a large firm overseeing real estate and contracts related to those type of deals."

"Well, then, you could come to work for Tyson Industries. That's exactly what we specialize in."

"What do we specialize in?" My father's voice booms from the doorway. He saunters over to my mother, putting his hand on her back and lightly kissing her cheek.

"Ted," my mother says stiffly and pulls away from him. "We weren't expecting you today."

Well, this sucks.

His gaze finds its way over to the couch where Meredith is sitting. He eyes her up and down like candy. Or a stiff drink.

"Dad." I walk into his line of vision to protect Meredith from his predatory stare.

"I'm sorry, I didn't know we were having guests today." He intentionally included me in that description since I barely come home. "And what's all of this discussion about Tyson Industries?"

"My girlfriend, Meredith, was telling Mom that she's studying contract law at Stanford and hopes to specialize in mergers and acquisitions. Mom mentioned that's what we specialize in." I walk over to the couch and sit next to Meredith, pulling her stiff frame against me protectively.

"It's nice to hear you include yourself in Tyson Industries, Seth. Someday, you and your brother will run this company." He strides over to the large sliding doors, looking over our vast property.

"Daddy, can I get you something?" Chloe asks hesitantly. It's hard to see her practically grow up right before my eyes. Unfortunately, my sisters are old enough now to see our father for what he really is.

"No, sweetheart. I just came from the club." He turns to me. "Played a round of golf with the Sullivans. You should come next time, Seth. They were asking for you."

I haven't seen any of the Sullivans for a long time, and he knows full well that Tim Sullivan and I had a brawl on the baseball field after he purposefully beamed a fast ball at my head when I was thirteen.

"Thanks, I'll pass."

Chelsea comes back into the room long enough to lure Chloe away with promised gossip and details of whatever happened last night with one of their friends. I'm glad to see them watching out for each other, especially when my father is around.

"So, Meredith, do you have any internships lined up for next year?" he ignores me and approaches the couch.

"Yes, I have two or three I'm considering," she answers hesitantly.

"Meredith, why don't you join me outside? I'd love to show you my garden." My mother takes her hand and guides her out through the sliders and onto our lounge patio.

"Sure," she says as she's being pulled away. While Meredith may be nervous about spending time with my mother, if she stayed in this room with my father, it might get worse.

"Her tulips are incredible," I encourage her as she leaves with my mother.

As soon as they're out of earshot, I turn to my father. "What the hell, Dad? Why are you even here?"

He chuckles and pulls a key from his pocket, unlocking a cabinet on the wall. He pulls out a bottle of scotch and pours himself a glass, quickly drinking it all and pouring a second. He secures the cabinet, tucking the key back into his pocket. "You know, we can't be too careful with your mother around." He smirks, and I have the urge to punch him.

"Why is that even in the house? You know she will get to it if she knows it's there. What is wrong with you?" My fists are clenched, and I'm on the edge of yelling.

"Your mother loves her time away at the spa. Besides, she doesn't drink scotch. It never was something she could stomach, even when she was binging constantly." He swirls his tumbler and takes a sip of the aged scotch, savoring it between his teeth.

"You're unbelievable. Disgusting," I say, turning to leave the room.

"Why did you bring her here?" my father asks, causing me to turn around on my heel.

"What?"

"Why did you bring your girlfriend to our home? What purpose do you think it serves? Are you here to show off your happiness?"

What the hell?

"Not that it's any of your business, but I brought her here to meet Mom and the girls. We've been dating for almost two years, and I thought it was time. We're going to move in together next semester." I don't know why I even tell him any of this.

He laughs and says, "Really? You're going to move in with her? Are you buying a new place? Let me guess, she wants to pick out a luxury penthouse with servants."

I clench my teeth and can feel my pulse in my temples. "What are you implying?"

"She's like every woman who comes in contact with the Tyson men. She's a gold digger." His accusation hangs in the air and I'm stunned.

"What the fuck are you talking about? You don't know her. How dare you say that."

"Why do you think your mother drinks so much? She never fit in with my money and lifestyle. She drinks to cope. She came from trash, and by the looks of it, your girlfriend is cut from the same cloth." I begin to rush across the room toward my father when I hear Chelsea's voice.

"Daddy, can you come to the library? You haven't heard my cello solo yet." Her timing is impeccable as my father turns on his heel and follows Chelsea out of the room.

I run my hands through my hair, trying to get control of the rage that he brought out in me. I'm pacing back and forth in the lounge as Meredith slowly walks through the door.

Her face is pale and she looks like she's about to cry. "Seth?"

I turn toward her. "I thought you were in the garden." *How much of that conversation did she hear?*

"We were on our way, but your mother got a phone call she had to take, so I came back into the house." She enters the room hesitantly. "When is he coming back?"

Assuming she's referring to my father, I respond, "I don't know. He's listening to Chelsea right now. Hey, I'm sorry if you heard any of that—"

She puts her hand up and says, "I need to leave. I don't belong here." The look on her face tells me all that I need to know. I need to get her home and talk her down from the cliff she's about to dive off.

"Okay, we'll go."

"No," she interrupts. "I need to leave. I need some air and I want to be alone. I'm overwhelmed right now and I just need to go." I walk toward her and she backs away. Her hands are shaking as she fumbles for her cell phone.

"What are you doing?"

"Calling Talia." *Her best friend.* "She can come pick me up."

"No, Bob can take you. Are you sure you want to leave alone? I can go with you. We can talk about what you just overheard. It's not—"

"I'm good. I just need to get out of here."

I turn and pick up the house phone on the table. "Bob, can you pull the car around? Meredith needs a ride back to Palo Alto. Thanks." I hang up and walk toward her. "Please talk to me."

She practically trips to get away from me. "I—I gotta go." She turns and bolts toward the front door. I chase after her, but by the time I reach her, she's in the car and it's pulling away.

Motherfucker.

I charge back into the house to find that asshole, and I hear Chelsea playing her solo feverishly. He must still be in the library, and I don't want to interrupt her.

"Seth? What's going on?" My mother's voice comes from the foyer.

"Meredith. She had to ... leave," I say, not wanting to explain any further.

"Oh? Was it something I said?" she looks worried.

"No. No nothing like that. She wasn't feeling well," I lie. I don't want her to know what my father said to get her so upset. He completely annihilated my mother, too. No wonder she can't keep it together.

"Bob took her home," I add.

"That's too bad. I would have liked to have gotten to know her better. She seemed sweet." She's talking in past tense, as if she knows that Meredith will never step foot in this house again.

"She's amazing. You'll see," I say, feeling desperate to go after Meredith and fix this.

My mother smiles tightly and walks toward one of the dual staircases in our foyer. "I'm going to lie down. I'm not feeling well myself. Will you be around for dinner, or should I tell Jane to take away another place setting?"

I should stay, but I'm afraid if I do, I'm going to kill my father.

"I have to go. Meredith may need me," I say feebly, and I know that my mother can see through my charade.

"Go, darling. Take care of your girl. Tell her that I think she's lovely." She ascends the stairs without looking back.

My heart is torn, but I make the only decision I can. I pull out my cell phone as I head out to my car, calling Bob's private phone in the limo. "Bob, are you taking her home?" I look at the clock on my dashboard and realize I'm about fifteen minutes behind them.

"No, she has me taking her to Molly MaGees on Castro."

Dammit.

"Fine, I'll meet her there." I'm about to hang up when I hear Bob say, "Don't take I-880 South. My GPS says it's jammed with traffic. I'm on I-280 and it's moving quickly."

"Thanks for the tip, Bob. And thanks for driving her. Talk to you soon."

I hang up and head to Interstate 280. I grip the wheel as I think about all of the vile shit Meredith overheard coming out of my father's mouth. How could he say things like that? Accuse her of being a gold digger? Accuse my mother of being a gold digger? That man is evil, and I vow to deal with him after I make sure Meredith is okay.

He has sealed it for me. I'm finished with him. If he thinks I'm going to join Tyson Industries and work side by side with him, he's certifiably insane. I need to get my shit together and talk to Sean. I can't do this anymore. Not after today.

As soon as I hit the interstate, I'm stopped dead in traffic. *What the hell?*

I thought Bob said that I-280 was clear? *Shit.*

I slam my hands on the steering wheel, unbutton my sleeves and power down the windows. It's going to be a long ride.

IT'S DARK AS I PULL UP to the bar three hours later. I talked to Bob after I got stuck on the interstate. He was just as baffled as me, since the trip only took him about an hour. He's already back home and taking Chelsea to cello practice.

"Sorry I steered you wrong," he said. I know he feels bad, but I also know how crazy and sporadic traffic is out here.

I find a parking spot on the street and park my SUV. I look in the rearview mirror and see that I'm a disheveled mess. *Fuck it.* I need to see Meredith now.

The bar is dimly lit and packed shoulder to shoulder with people. Irish music is blaring through the speakers, and the roar of singing voices is deafening. I crane my neck to try to find Meredith, but she's not anywhere in sight.

I push my way through the crowd and notice her wild, dark hair from behind. As I get closer, I see that she's draped over some dude wearing a white, green and orange rugby shirt. *What the fuck?*

"Meredith?" I say as I walk up behind her. She's in the middle of whispering something into Rugby Dude's ear. She doesn't hear me, and she giggles as she throws herself into him.

I grab her arm and try to pull her away. "What the hell is this?" I ask, and Rugby Dude stands. Fuck, this guy is like seven feet tall and as wide as a truck. "Can I help you?" he bellows, protectively throwing his arm around Meredith.

"Seth!" she slurs and pulls away from the behemoth.

"You're drunk?" Clearly, this should be the least of my concerns, but she has never touched a drink since I've known her, and she reeks of booze.

She hiccups and nods her head slowly. "Liam said I would like the whiskey and he was right!" She smiles crookedly and wobbles a bit.

This is a disaster. How could she do this? She's terrified of alcohol and what it could do to her. She's seen what it's done to her mother, and now she's completely wasted. Not to mention hanging on *Liam*.

"It's time to go, Meredith. Now." I grab her hand and attempt to pull her away from him.

"No!" she shouts and pulls away. "Don't let him take me," she begs Liam.

"Meredith, I don't know what's going on, but you need to come with me now. We need to get you out of here, away from all of this. You don't belong here, and we need to talk about what happened today." Liam squares his shoulders and pushes her behind him.

"You heard her, buddy. She's not going anywhere with you."

My eyes lock on hers, pleading with her. "Meredith?" I say weakly as she turns away from me. Liam waves his hand in the air and before I know it, two bouncers are lifting me backwards toward the door. "What the fuck?" I yell as I try to pull myself out of their grasp.

I'm literally tossed out the door and barely land on my feet. I balance myself next to my car and look back toward the bar, expecting Meredith to come chasing after me, realizing the huge mistake she's making—or is about to make. I slide into the front seat and wait. And wait.

My mind is racing with all sorts of scenarios and disbelief. I should have never taken Meredith to my family's home today. It was too much for her, and she was clearly uncomfortable. Then, to overhear what my father said about her and my mother? I can't believe I subjected her to that.

But it's clearly shown me something about her that's been hiding. She lost her shit. Jumped off the deep end and did it without me. She's drinking. And hanging all over some guy? She's always told me how her impulse control is constantly hanging in the balance. Well, the scales have certainly tipped, and she obviously doesn't give a fuck about me or us.

After waiting for over an hour, I slam the car into drive and press my foot to the floor. As the entire day plays back in my mind in slow motion, I realize that I need to get away from all of this rotting shit.

Away from my father and the poison that he spews.

Away from Meredith and her uncontrollable 'impulses.'

Over the two years we've been together, she's struggled with allowing her urges to get the better of her. We've almost split three times, and every single time, my heart got in the way and I went running back, trying to help her. We actually took a break a few months ago and *she* came back, crying and saying that she couldn't live without me. She's never cheated on me, *that I know of,* but she's come close. She claims her flirting is a side effect and that she's been seeing a therapist. Clearly, her therapy and all of the support I've given her aren't working. I'm sick of it.

I can't handle my life. I've forced it for too long and I need to get away.

I hit the first number on my speed dial and immediately hear a voice.

"Seth?" Juliet answers.

"Hey," I pause and think about what to say. "What are you doing this weekend?"

"What? Oh. Ryan and I have dinner and tickets to a show tomorrow. Why?"

"I'm about to get on our plane and fly to Philly," I respond. "I need to get out of town for a few days." *Or forever.*

"Oh! We'll make it work. Come straight to my place and we'll figure it out." She holds the phone away from her mouth and yells,

"Ryan! Seth is coming." I hear a mumbled voice and she's back with me on the line. "We can't wait. Safe travels and let me know when you get here, okay?"

"Yup, see you soon."

I'm about to hang up when she says, "Are you okay? You don't sound yourself." There's concern in her voice, but I shrug it off.

"I'm fine, Jules. I can't wait to see you. And meet Ryan." *Do I really want to meet Ryan?* As long as Jules is there, I can stomach meeting her boyfriend, I guess.

"Is Meredith coming with you? Do you have a place to stay?"

"No, she isn't, and I haven't even thought about where I'm staying."

"Oh, well, plan on staying with us for at least one night, and we can set you up in a nice hotel for the rest of the time that you're here."

"Sounds good. See you sometime tomorrow morning." I hang up and quickly dial Clark, our pilot.

"Clark, can the plane be ready in a few hours? I'm going to Philadelphia."

"Yes, sir. Give me an hour or two, then she's all yours. I'll have the crew ready when you arrive."

"Thanks, Clark." I hope that he doesn't tell anyone that I'm taking the plane, especially my father. I don't want him to try to stop me, not that I think he would, but he could make it difficult for me to leave.

I make it back to my apartment and pull out the two biggest suitcases I can find. I load them up with clothes and whatever personal belongings I can grab. I slide my laptop into my backpack and toss that over my shoulder. Pulling the two suitcases behind me, I look back at my apartment before I head out to the airport.

While I haven't been here for too long, Meredith and I had started to make a life together. Memories. We were talking just this morning about moving in together permanently.

Son of a bitch.

That will never happen. Ever.

I don't even want to think about where she is right now, but a vision of her on top of Liam causes bile to rise into my throat.

My phone rings, and I see Meredith's number on the screen. *She's seriously calling me right now?*

I hit the Bluetooth. "Meredith," I say coldly.

"Seth," she slurs.

I hear a male voice in the background say, "I told you not to call him. It isn't worth it."

"Who's that?" I ask.

"Liam," she says softly.

"Why the fuck are you calling me with Liam there?"

"I don't know. I just wanted to say I'm sorry, I guess."

"You guess? Seriously, Meredith, this phone call is fucked up, even for you."

"I didn't want you to find out that way, believe me," she pleads.

"Find out what?" I ask, curious. Confused.

"Liam."

"You and Liam?" I yell into the phone. *What the fuck?*

"Yes...I mean, no. When you and I took a break, I met him, and he made me feel better."

My mind is reeling right now. Just this morning we were talking about moving in together. Starting a life together. Sure, we've had our ups and downs, but hearing this right now is making my blood boil.

"How long?" I blurt out, realizing that I don't even want to know. I don't fucking care.

"We've been talking for a while. He doesn't come from all of the money that you do. He's normal, like me." *Normal?*

I need to calm down before I drive off the road. "Goodbye, Meredith." I end the call.

I can't believe her. She's thrown away everything for a *normal* guy. *What am I?* I've been nothing but giving, understanding, protective. God, I'm such an idiot.

I press my foot to the floor and speed up the interstate.

By the time I get to the air strip, the plane is ready and Clark welcomes me aboard. "We should have a nice, smooth flight, Mr. Tyson. The crew has prepared the cabin, and you should be able to sleep comfortably most of the way." He looks at his watch, and I note that it's almost ten o'clock. "We'll be on the ground in Philly before seven o'clock local time."

"Thanks, Clark."

The crew takes my bags, and I slump into the large leather seat. I'm anxious and can't wait for the plane to lift off and get me out of this fucking city.

I don't know what awaits me in Philly, but I don't plan on coming back here for a long time.

If ever.

chapter eighteen

Juliet

Past
Philadelphia, Pennsylvania
Age 19

"OH, ROMEO, ROMEO?" I say as I nuzzle into Ryan's side. After Seth arrived early this morning, he looked exhausted, so he went to sleep in the guest room and Ryan and I went back to bed ourselves. It's now eleven o'clock, and we have so much to do today.

"Hmmm," he squeezes me, kissing my neck. "I want to stay in bed all day." He rolls us so I'm on my side and he's behind me. He drapes his leg over mine, pinning me to the bed.

"No," I insist, wiggling out of his grasp. "We have dinner and a show tonight with Holly and Drake. And you promised we'd go find some travel books about London." I turn to him and bat my eyelashes.

"You know I can't resist you when you do that," he mocks me, throwing the covers off of his body.

"You can't walk around like that," I gesture toward his almost naked body. He's wearing boxer briefs and nothing else.

"Seth won't care. He's a guy." He grabs me from behind and wraps his arms around my belly, nuzzling into my hair. "You, on the other hand, are far too naked for anyone other than myself to see."

He slides his hands under my tank top, grazing the bottoms of my breasts. I shiver and try to pull away.

"Ryan," I scold. "Get dressed." I wink at him and run into our bathroom, grabbing my clothes on the way.

After my shower, I hear Ryan and Seth's voices coming from the kitchen. When I walk in, Seth's eyes light up.

"Jules, sorry I was so out of it this morning. Look at you." He stands up from the stool and immediately lifts me off the ground, spinning me around. "Philadelphia has done wonders for you. You're stunning." He places me back on my feet and kisses the top of my head.

Ryan shifts a little on his stool, but doesn't seem to mind Seth's affection toward me. He knows our history and how close we've been throughout our lives.

"Stop. I'd say the same to you, but you look exhausted!" I tease and playfully mess his hair.

"So, why didn't Meredith come with you? I emailed her last night and she didn't respond. What's going on?" He frowns and shifts on his feet, clearly uncomfortable.

"Let's not talk about that now, okay?" He changes the subject. "What are we doing today before you guys go to dinner?"

"You're welcome to join us for dinner, Seth. I already added you to our reservation. Unfortunately, we don't have another theatre ticket. Maybe we can scalp one?" Ryan is graciously trying to make Seth feel included and my heart swells. Besides my father, he hasn't met anyone else from home.

"Thanks, but I'll pass on dinner. I'm thinking I'll get something quick to eat and come back here and crash. I had a long night." My heart grabs. I wonder what's going on and if he's okay.

"Hey, are you up for doing a little running around with us today? We need to get some things to start planning for our year abroad." I look toward Ryan and silently ask for his approval for a tagalong today.

"How about this—why don't you two go out and catch up for the next few hours. I'll meet you later and we can make a few stops before dinner. How does that sound?"

"I'm good with that," Seth agrees, and I clap my hands.

I grab my purse, kiss Ryan on the lips and head toward the door. "Let's go, Seth. I have the perfect place in mind to grab a quick late breakfast." I turn toward Ryan. "I'll text you in a couple hours and let you know where to meet us."

We make our way to a small café about two blocks from our apartment. Seth slides into the chair across from me and we stare at each other silently. "How long has it been since we've seen each other?" he asks. "Two years?"

It seems longer, but that's about right. "Yeah, wow. That seems like forever, doesn't it?" I respond. It's not like we don't know what's going on with each other, because we email every few weeks, if not more. For one reason or another, we haven't been able to see each other during my various trips home for holidays and breaks. But at least we chat frequently over email, and I even keep tabs on him through Meredith.

Meredith. That's why he's here.

"So, do you want to tell me, or am I going to have to put you under a light? What happened, Seth? Why are you here?"

He shifts uncomfortably in his seat and looks everywhere but at me. He flags down the waitress. "Can we have some menus, please?"

"Sure, be right back. Hi, Juliet. Great to see you again," Mandy says before she walks toward the back of the restaurant.

He smiles at me and says, "So, you really must be a regular here, huh?"

"Yes, Ryan and I come here every Sunday for brunch. They have the best croissants and fresh fruit."

Mandy returns with menus and a cup of chamomile tea for me.

Seth nods at my tea and his smile grows bigger. "I've missed you, Jules."

"I've missed you too. I can't believe you're here." I reach across the table and squeeze his hand. His hand lingers and I don't want to break contact.

"Is there anything I should know about?" Mandy says, standing at our table, ready to take our order.

I laugh, pulling my hand away. "No! Oh no. No. Seth and I have been friends since we were kids. He's from Sausalito. Back home."

Mandy jokes, "Oh! Good to know. I was about to carry my 'Team Ryan' flag over here, just to make sure you knew where I stood." She turns to Seth, "Not that you wouldn't be a great choice, but Ryan." She smiles, and I understand her joke completely. She constantly talks about Ryan and me and what a great couple we are. She's practically planned our wedding, and we haven't even graduated college yet.

Seth looks confused and a little uncomfortable. "Trust me, I'm no threat." He puts his hands in the air as if to surrender.

We order our food and sit in silence for a few minutes. "Don't make me keep asking you. What's going on?"

He lets out a deep sigh and pushes away from the table a little bit. "Where do I start?" he says and looks out the window.

"I'm confused, Seth. What could have happened between yesterday morning and last night?" Assuming this has to do with Meredith, I press. "What happened with her?"

"She met my family yesterday and freaked out. As soon as we pulled up to the house, she couldn't contain herself over the opulence of it all. She was extremely uncomfortable around my mother, and then my father..."

I bring my hand to my mouth. Ted Tyson is a force to be reckoned with, and I can't believe he *actually* brought Meredith home.

"Yeah. So I thought Meredith was finally calming down, and she and Mom went out to the garden. This was after my father visually assaulted her, making her squirm in her own skin. When she left the room, my father, in typical Ted fashion, said some truly horrendous things about her and my mother, accusing both of them of being gold diggers. He blamed my mother's addictions on her weakness as an individual. He said truly hideous things. I almost attacked him, but Chelsea lured him out of the room. She saved his life." Seth's pained expression is making my heart hurt.

"Oh God, that's awful. I'm so sorry that happened. I know how much your father upsets you."

"It got worse. Meredith overheard everything he said and bolted. She wound up in a bar back in Palo Alto, hanging on some seven-foot rugby player, practically assaulting him with her tongue. Apparently, it wasn't the first time she and *Liam* had been together." He places his head in is hands and slowly rubs his face.

"I don't know what to say." I reach across and grab his hand. "How can we fix this? There must be some misunderstanding."

He abruptly pulls his hand away and glares at me. "There's nothing to fix, Jules. She couldn't handle meeting my family and she flaked. She lost it and let her impulses get the better of her. I'm done with her. With all of them." He looks out the window. "This was a bad idea. I shouldn't have come here."

"Stop it, Seth. Just stop. Where else would you go? We're practically family. You've always been there for me, so it's about time I return the favor."

He looks away and our food is delivered. We eat in uncomfortable silence. I feel all of the pain that he's feeling. He's lost, and I feel the need to help him find himself. I *have* to help him.

I break our silence. "I want to help. Please tell me how." I realize we aren't used to having open and frank face-to-face conversations. Everything important we've ever discussed has always been over email.

"I need to figure it out on my own, Jules. But thanks. I'll be fine." He smiles thinly and takes the last bite of his food.

"Not acceptable," I state sternly. He raises his hand to stop me from continuing.

"Just be my friend, okay? That's all I ask." His eyes plead with me to stop, so I do.

We sit quietly for a few more minutes. "So, London?" he says, breaking the silence. "McKinsey? I know this has been a huge dream of yours. I'm so happy for you."

I wish he would just talk to me, but I'll go through the motions and play along with this two-dimensional conversation.

"Yes, London is going to be incredible. I still can't believe I got the internship at McKinsey."

"And Ryan will be with you. That's great." He seems to force out this statement, and I raise my eyebrows.

"Can you believe it? We both got into the program, and I couldn't be happier." I smile, thinking about spending a year abroad with him.

"You guys seem so happy. In love." His voice trails off and I shift in my seat. We've never said those words to each other, honestly. "Sorry, did I say something wrong?" He notices my discomfort.

"No, it's just... We've never defined our relationship in those terms. We're happy, so I guess you can say that's love. I guess." *Is it?*

He laughs. "I'm glad you're happy. It shows." His eyes lock onto mine, and I see so much pain and hurt in them.

His brows furrow and he looks pained. "Do you think about them?"

"Every day," I whisper.

"I know it's only been a few years, but I forget what Jeremy looks like. That's bad, isn't it?" he says, raising his water to his lips.

"Really? I see him in my dreams. I could never forget his face." I turn on my phone and swipe to the pictures stored on there. I tap on our graduation picture and hand the phone to him. "I look at this picture at least once a day. To remember." Tears sting my eyes and I look down.

I watch his cheeks drop and the corners of his eyes seem to turn down at the same time. "This was the greatest yet worst day of our lives," he whispers and shuts off the phone. The tears spill and I can't stop them.

"Hey, don't cry, Jules," he says tenderly as he touches my hand. I sniffle and nod my head, wiping the tears with the back of my other hand.

"It's been a long process, you know? I've gone through so much anger and hate over what happened to them. They left such a huge hole in our lives, and I wish I could trade places with either of them at any given moment."

"No!" he interrupts. "Never say that. What happened to them is awful. Terrible. Unthinkable. But *never* wish it had been you instead of them. You belong here, Jules."

I shrug my shoulders, trying to shake off the sadness that's weighing on them right now. "Okay, enough tears and sad faces. We've had plenty of that for a lifetime, don't you agree?"

"Agree." He lets go of my hand and pulls money out of his pockets. "Brunch is on me, and don't argue." I let him leave the money on the table and we get up.

"Bye, Mandy. See you next Sunday," I call out to her as we walk through the door.

I look at my phone. It's two thirty. I send Ryan a quick text to meet me at the bookstore a few blocks from our place. "Are you going to join us? We have some research to do for London."

"I'll walk you there, make sure you get there safe. Then I'm going to see if I can get a room at the Ritz."

"No! You're staying with us and that's not up for debate."

"Sorry, but I need some alone time. To think about what's next for me. I promise, you're not getting rid of me anytime soon. You never know, I may stick around in Philly for a while. I like having friends around." He pulls me against his chest and hugs me tight. He whispers into my hair, "I've missed you so much."

I squeeze him back. "I've missed you more."

I loop my arm through his and we walk silently over to the bookstore. I love this place. It's so quaint.

"Ryan." I let go of Seth and lean in to give Ryan a kiss. His lips linger on mine and he smiles.

"How was brunch?" he asks, looking between us. I wonder if he can tell that I'd been crying.

"It was great," Seth says immediately. "Although I wasn't as welcomed by Mandy as you are, apparently. You have a huge fan there."

Ryan laughs and pulls me against his side. "Yeah, Mandy and her croissants were instrumental in me winning this girl over." He nods his head in my direction. "She feels personally invested in our relationship."

Seth smiles and begins to walk backwards. "Alright, it's time for me to go blow some of my father's money on a ridiculously priced suite at the Ritz." He waves his hand in the air and points toward Ryan, "Have fun with our girl." He flashes his smile and then disappears around the corner. Ryan's grip on my hand tightens, and I wonder if it's because of what Seth just called me.

"Is everything okay? Why isn't he staying with us?" Ryan seems concerned.

"He and Meredith broke up, and he had a bit of a falling out with his father. Which isn't unusual, but it was a big one this time. He's here doing some soul searching of sorts and made a pretty good case about why he needs to spend some time on his own. I think I understand," I say.

He shrugs his shoulders. "Well, he knows where we live if he needs anything." He reaches across me and opens the door. Chimes ring as we walk in.

The store is small and welcoming.

"Hi, can I help you?" A girl walks out from the back room, carrying a box.

"Yes, we're going to London for a year, and we were hoping you had European travel guides."

She places the box on the counter near the front of the store and gestures toward the back corner. "Most of our travel guides are in that back section. The last time I checked, we definitely had England, Ireland and Scotland. And maybe France and Italy. If you want any other countries, I'll be happy to order them for you."

Ryan is already in the corner, pulling books out and tucking them under his arm. "There are some good ones here, Jules. But I definitely want Spain."

I nod and turn to the girl. "Can you order one for Spain?"

"Of course! You'll have to come back in here and tell me all about your time in Europe. A year sounds like so much fun. I'm super jealous." She opens up her computer and starts clicking away on the keyboard.

"What about this one? It looks like it's from the same travel company that published the ones that you're already holding." She turns her screen so I can see.

"Perfect."

"I can have it shipped here or to your house, your choice. Either way, there are no extra charges."

"Here's fine. It will give me an excuse to come back and browse your shelves."

"Great!" She clicks a few more times and says, "Ordered!" She pulls out a notebook and asks, "What's your name and number? So I can call you when it arrives."

"Juliet Oliver or Ryan O'Malley." I give her both of our cell phone numbers, and Ryan hands her his credit card to pay for the books that are stacked on the counter. She pulls a canvas tote out from underneath the counter and carefully arranges the books into it.

"Thank you for your business, Juliet and Ryan. I'll see you soon." She smiles. "My name is Kirsten, so if you get a message from me, you know that Spain has arrived!"

I wave to her as we leave the store. "I can't believe I've never been to this place. It's lovely, isn't it?" I ask him.

"I guess?" he says with a smile on his face. "You know, for a bookstore."

"Well, I'm glad we found this place. Just saying."

Changing the subject, I say, "You know, I'm really glad that Seth is here. It feels right having him in Philly. I'm excited for you to get to know him."

"I'm happy too, Jules. You're different around him, and I like that one of your best friends is here." He sounds sincere and I'm relieved.

"Holly and Drake should be meeting us at the restaurant soon. Do we have time to drop this bag off at home?" I ask, and Ryan glances at his watch. "I also need to get dressed for dinner and the show."

"We have plenty of time." He bends down and pecks me on the lips. He grabs my hand and we jog the couple of blocks back to our place.

In the cab on the way to meet our friends, I picture Seth's face when he saw the picture of us with Jeremy at graduation. He was so sad. I hope I can help pull him out of whatever he's going through before I leave for London.

I owe it to him.

chapter nineteen

Seth

Past
Philadelphia, Pennsylvania
Age 21

I LOOK AROUND JULIET'S APARTMENT after I unpack the last of my bags. She and Ryan left for London a week ago, and they insisted that I move in here while they're away. I've spent a small fortune at the Ritz these past few months, and it's time to give my trust fund a break.

As much as I appreciate that I can crash at their place, I'm going to make sure I leave it 'as is.' I know they'll be back soon enough, and I don't want to disturb their home.

I open the refrigerator and see that it's completely empty. Juliet cleaned it out before they left and profusely apologized for not at least providing staples of milk and bread. I'm in the mood for diner fries, so that's what I'm going to eat.

Before I leave, I open my laptop to check for messages.

Seth,

We're here! Our flight was a bit bumpy, and Ryan had to hold my hand the entire way. But we made it. London is amazing so far. We're getting settled into our flat. I like it more than Ryan does. He likes our place in Philly so much better because we have more room. He can adjust. LOL.

We check in with our advisor at McKinsey next week, so we have the rest of this weekend to start exploring. You should see the London guide book. I have practically every single page dog-eared to visit.

Oh! I almost forgot. I totally forgot to forward our mail. Can you try to send it over to us every few weeks? I would really appreciate it.

I think that's it. I miss you already, and I can't wait to hear all about the fun you're going to have while we're gone. Try not to get into too much trouble.

Yours,
Juliet

I close the laptop and smile. I missed her as soon as she boarded the plane. I grab a Post-It note from the desk and make a note to ship their mail to them. I stick it on a conspicuous place on the desk where I'll see it often so I won't forget.

Chuckling to myself, I swipe their keys from the desk.

Time to eat.

I NOTICE THAT THE DINER is empty as I walk through the door. I turn around to confirm that the sign hanging in the window says

'Open.' I slide into the last booth in the row and look around. I haven't been in Philly that long, but one thing I've come to appreciate is the great diner food. But I've never been to this one, so I'm excited to try it.

That's when I see her. The waitress didn't notice me come in, despite the bells that jarred when I opened the door.

She looks like she's daydreaming, and I watch her. I'm not sure she's noticed me yet. But damn, I've certainly noticed her. She's tall, around five foot eight, and very slender. Her hair is black and pulled back behind her ears, and strands have fallen around her cheeks. She's beautiful, in a simple way, if that even makes sense. She almost seems disinterested in her surroundings.

I'm starving, but I don't want to disturb her from her moment. I let my own mind wander, and I wonder how Jules and Ryan are doing. I bet they're having a great time.

While I'm waiting for daydream girl to notice me, I try not to think about why I'm here in the first place. When I officially withdrew from Stanford, Chloe called me to relay how angry my father was. She said that he went 'nuclear,' and I laughed out loud when I heard that. After what he said about my mother and Meredith, he doesn't deserve to be a part of any of my decisions, ever.

An older woman comes to my table. "Hi there, what can I get you to drink?" she asks. I look past her, toward the girl behind the counter. "Um, this may seem weird, but can you pretend like you didn't come over here? I'd like the other waitress to help me." I suddenly feel bad about asking this waitress to give up her only table and slip her a ten-dollar bill.

Shit, I feel like a creeper.

She winks at me. "Sure thing. Tabby's a doll." She pushes the money back toward me and says, "She needs this more than I do, but thanks, hun." She walks away, and I see her smiling and whispering to her. I drop my head when I see Tabby roll her eyes.

She walks toward my table and I freeze in my seat.

She's stunning.

And the glint in her eyes tells me that she's trouble.

Part Two

Present

Five Years Later

Suggestion: If you haven't read Dear Emily or Dear Tabitha yet, now is your chance. Part Two will be confusing for you if you haven't read these books.

You've been warned ;-)

chapter twenty

Juliet
Philadelphia, Pennsylvania
Age 24

Five Years Later

"DO YOU LOVE ME?" Ryan asks, as he does almost every day.

Every single God damned day.

He's asked me to marry him three times since we graduated Wharton and moved back to work at McKinsey's Philadelphia offices. The last time was six months ago, and I once again said no. I wish I could make him understand, but I've lost so much of myself over these past few years. I'm a shell of the person that I strove to build up and make stronger after I lost Jeremy and my mother when I graduated high school. I was so happy when I first met Ryan, but I feel lost now. I've lost my purpose, my strength.

And I blame him.

"Juliet. Do you love me?"

There's an urgency in his voice that I haven't heard before, and I can feel the tension in his body as he wraps his arms tighter around my waist.

I turn my head away from him and shrug, almost involuntarily.

"Dammit, Jules. You should know right away if you love me or not, right? It should be a gut reaction. I'm not asking you to marry me again—I've given up on that hope— but every time I see you. Breathe you. I *know*. I love you so damn much. I'm *begging you*."

A tear slides down my cheek, and several more follow as I close my eyes and shake my head. "No."

That word hangs in the air like poison.

He lets go of me and my body goes limp.

"Dammit. What the fuck are we wasting our time for, then? After all of these years! What happened to us? Are we even friends anymore?"

He's pacing back and forth through the kitchen, fists clenched. He slams his open palm on the counter and shakes his head. The moment that I feel is imminent has been building for a long time. We're no longer the happy couple who spent a year abroad together. I'm a stranger to him, to myself. I left a piece of myself in London and have been deteriorating emotionally ever since. I've used him for comfort and he's let me. I brace myself for what he's about to say.

"I can't do this anymore, and I certainly won't sit and wait for you to finally give me something that you're clearly incapable of giving to me or anyone else." The words leave his mouth as if he's been rehearsing them for a while. Like he's been waiting to finally confirm my true feelings so he can cut the cord. There's no surprise in his voice. No sadness. Only anger.

I nod, fully accepting his closure of our relationship. If I were stronger, I would have ended this before it even began, but I was lonely and I wanted companionship. I wanted something. Anything. I was selfish.

I am selfish. Like Lily.

Ryan turns to leave and looks over his shoulder. "I found a new place to live a few months ago. I'll be back for my stuff when you're not here." This too should surprise me, but it doesn't. I only feel numb. He looks down at his feet, as if mustering the courage to say the last words that he'll ever speak to me, "We could have been forever, Jules. We should have been."

He hesitates before opening the door, as if he's hoping I'm going to run into his arms and declare my undying love for him. Make promises that I know I could never keep. He doesn't deserve the emptiness that only I could give him. He drops his head and walks out of the apartment, slamming the door behind him.

I keep hearing his words in my head as I walk aimlessly into my bathroom.

"We should have been."

So much could have gone right in my life to give me the strength to be able to be someone's forever. But in truth, I've just been going through the motions.

Living life on autopilot.

This void in my heart has been tearing me apart from the inside out since the day my mother and Jeremy were ripped from my life. No, even before then. The day that I found out about Lily's letter. There is a burning hole in my chest. In my gut.

I'm empty.

I've been a hollow shell for too long, and I don't want to feel empty anymore.

I find myself in the bathroom, unsure of how I even got here. I look into the vanity mirror and a ghostly image of a woman stares back. Cold, sunken, sad eyes. Eyes that I don't even recognize. Eyes that tell me everything and nothing about who I really am.

Without thinking, I pour the remaining contents of two prescriptions into my palm. I was prescribed these when I started suffering anxiety and insomnia in London. These pills are supposed to help me sleep and cope. Ambien and Xanax. I don't count them as I toss them back, chewing and swallowing them dry. Bitterness fills my mouth as the powder from the pills causes me to gag. I bend down and open my mouth under a stream of water from the faucet. Lukewarm, but it does its job as the powder and half-chewed pills are washed down my throat.

I look back up to see the broken girl in the mirror again and say, *"Goodbye."*

Because that's what I really want, right? I don't want to be here any longer. There's a better place. There has to be. I'm sick of the ups and downs in my mind. The emotional rollercoaster I've been living on for too long. I was at the peak of my happiness in London, and it quickly disappeared and became out of reach. I felt my happiness melting away, and every time I looked in the mirror, my face looked distorted. Ugly.

I can't put my finger on the exact moment when I realized that I couldn't give Ryan everything he wanted, but it was a long time ago. I think he knew this all along, hoping I would change.

Why did I wait?

If I'd left him sooner, would I be happier now? Would I be better?

I don't know how long I've been staring into the mirror, but my reflection suddenly morphs, almost terrified. My own green eyes peer back and seem to plead with me.

"Why? Why are you doing this, Juliet?"

I must be hallucinating because my reflection just spoke to me. *Or did it?* But I can't answer her. I'm frozen as her fear suddenly becomes my own.

My heart begins to race and panic sets in. *What have I done?*

I look back at the pleading eyes in the mirror. *My eyes.*

I can't do this. I don't want to do this. But I feel so heavy. My arms and legs weigh me down and are tingling. My ears are ringing so loudly I can't hear my own voice, but I know that I'm moaning. I can feel it in my chest.

My legs can no longer support my body, and I barely make it into my bedroom. The room is closing in around me and I can't feel anything.

I begin dreaming before I'm even asleep. I see a familiar church and a solemn ceremony taking place. *Jeremy's funeral?* But something is… different. My father is standing at the podium in Jason's place. His mouth is moving, but I can't hear his voice. He's crying and keeps looking at a picture to his right. The picture is blurry, but I think I know who it is.

Is it me?

I'm suddenly transported into my vision.

I walk toward the open casket in the front of the church. I don't want to look, but my body is floating down the aisle and I'm unable to stop.

I'm cold. So cold.

When I reach the casket, a tremor rattles me as I see my own lifeless body.

I try not to look, but I can't help it. The face that stares back at me is frozen, almost in fear. There is no peace in the expressionless corpse in front of me. I try to reach out to touch her, but my arms are frozen at my sides. She's looking at me. Through me.

My eyes travel to her mouth and it's moving. She's whispering something in her eternal sleep, but I can't hear what she's saying. I can't get close enough to hear the whispers coming from her cold, ashen lips.

Silence.

Stillness.

Her mouth stops moving, and her eyes seem to become encased in ice, staring into nothingness. Her body vaporizes before me, and I reach out, swiping at the smoke that was once her.

I look around the church in an attempt to find her. Find anyone. But it's empty. My father is gone. The congregation is gone.

I'm alone. And tired.

And so very cold.

I crawl into the now empty casket, trying to get warm. I need warmth.

And sleep.

Then I feel nothing.

chapter twenty-one

Seth
Philadelphia, Pennsylvania
Age 26

I PUSH THE DOORS OPEN and walk out of the church. *I'm glad that's over.* I keep walking until I reach the block where my car is parked, and by time I turn the corner, my mind feels free.

I needed that.

I needed to say goodbye, and that was the best way, right? Hiding out in the balcony of a church, practically stalking Tabby on her wedding day?

I'm such an idiot.

By the time I reach my car, I'm laughing hysterically and I must look ridiculous. Or crazy.

Did I really just do that?

And Alex. Holy shit, what must he think? And why am I still laughing?

I'm free now. And so is she. Well, she's been free for a while, but now I can finally let her go. The sad girl that I met in the diner. Closed off and afraid to give herself to anyone. Tabby and I had many ups and downs, but the thing that I'm most sad about above all else is that our friendship is gone. We were friends first, before anything. We should have stayed that way.

My cell phone rings, and I see Juliet's name on my screen. I slowly relax as I swipe to answer, waiting to hear her soothing voice in my ear.

"Hey, Jules. You'll never believe what I just did." She doesn't respond, and I look down to see if I've lost my cell signal.

Full signal.

"Jules?"

"Hello?"

I chuckle, thinking about all of the times that she's accidentally dialed me from her phone.

"Jules. You butt-dialed me again."

I'm about to hang up when I hear a soft voice whisper, "Help. Cold."

My laughter immediately turns to panic as I yell into the phone, "Jules! Can you hear me?"

Nothing

"Jules? Please answer me," I plead.

Nothing.

Shit!

Something is very wrong. She's not responding, and the silence is deafening.

Thinking fast, I tap the call button on my phone and dial 9-1-1. Before the operator answers, I tap the call button again, conferencing the two calls together.

"9-1-1, what's your emergency?"

"My friend is on the other line, but she's not responding. I think something's wrong."

"Okay, where does your friend live?"

I give the operator Juliet's address and say, "I'm on my way there right now." I turn around in the middle of the street and head in the direction of her apartment.

"Sir, please stay on the line with us as we dispatch help to the location. What's your friend's name?"

"Juliet."

I hear the operator dispatch emergency services to her apartment, and then she's back on the line with us. "Juliet? Can you hear us? Help is on the way."

My heart is racing as I hear Jules gag and gasp for air.

The operator says, "Juliet, please remain calm. Can you hear us?" Her line is silent once again, and I press my foot to the floor. I hear the operator communicate with the emergency team already en route. "Patient is on the line, unresponsive, and breathing is erratic. What's your ETA?"

"Sir, the emergency team is about three minutes out." I grab my chest. She could be dead in three minutes! Not fast enough, and neither am I.

"I think I'm about ten minutes away." I see car lights blur in my peripheral vision as I fly through the streets.

Twelve minutes later, I pull into the parking lot to see an ambulance and police cars scattered throughout. I see a stretcher being wheeled quickly across the parking lot to a waiting ambulance. A paramedic is straddling her, working on trying to revive her.

Desperation overtakes all of my senses and I rush toward her.

Another paramedic is on his walkie-talkie, giving her vitals to someone, as the other one places oxygen over her face. "She was unresponsive when we got here, faint pulse, shallow breathing. We'll be there in two minutes."

Faint pulse.

Shallow breathing.

Fuck.

I watch them lift her limp body into the ambulance as they try to keep her alive. A police officer emerges from her building with a large plastic bag containing what looks to be empty prescription bottles. He speaks into the walkie-talkie on his shoulder. "Two empty prescription bottles. One Xanax. One Ambien. Possible suicide attempt."

Suicide?

The ambulance carrying Jules is already pulling out of the parking lot. I run back to my car and attempt to follow. One of the police officers flags me down to stop me. "Sir, this is an emergency. You'll have to wait until all of our vehicles are cleared out."

"No!" I yell and his face becomes stern. "That's my friend in there. I need to follow that ambulance." He looks around and steps aside. "They're on their way to University Hospital." He pauses and then says, "I'm sorry."

I quickly drive past him onto the city street and don't look back. I've lost sight of the ambulance, but University Hospital is only about twelve blocks from here. I grab my cell phone and notice that I'm still on the phone with Jules. I can't hear anything on the other end and realize that her cell must still be in her apartment. But she's still connected to me. I don't want to disconnect, but I have to.

My mind is racing and I know I need to call her father. This is going to destroy him. I hesitantly end the call with Juliet's phone and dial his number.

"Hi, Seth. How are you, son?"

I hesitate and say, "Mr. Oliver, it's Juliet. Something's happened."

"What? What's going on? Is she okay? Please tell me!"

"I don't know, sir. I'm almost to the hospital. But I don't think it's good."

"I'll be there as soon as I can. Stay in touch." Our connection ends abruptly and I suddenly regret calling him. I don't have any answers yet. I don't know what's going on.

She could be okay.

The paramedics could have revived her.

Right?

೧೨

"MR. OLIVER?" I HEAR a voice echo in the cold, dark hallway.

"No, he isn't here yet."

The last text message that I received from Kevin Oliver was about four hours ago, when he boarded the plane from San Francisco. I don't expect him to be here for at least another two hours.

"Are you a family member?"

"Yes," I lie easily.

"Please come with me. Dr. Geddy would like to speak with you."

I numbly stand up and follow the nurse through the doors. I shouldn't be doing this, but I have to do what's right for Juliet and her father. Maybe I can soften the blow by finding out what happened and what the medical staff could piece together.

"Mr...?" the doctor tries to address me.

"Tyson. I'm... family." Deep down, I know that I *am* family. Really, her only family on the East Coast.

"Juliet took a lot of pills. Based on the empty bottles the emergency team found in her apartment and the number of pills prescribed by the physician, we estimate that she took about eight each of Ambien and Xanax. This unfortunately is a very serious and deadly combination. As you know, the paramedics found her unresponsive and barely breathing. Their immediate attempts to revive here were unsuccessful."

My chest tightens and I feel light-headed. I press my hand into the wall beside me. The cool cement draws in my fingertips and begins to balance me. The doctor's voice trails off.

A sob gets stuck in my throat, and I suddenly want to run out of this fucking place.

Attempts were unsuccessful.

How am I going to tell Mr. Oliver?

She's gone. I've lost one of the most important people in my life, and all I keep hearing is...

Attempts were unsuccessful.

"Mr. Tyson, do you understand all that I've told you?" the doctor asks.

"Yes, I understand," I whisper.

"So the next few days are going to be critical to her recovery."

Recovery?

"What?"

The doctor continues, "Yes, as I said a few minutes ago, our initial attempts to revive her were unsuccessful, but once the paramedics got her into the ambulance, they were able to use paddles to shock her heart into a sinus rhythm and provide oxygen to her. We were able to pump the contents of her stomach, but are unsure how much of each of the medications made it into her blood stream. We need to keep a close watch and be sure she doesn't take a turn for the worse and that no major organs were affected. She's in a coma right now. We need to monitor her closely."

This is too much information to digest, and I just say, "Thank you. Can I see her?"

He moves aside, gesturing toward the glass room to his left. "You should only stay for a few minutes." He then nods and walks away.

I feel like I'm glued to the floor where I stand.

I want to see her but I can't move.

chapter twenty-two

Juliet
Philadelphia, PA
Age 24

"SAY CHEESE!" MY MOTHER'S voice echoes in my ears.

Jeremy's arm is around my waist, and I smell the flower that he's wearing on his suit jacket. I look down and see that I'm wearing the complementing wristlet that he placed on me a few minutes before.

Mom's face is blurry, but I can hear her sing-song voice. "Juliet, Jeremy. Smile."

I try to smile, but my face feels frozen in place. I'm unable to speak and I feel woozy. Almost like I'm floating.

Jeremy's arm squeezes tighter, and I feel his breath near my ear. "Smile, Jules. We're all together again."

Together again? What does he mean?

I raise my free hand into view and see that the flowers in my wristlet are all white. This couldn't be my prom, because my corsage was made of pink carnations.

Not white.

Where are we?

A breeze tickles my toes, and I realize that I'm barefoot. Where are my shoes? I look down and see that I'm wearing a long, flowing white gown.

I can't feel anything beneath my feet, and I grip Jeremy tightly. Am I floating?

"What's happening?" I ask them, but my words are jumbled and slurred. Their smiles remain on their faces.

"I want to capture this moment, Juliet. Isn't it beautiful?" My mother raises the camera to her eye and begins to focus the lens.

Jeremy's lips brush my hair and he says, "Please smile. We won't be together much longer."

"I don't understand," I respond, but strangely, I don't panic. Although I feel like I should.

Mom's face becomes clearer and she's stunning. She's wearing a similar white gown, and her brown hair has a sheen to it like I've never seen. Almost glowing. Brilliant.

"Juliet, do you know why you're here?" Jeremy asks, sounding worried. "You aren't supposed to be here."

His arm falls from my waist, and I feel like I'm about to float away from him. I grab ahold of his arm and try to stay next to him.

"Please smile for the camera, Jules." Mom's tone changes as she begs me to smile.

"What are we doing? Where am I?" I ask, but they don't seem to hear me. "Jeremy? What did you mean? Why shouldn't I be here? Talk to me, please!" I beg him to hear me, to respond.

I hear a muffled voice coming from all around me, but nobody else is here.

"Please don't leave me, Juliet."

"What did you say?" I turn to Jeremy, and he's looking off into the distance as he releases my hand.

"Mom? Was that you?"

"Come back to me, please," I hear again.

My mother moves to stand next to Jeremy and she smiles warmly. "Mom." I try to reach out to her, but she begins to fade as if she were just a vision. "Jeremy!" He's almost transparent now, but his warm smile remains. "NO!" I yell. "Don't leave me. Please don't leave." I'm sobbing and can barely breathe.

DEAR JULIET

"PLEASE STAY! I need you. Oh my God, what's happening?" They have vanished right before my eyes, and I'm screaming so loudly I can't even hear myself.

I feel so heavy. My dress pools around my legs as I collapse onto the ground. I feel my heartbeat throughout my body, and everything is pulsating around me.

I hear the voice again, and now it's all around me.

"I'm so sorry. I need you to wake up so you can forgive me."

Where is that voice coming from? Mom and Jeremy are gone. Disappeared.

The voice says one final thing, and I finally realize who it is.

"Olive juice."

chapter twenty-three

Seth
Philadelphia, PA
Age 26

I STAND IN THE DOORWAY, listening to the sporadic beeps from the intensive care equipment that surrounds Juliet.

A nurse looks up and smiles warmly. "She's breathing on her own, so you won't see anymore scary tubes." She looks up at me with sympathetic eyes, "That's a good sign, you know. If she's breathing on her own, it means her brain is sending the right impulses to her lungs. She's fixing herself." She squeezes my arm as she passes by and leaves the room.

I walk tentatively to the side of her bed and instinctively grab her hand. It's surprisingly warm and I squeeze harder.

Her face, however, is pale, and her eyes look sunken into her head with dark charcoal circles underneath. Dark marks and smudges surround her lips, as if they're bruised, and I remember the doctor telling me that they pumped her stomach.

"Jules," I whisper and squeeze her hand tighter, hoping she can hear me.

"What did you do? Why? God, please come back to us," I plead with her through my own tears, choking on my words. "Heaven isn't ready for you yet."

I watch her face as her eyelids flutter.

Is she dreaming?

Is she trying to wake up?

Is she having a seizure?

Panicking, I press the call button and the nurse reappears quickly.

"Look at her eyes. What's happening?"

"I'll let the doctor know. He'll probably order an EKG and an MRI. I'll get him right away." She smiles and rushes out of the room.

Seeing her eyelids move gives me so much hope, and I get a bit more aggressive.

"Jules, you better be coming back to us. To me. Do you hear me? And when you wake up, I'm going to make you swear in blood that you'll never do this again." I place my lips close to her ear. "Come back to me. *Please.*"

A medical technician enters the room, rolling a cart with what I assume to be the EKG equipment. "Excuse me, sir, I'll need you to leave for a little while as we hook her up to the machine. You can come back in about a half hour. She's scheduled for an MRI right after this."

I squeeze her hand one last time before I leave the room. I walk past Mr. Oliver, who is huddled with the doctor in the family lounge, and hope their discussion is positive. I make a mental note to devise a game plan with her father about what's next, presuming she walks out of here, healthy and alive. I will promise him to devote everything to helping her live a long life, free from whatever demons are haunting her.

"Seth?" Ryan appears from around the corner and stands in front of me, voice shaking. "How is she?"

I clench my fists, remembering the conversation that I had with him last night. I called him after Juliet stabilized to let him know what happened. I was concerned and wondered why he wasn't there. After he told me what happened between them, that they broke up right before Jules took all of those pills, I wanted to kill him. His guilt was tangible, and he's blaming himself for everything. His face in now drawn, worried.

"She's still in a coma, but they're running tests right now. Her eyes were moving. I hope that's a good sign." I start to walk past him, and he reaches out to stop me.

"Please listen to me. I didn't want this to happen. God! I would trade places with her in a second, you have to believe me. I love her more than anything."

"Then why did you leave her? You told me last night that you broke up with her. What the hell, Ryan?"

"You don't understand. She's been on this downward spiral for so long. It started in London and she's been pulling away from me since. The only thing she has put any energy into is work."

I know that her job is demanding, but I can't imagine it would cause her to dive into a pit of despair. "I don't get it. You guys were in love, so happy. What happened to tear that apart? What was so bad that she would want to end it all?"

"I'm in love with her, but she doesn't love me. She never did. I told her yesterday that I couldn't live like this anymore. Did she tell you that I asked her to marry me? Three times."

Shocked, I turn back to him. "What? She never mentioned that you proposed."

"I'm not surprised. She barely acknowledged the proposals to me. She just kept saying no. I should have realized that there was something so much worse going on inside her head. I just loved her the best way that I could."

"I need you to help me understand, because I can't figure it out, and I need to help her." We sit in the coffee lounge and my mind begins to race. And suddenly I remember something that causes me to catch my breath.

"Seth, are you okay?" Ryan leans forward, concerned.

Piecing together some of the correspondence that we've had over the past couple of years, I start to see something that I didn't before.

Could this be my fault?

"Seth?"

"Fuck, Ryan." I put my head in my hands, trying to restore my breathing to normal.

"This is my fault," I whisper into my palms.

"What?"

I take a deep breath and sit back in the chair. Months and years of emails seem to float before my eyes, and it occurs to me that *I* could have triggered her depression.

I turn on my phone and scroll to the email archive folder titled JULES. I click on the email I got from her after I told her about Tabitha and the baby that we gave up for adoption.

Seth,

I don't know what to say to you right now. I'm beside myself and sick. Seriously sick and full of bile. You OF ALL PEOPLE should know what it feels like to be a child adoptee. YOU watched me go through shit tons of HELL when I was younger. What I STILL struggle with on a daily basis. How could you make this decision without thinking it all the way through? What you and your girlfriend are doing is going to affect that child FOREVER. Don't you realize that??? Do you care? You're selfish. SELFISH! Why are you doing this? Give that baby a chance and choose to be a parent, for God's sake. Don't force her into the life that I've lived for so long. Dammit, Seth. Do the right thing.

The email ended abruptly without a signature. My response was simple. Angry.

Jules,

I am doing the right thing. I wish you could see it from my perspective. Maybe if you could, you would finally be able to get over your own issues about Lily. How about trying?

After that note, she and I didn't speak again for at least six months. I remember trying to pour my heart out to her about Emily and all of the doubt that I felt when we made the decision that we did. But she wouldn't listen, she couldn't understand. I tried to convince her and myself that it was for the best. Tabitha moved on and eventually found true happiness, with Alex. It's all I would have ever wanted for her, and it's easy to see now that she and I were never meant to be.

But Juliet was so upset with me, almost as if she couldn't forgive me for a decision that was mine to make.

"Hey, what's going on?" Ryan asks, concerned.

I flip my phone around to show him the emails. He reads them quickly, shaking his head. "When did this happen?"

"I don't know, maybe right before you finished your internships in London. Just after? Look at the date and timestamp on them." Ryan scrolls up and sees the date I sent that email.

He sighs. "This explains a lot." He hands me back my phone. "I remember when she got your email, because she threw her laptop across the room. But she never told me why, only that you and she weren't seeing eye to eye on something. She was sick over this and couldn't snap out of it for a while. I never knew until now what you both were emailing about. She wouldn't tell me."

"It's my fault," I say again in disbelief.

"Stop. That was years ago. You can't think like that," he says, and I wonder if he even believes the words coming out of his own mouth.

"Besides, I was the one in a relationship with her. I need to take responsibility for not realizing how to help her through. I should have been able to help her, but I didn't know how." His regret hangs in the air, and I don't have it in me to lie to him and tell him that he's wrong. Because he's not. He *should have* done something. Picked up the phone. Called me. Called her father. Done *something* to let us know that Jules was spiraling out of control.

Because of me.

I push away from the table. "I need to get back to see her. She should be back from her MRI by now."

Ryan stands, shoving his hands into his pockets. "Should I come too? Can I?"

"That's up to her father. He's not thinking too straight right now, and the only thing he knows is that you broke up with his daughter minutes before she overdosed." I don't mean to sound stern, but it comes out that way.

"Oh." He looks down at the ground. "Call me as soon as you know anything. Please?"

"I will."

"I still love her. That hasn't changed, and I would do anything to turn back the clock."

DEAR JULIET

"Me too, Ryan. Me too." I walk away toward the Intensive Care Unit.

Her father is standing outside the room, pacing back and forth.

"Mr. Oliver, is everything okay?" I ask nervously.

"Oh, hey, Seth. Things are good, I think. Her EKG showed normal brain activity and she just got back from the MRI. The doctor thinks she'll wake up any time now."

My heart leaps in my chest at this good news. "Thank God." I feel as relieved as I can until she actually opens her eyes.

"Ryan's here and wants to know if he can see her."

He tenses up, shaking his head. "No. I don't want him near her right now."

"Okay, I'll update him myself and when you think it's a good time, I'll let him know to come by." "There won't be a good time. Not for the man who broke my baby's heart." His words grip my chest, because I know the truth. Ryan may have ended their relationship yesterday, but I was the one who triggered her depression.

Guilt overwhelms me and I say, "I think Ryan really wishes he could change everything that happened yesterday, Mr. Oliver. To turn back the clock and never do what he did."

Is this Ryan's wish or my own?

"We all have regrets, son. But his actions are what pushed her to do this. I won't forgive him or allow him near my daughter."

Would he allow me near her if he read my email?

I nod and follow him into her room. The nurse is smiling as she adjusts her fluids and presses some buttons on the machines. "She's resting comfortably. The radiologist is reviewing her MRI right now with the neurologist, but so far so good."

We both sit down on either side of her bed in silence. He brushes her hair away from her face with his hand, leaving his palm on her cheek. "We're here, Juliet. Please come back to us."

"Mr. Oliver?" The nurse comes back into the room. He turns to face her. "Dr. Geddy would like to see you. Can you come to the patient conference room now?"

He looks worried. "Is everything okay?"

"Yes." She smiles. "He'd like to talk about what's next, after Juliet wakes up. She's going to have a long road ahead of her, and he wants to talk to you about what to expect. Our social worker and therapist would also like to talk to you about her support network and the road to getting her well."

After Juliet wakes up.

He stands to follow her out of the room and turns to me. "Stay with her, please, and let me know if anything changes."

I nod and grasp Juliet's hand. I'm alone with her again, and I have so much that I need to say. I'm desperate to tell her, even if she can't hear me.

Tears threaten to spill down my cheeks. "I'm so sorry. This is all my fault. I don't know what to say, but you wouldn't be here if it weren't for me. I shouldn't have burdened you with my decision about Emily. I shouldn't have told you the way that I did. I should have been more sensitive to what you've gone through, trying to cope with your own adoption. It was wrong of me, and I'm so very sorry."

I press my lips to her ear and say it again.

"I'm so sorry. I need you to wake up so you can forgive me."

I rest my head next to hers and whisper something in her ear that makes me think of a time when we were younger.

"Olive juice."

I smile after saying that, remembering when she slurred those words to me at Jeremy's party so many years ago.

Her fingers move in my hand and I sit up quickly.

"Jules?" I scan her face for any signs of movement. Something. Her eyes are fluttering and her breathing becomes erratic. I slam my thumb repeatedly into the call button and repeat the nonsensical words again. "Olive juice, Jules. Olive juice."

Several nurses come in and usher me away from her bed. One grabs an oxygen mask and holds it over her nose and mouth. "What's happening?" I ask.

"Juliet, can you hear me?" One nurse says loudly into her ear, while holding her hand, and the other is running a metal tool under her feet.

Juliet begins coughing uncontrollably, and I see her eyes suddenly open wide. Her father runs into the room past me, and the doctor moves to her bedside. "Juliet?" the doctor says as he starts checking her vital signs and tapping lightly on the center of her chest.

Her breathing starts to regulate, and they raise the head of her bed slightly. Her eyes are darting all around the room and she looks terrified. I rush to the foot of the bed and she sees me, I think. I smile nervously and touch her foot.

She coughs and chokes a little bit more and says, "I'm alive?" Her voice is hoarse and raspy. I exhale heavily, realizing that I'd been holding my breath.

"Juliet!" her father says, his voice filled with relief. "Thank God you've come back to us. Thank God." He's weeping and presses his lips to her forehead.

"You've given everyone quite a scare," the doctor says. "Do you remember what happened?"

She turns her head slightly to look at him and pulls her hand away from her father to remove the oxygen from her mouth. "I remember." She makes eye contact with me. "How am I alive?" She seems confused.

The doctor speaks up. "You took a lethal combination of pills, but your friend alerted the paramedics very quickly, and we were able to pump most of them from your stomach."

"How?" She looks at me perplexed.

I clear my throat. "You called me."

She blinks repeatedly and our eyes remain locked on each other.

"But I was... I saw *them*," she stammers, and her breathing becomes quick and shallow.

"Thank God you're awake," her father says, throwing his arms around her.

"We're going to examine Juliet some more. Can everyone but medical staff leave for about twenty minutes?" the doctor politely asks.

Her father and I leave the room, and as soon as we pass through the doors into the hall, he pulls me into a tight embrace and weeps into my chest.

"Thank God she's back. She's alive," he says, and I let him hang on to me for a minute.

He releases me, looking a little embarrassed. "Sorry about that."

I laugh, feeling the same relief he is. "It's okay. There's never anything wrong with a bro hug, especially when we have something to celebrate."

He chuckles and wipes the tears from his face.

I pick up my phone and gesture toward the waiting area. "I'm going to let Ryan know she's awake." He frowns but nods in agreement.

"Seth?" Ryan's voice is hoarse and desperate. "Is she okay?"

"Yes, she just woke up a little while ago. They're examining her now, but she's awake." I smile and breathe another sigh of relief.

He exhales loudly. "Good. This is good." He pauses and then says, "Please tell her that I'm thinking about her."

"Of course. I'll keep you posted."

"Thanks, Seth." He disconnects, and I shove my phone into my pocket. I lean my head against the wall behind me and close my eyes.

***

"SETH, WAKE UP."

I suck in some air and my eyes pop open. "Mr. Oliver, is everything okay. Jules... is she...?"

He smiles warmly. "She's perfectly fine. Just fine. You fell asleep a few hours ago, and I didn't want to wake you. I spent a lot of time with her and the therapists. We're all exhausted." He sits down on the other couch and puts his feet on the ottoman. "She's resting right now, but she's going to be okay, Seth."

I stand up, running my hands through my hair. "Can I go see her?"

"Sure, but let her sleep. She's had an emotional few hours."

I open her door quietly and sit in the chair next to her bed. The color has returned to her cheeks, and she's sleeping peacefully. I watch her chest move up and down, and I wrap my hand around hers.

DEAR JULIET

My heart pounds in my chest, and I whisper a vow.

"I promise I'll make everything better for you. I need to see your smile again."

chapter twenty-four

Juliet
Philadelphia, Pennsylvania
Age 25

"THANK YOU, DR. GRANT." I say, closing the door as I leave her office. We just had a little celebration together, celebrating my fiftieth session with her.

Three sessions a week.

For sixteen weeks.

Four months since I tried to end my own life.

We've delved into every crevice in my brain, trying to help me understand what brought me to her in the first place. Several themes swirl around why I dove off the deep end, including acceptance, regret and loss.

I've learned that I have a difficult time dealing with any of these things, and I spiraled into a perpetual state of anger and apathy over things that were completely beyond my control. The grief and anger that I felt pushed me to a dark place that no one should ever venture to. She says that I'm only allowed to feel regret for one thing, and that's my suicide attempt. She wants me to feel that regret and remember what suicide means.

It's final.

Our sessions have opened my eyes to so many things, and I'm driving on a slow, uphill road to recovery. I'm incredibly blessed to have so much support. My father, Seth, Holly, Summer and even Ryan. I smile as I walk into the waiting room and see my biggest supporter sitting on the couch.

"Hey," he says, smiling as he stands.

"Thanks for taking me here today, Seth. It really means a lot. Dr. Grant says hi."

He chuckles. "I thought there was supposed to be some doctor-patient confidentiality going on." Seth spent some time with her on his own, working through so many things, including his intense guilt over my suicide attempt. He blamed himself, because he thought that he triggered my depression. It went so much deeper than that, and stemmed from my lack of acceptance of my life and everything that was right in front of me. She helped both of us recognize the true gifts that we have and not dwell on things that we can't control.

Some of our sessions were together, which was especially difficult for me. It was so hard to share things with Seth that I've only ever put in writing. For the first time in years, we were both able to confront our grief, face-to-face.

Seth and I have been getting much closer, in a way we have never been before. I confided in Dr. Grant a few sessions ago that I was developing feelings toward Seth. Feelings that I'm afraid he's not able to reciprocate, or wants to. I explained to Dr. Grant that I feel immense guilt for allowing myself to *feel* the way that I do about Seth. She explained that it's natural to feel this way, and I should just be honest with him. I don't know if I'm ready, but I *feel* something developing between us. *Does he feel it too?*

"Let's get out of here, shall we?" He offers his arm, and I loop mine through it, leaning my head on his shoulder.

We slide into his SUV and he looks over to me. "I'm proud of you, Jules." My heart swells.

"I'm proud of me too." My phone buzzes in my lap, and I see a text message from Ryan.

Thinking about you. Hope you're doing great.

Ryan's support has been integral throughout my recovery. I needed him to forgive me for disconnecting from him for so long and not being able to reciprocate his love. For not being able to give him what he gave to me. It was one of the harder sessions that I had with Dr. Grant, but she helped me understand that it was okay to not feel the same for Ryan as he did for me. It was hard for him to finally let go of what we had, but we've remained cordial, friendly. He still blames himself for my suicide attempt though, and I wish he would move past that. We care deeply about each other, and that will never change.

I'm great ;-) Thanks for thinking about me. ;-)

I smile and place the phone into my purse.

"Did you talk to Dr. Grant about your idea?" Seth asks, sounding mildly concerned.

I want to find my birth mother. I *need* to.

"Dr. Grant thinks it's normal and healthy for me to want to find Lily. She's concerned that I don't yet have all of the necessary coping mechanisms to handle what I might find. But I disagree. I'm ready." Finding Lily will help me with my acceptance of my life. Who I am and why.

I turn to Seth. "Are you ready to help?"

"I don't know, Jules. I tend to agree with Dr. Grant on this one. Why now? Maybe we can start looking in a few months?" The concern in his voice is evident, and he frowns while looking through his windshield.

"I can't do it without you." Sean's wife, Tiffany, is a private investigator in San Francisco. She promised she would be able to find Lily Todd for me as soon as I'm ready.

"I don't know…" His voice trails off and I huff.

We drive the rest of the way to my apartment in silence.

"We're going to find her, I promise. But let's just wait a little bit, until Dr. Grant gives you the green light, okay? You've come so far. Let's not go too fast, okay? When are you going back to work?" he changes the subject.

"I don't think I'm going back," I state and smile.

"Really?"

"I want a fresh start. Find something that ignites my passion. I'm thinking about social work, but I'm still exploring options." I can't go back to the high-stress, high-pressure job that I had before. It was too intense for me, and I realized that I need to find something that I'm passionate about and apply my experiences to helping others. Social work is definitely stressful, but it's the kind of stress that I can handle, I think.

"That's awesome. Good for you." He places his hand over mine and squeezes.

We pull up in front of my apartment and sit silently for a few minutes. "Are you coming up?"

"Sure." He turns off the ignition and we walk quietly into my apartment.

We flop onto opposite chairs and simultaneously exhale. I look at him nervously and wipe my palms on my jeans. There's something that I've been wanting to ask to him for months, and it seems so ridiculous that I've waited this long.

"Are you okay?" he asks, concern taking over his expression.

I shift in my seat, wanting to talk about us and how I feel. Nervously, I make eye contact with him, "I heard what you said."

He looks confused, "What do you mean?"

"I heard what you said to me when I was in the hospital."

"I said a lot of things to you in the hospital, Jules. I was begging you to wake up. To *live*."

"You said 'Olive Juice.'" I smile and his eyes beam.

"I did say that." His smile spreads across his face and becomes infectious.

I'm laughing when I continue. "Why did you say that? Of all things, what does it mean? Did I hear you correctly?"

He shakes his head and runs his hand through his hair. "You're telling me you don't remember 'Olive Juice'?" His eyes are twinkling and he starts to laugh.

"I remember that you whispered it into my ear when I was in the hospital," I respond defensively. *What does he mean?*

He stops laughing and leans forward in his chair, placing his hands on my knees. "At Jeremy's party before graduation, you got really wasted. Do you remember that?"

"Yes..." I respond, wanting to know where this is going.

"You were puking and started to pass out on his bathroom floor, so I moved you into bed, and you were babbling about what a great friend I am. You were pouring your heart out to me." He winks and squeezes my knees, causing me to squirm.

"Hey, that tickles!" I say, playfully slapping his hand.

"As you were about to pass out, you slurred—really slurred—the words 'Olive Juice.'"

I raise my eyebrows. I still don't get it.

"Think about it." He smiles from ear to ear. "C'mon, it's not that hard if you really think about it."

I *slurred* 'Olive Juice'?

Ohhhhh...

"I get it now," I say, embarrassed. *I told him 'I Love You.'* He leans back in his seat and grins.

"But why did you say it to me when I was in the hospital?" *I need to know.*

"Because it's ours," he responds without hesitation.

My heart jumps in my chest over this admission. "I see," I say softly. *Does he feel the same way that I do now?*

He continues, "It was the first time you told me how much I meant to you. So I kept it. It's ours." He stares into my eyes, and I'm beginning to realize that it *does* mean so much more now.

I smile and say jokingly, "Only to be said when drunk or in a life-changing situation?"

"Why limit it to that, Jules? I could walk the streets, yelling 'Olive Juice, Juliet Oliver!' all day long." His eyes become heavy, and I know he's definitely not joking about this.

"This is a ridiculous conversation. You know that, right?" I say.

"Hey, you brought it up." He laughs and stands up.

"I suppose I did," I say, feeling silly. He offers his hand to me, pulling me to my feet and into an embrace, hugging me tight. I'm tense at first, but quickly relax into his chest.

"Why are we afraid of those words? The *real* words?" he asks into my hair.

"Because the only people that I've said them to have died," I whisper.

"I'm sure you've said it to your father tons of times, and he's still alive." He pauses. "You said it to me, and I'm still here."

Yes, you are.

I smile again and hug him tighter. "Don't be afraid to say the words, Jules. But if you can't bring yourself to do it, just use our code." I laugh and start to shake in his arms.

"Thank you, Seth. You know I love you. You've been the best—" I stop. *No, he's so much more.*

He's been everything to me throughout the years. My confidant, my savior, my friend. Someone who was looking out for me when I didn't even know it.

"You've been everything," I say breathlessly.

He stiffens and pushes me gently away from his chest so he can look into my eyes. "I've only ever wanted happiness for you. I've wanted you to be free of the sadness and grief that you carried around for too many years." He softly touches my cheek and runs his finger along my jaw, stopping below my lips. I lean into his hand and close my eyes.

"Look at me, please. I need to know that you're hearing me. Seeing me."

I slowly open my eyes and look into his.

"Jules," he says, lowering his lips toward mine, "Olive—" he stops and smiles "—I love you." His lips softly brush mine, and I'm still staring into his eyes.

He backs away but doesn't break our gaze. I bring my hand to my lips and touch where he just kissed me. *That was so... different. Good?*

"Seth," I exhale. I want to say so much more, but I need to process this. We've been *friends* since we were kids. Friends. Never anything more. *Or were we?*

Why now?

This feels right.

He places his hand on my cheek and traces his thumb over the same place I was just touching.

We're both startled by a loud buzzing sound coming from his jeans. I step back as his hand falls to grab his phone.

"It's Chloe. Do you mind if I take this?" I shake my head slowly as he swipes to answer the call.

"Hi, Chloe." The smile from his face disappears immediately as I hear Chloe's muffled voice through the phone, sounding frantic. "What?" he says as his hand tenses around his phone. I hear her cries and assume that whatever she's telling him is awful. I move closer to him and take his other hand in mine. "I'll be home tonight," he says and disconnects the call.

I squeeze his hand, afraid of what he's about to tell me. His mouth is open, almost in disbelief. Shock.

"What is it?" I ask.

He lets go of my hand and turns, looking out the window.

"He's dead."

"Who, Seth? Who's dead?" I move behind him, grasping my hands in front of myself.

"My father."

chapter twenty-five

Seth
Sausalito, California
Age 27

"WE'VE REACHED OUR CRUISING altitude of thirty-five thousand feet. We're anticipating a smooth flight and should be on the ground in San Francisco by eleven o'clock local time." Our pilot's voice cuts off and the cabin is silent.

Sean is sitting across the aisle from me, looking out his window. He was in Milan on business and had the plane stop in Philly to pick me up on his way home.

"How's Mom?" I ask Sean. Things happened so fast after Chloe called me, I didn't have time to call to check on her.

"I spoke to her when we landed in Philly. She sounded—" he pauses, furrowing his brow "—a bit out of it." That can't be good. It means she's heavily medicated or worse.

"She's going to be okay, Sean. She has to be, right? I mean, without him around, she can only get better."

"How can you say that?" He scowls. "He's our father. Yes, he was an asshole, but he was still our father. And her husband."

I grip the armrests tightly and hold my breath. "He was never her husband," I spit out. "He treated her like shit. There isn't an intern he didn't have bent over his desk on any given day, not to mention all of the other women we don't even know about. He was a philandering pig, Sean. And he didn't respect Mom one bit. Don't call him a husband or a father."

He turns to look at me and his expression is pained. Sad. "I just want to believe that there may have been something redeeming about him. There *has* to be."

"There isn't, and I came to terms with that a long time ago. The things that he said about his wife, our *mother*, were despicable. Disgusting. You would have torn him to pieces if you were there, trust me. That was the last time I saw him, and I'm glad that memory is still fresh in my mind. Because when we bury that fucker in a few days, I'll be able to look down on his grave and make a vow to never follow in his footsteps." I'm shocked at the words that come out of my mouth, never thinking I'd utter them to anyone but Dr. Grant.

"How can you have that much hate?" he asks.

"I don't know, I just do." I lean my head back into the headrest. "She's better off without him and so are we."

He slowly nods his head, and I'm not sure if it's in agreement or disgust with me.

"How's Jules?" he asks, changing the subject.

I close my eyes and try to remember what her lips felt like on mine just a few hours ago. I'm unsure if what happened earlier today was a mistake or if it was meant to be. Seeing her emerge from the darkest period of her life has been the most rewarding thing I've experienced in a long time. I realized that I've fallen in love with her over these past few months.

Haven't I always loved her?

"She's doing great," I smile. "Really great."

"Oh? Do I detect something more?"

"Are we really talking about this?" I ask him.

"Seth, I haven't seen you happy in a relationship, ever."

"You've never met any of my serious girlfriends, so how would you even know?" I say defensively.

"Because you've never spoken about any girl with our family, except Jules." He smirks and adjusts his seat to recline.

"Not true. You all knew about Meredith, and she even met almost everyone." I stop myself from arguing further, because I know what he's getting at. Meredith met our family *once*. Jules has practically been part of our family since grade school.

He raises his eyebrow. "You know what I mean. Now, what are you going to do about it?"

I already did something.

But I shouldn't have kissed her today. She almost died four months ago. How could she possibly be ready for a relationship—or anything—with me?

"I'm going to let her decide what's next."

Sean stares up at the cabin ceiling and says, "You can make each other very happy. You belong together."

Maybe we do, but I can't push her.

I nod and he suddenly speaks up. "I should have told you about this last week, but I had to be in Milan suddenly. Tiffany found Lily Todd."

What?

"Really?" When Jules told me she wanted to find Lily earlier today, I didn't want to tell her that I had already asked Tiffany to start looking. Because I'd had ulterior motives.

I actually reached out to Tiffany four months ago, just after Jules's suicide attempt. I wanted to find Lily on my own and confront her about how her letter completely destroyed Juliet's life. I vowed that I was going to make Lily feel the pain that we all were living during those days when Juliet's life hung in the balance. Part of me still wants to rip her to shreds, but Dr. Grant has helped me control those urges. She helped me see the parallels between the decisions that we both made to give up children.

My chest twinges, thinking about Emily and that day so many years ago. The day that I said goodbye to her.

Emily squirms in my arms as I hold her uncomfortably. Her eyes are open and her arms and legs are in the air. I bend down and place my lips on her forehead, inhaling her baby scent. Her hand swats me on my cheek and I jerk away. Am I hurting her?

"Hey, you're a feisty little thing. Just like your mama." She looks toward my face, trying to focus on where the voice above her is coming from. I study her features and the curves and contours of her face. I try to see myself in her, but I can't. She looks nothing like me, and I'm not sure if I'm relieved or sad. Everything that I've said to Tabitha is true. I can't be a father. My own father is despicable, and if I turn out anything like him, I belong in Hell, not at the head of a table. This child is an angel and belongs with a loving, perfect and normal family.

I look down at Emily one last time and awkwardly place her into the bassinet. My chest tightens as I pull my finger from her grip and softly say, "Goodbye."

I sit in the waiting room, waiting for Michelle to find me to sign the papers that I need to. I find a piece of paper and write a note to Tabby. I need to tell her how I feel and let her know her decision to give up Emily was the right one.

"Seth, are you ready?" Michelle, the hospital social worker asks.

"Yes." I fold the letter hand it to Michelle. "Can you give this to Tabby when you get a chance?"

"Of course," she says

I follow her into a small conference room where the adoption attorney and his paralegal are sitting at the table, pens ready.

I go through the motions, signing similar documents that I did before Emily was born. I haven't seen Tabitha since the morning we broke up a few days ago. The day she gave birth. She was very clear that she never wanted to see me again, and I needed to respect her wishes.

I walk out of the conference room, looking back at the nursery. "Goodbye, Emily."

"Seth?" Sean asks hesitantly. "Are you okay?"

"Yeah." I bring myself back to the present and realize that I need to figure out how I'm going to tell Juliet that I started this search months ago and the reasons why.

"Tiff has all of the details back home, but I think she'd prefer to give them to Jules directly. You understand, right?"

I nod. "That's probably for the best."

"We have to talk about Tyson Industries. One quarter of this company is yours now."

"I don't want it," I blurt out.

"Don't be ridiculous, Seth. We'll talk to the lawyers in a few days, but you need to know what's been going on and what vision the board has for taking us into the future. I think you're going to like what you hear." He turns to face the window, pulling his blanket up to his shoulder. "Get some sleep. We have a long week ahead of us."

My thoughts are consumed by one thing right now.

How am I going to tell Jules about Lily?

A COOL BREEZE BLOWS THROUGH my hair, and I look out across the vast cemetery. Father Cavanaugh is finishing his interment speech, but I've tuned out his voice.

It's finally over.

That's all I can think about. My father is about to be lowered into the ground where he can never inflict pain on my family ever again. Now it's time for us to pick up the pieces and pave a new path to repair the damage that he's done to us. My mother sits to my left and squeezes my hand. Chloe and Chelsea are to my right, sobbing. Sean sits on the other side of my mother and stares stoically at my father's casket.

Father Cavanaugh gestures toward us to begin our final goodbyes. The procession of mourners begins from behind as we watch lifelong family, friends and colleagues drop a red carnation onto his final resting place. Some linger, touching the casket, while others drop their flower without regard. So many people are here to say goodbye, and I wonder how many are as relieved as I am. I don't notice a plethora of young, single women and I'm thankful for that. It would kill my mother to see any of his mistresses here.

Thirty minutes have passed as our family sits and waits for the final mourner to leave. Chloe elbows me lightly in the ribs and whispers, "Seth, look."

I look up and see Juliet standing in front of my father's grave, her eyes closed in what appears to be a silent prayer. My heart jumps in my chest. I want to go grab her hand now and leave this place immediately. After about a minute with her head bowed down, she walks away without looking back.

Father Cavanaugh makes a blessing and he too walks away.

Sean stands and pulls my mother to her feet. I help him escort her to his grave and I hear her suck in a breath. Chloe and Chelsea each quietly sob, dropping their flowers and quickly walking away. Their cries get louder as they ascend the hill toward the limousine.

"Ted," my mother says quietly but with force. "You motherfucking no-good bastard." I stiffen and squeeze her hand tightly. "You're done making a fool of me and a mockery of our lives. You're done demeaning our family and me." She drops my hand and tosses the bouquet of red roses across the grass, landing near another grave. She lifts her head high, squares her shoulders and walks toward the car.

Sean and I stand there, dumbfounded. I don't ever recall a time hearing her speak like this.

"He deserved that," I say, smirking.

Sean breaks his silence and exhales deeply. "I suppose he did."

We both toss our flowers in the same direction that our mother did, gracing someone else's grave.

I see Juliet hugging my sister when I reach the car. "Thanks for coming, Jules," Chelsea says as she slides into the car next to my mother, who's comforting a sobbing Chloe.

Jules turns to me and grabs my hand. "Need a ride back to the house?" she asks.

"Sure."

"See you at home," I say to my mother and sisters. Sean and Tiffany are in their own car behind the limousine.

We walk quietly to Juliet's car, and I feel relief with each step that I take, happy that this is behind us.

"How are you?" she asks while pulling out of the cemetery.

"I'm good."

"I'm so sorry, Seth. I can't imagine how hard this is for you and your family."

"I'm relieved, actually. Happy that it's over. We'll get through this and come out stronger. I'm sure of it."

I grieved Jeremy's death. Grieved the loss of Mrs. Oliver. I'm not grieving now and don't plan to. I'm not sure she would agree with my attitude or even understand it, so I keep it to myself.

"Can I ask what happened?" she asks hesitantly.

"What do you mean? How he died?"

"Yes."

"Massive heart attack. He collapsed in his office and was apparently dead before he hit the floor. I was told that Heidi Cross was the one who found him. But if I were to guess, she was with him when it happened." Heidi is the head of Human Resources for Tyson Industries and rumored to be one of my father's fuck buddies.

"Oh."

"I'm really fine, Jules. Please don't worry about me." I look into her sad eyes. "You shouldn't have come back here. You don't need to be subjected to any of this depressing shit."

She huffs in silence, and I realize I shouldn't have said that out loud. I'm worried about how another death may affect her. I don't want to see her in pain.

"Are you being serious?" Her voice raises and I know she's mad. "I would go anywhere to support you and your family. Chloe and Chelsea are the little sisters I never had. Your mother has always welcomed me warmly into your home throughout the years."

"Yes, but—"

She cuts me off. "But more important than them, Seth, I'm here for you. I know what it's like to lose a parent, and I am here to help you. Please let me."

"It's different for me. I'm not sad that he's dead. The only loss that I feel is the fact that I never had a real father," I say too harshly.

"Bullshit," she retorts.

I refuse to argue and try to convince her that I'm glad that my father's dead. So I relent, "Thank you. I'm glad you're here. You have no idea how much it means to me." I'm sincere in this statement and I hope she believes me.

We pull up to my family's home, and there are cars parked along the vast driveway. I completely forgot about the post-funeral party.

"You can pull into the garage. No need to park all of the way out here." When we make it to the top of the driveway, the valet waves me past.

After we're parked, I turn to Jules. "Can we take a walk? I really don't want to go inside."

Her eyes soften. "Of course."

We walk silently through the grounds and stop at the pool house.

"Seth, why do you hate your father so much? Can you find *anything* positive?" I know she's trying to understand the differences between our families. Why I can be so cold toward the man who brought me into this world. She would give anything to have her mother back.

"He didn't deserve our family."

"But maybe there's something he could have done to change?" She's grasping at straws.

"My sisters are grieving hard, and maybe someday I'll ask them why they miss him so much. But I never saw the side of him that they did. The only thing that he did to redeem himself is that he didn't treat my sisters the same way he treated my mother. *That* is the *only* positive thing I will say about that man."

"If you could go back and change one moment with him, from any point in time, what would it be?"

I don't hesitate. "I'd want him to see me play in my first ball game and be proud of me." She knows firsthand that he never came to a single game, since she was there all of the time cheering me on. And Jeremy, too.

"I'm sorry that you can't have that back," she says softly.

"Thanks, Jules."

"Can we talk about the other day?" she asks hesitantly.

Oh boy.

I'm afraid of where this is going to go. *Our kiss.* I'm worried that she's going to say that is the one moment she wishes she could go back and change.

"I'm sorry about that. I shouldn't have kissed you."

Her face suddenly falls and she looks down at the grass.

"Oh."

Is she disappointed?

"Jules, talk to me. What are you thinking?"

"We said a lot to each other and I thought... I just thought that your kiss meant more."

"I know what it meant to me, but what did it mean for you?" I ask, taking a step toward her. She doesn't move and looks back into my eyes.

"I told you," she says softly.

"Tell me again."

She hugs herself with her arms and her eyes glisten. "It meant everything to me, Seth. *You* mean everything to me."

"Jules." I pull her toward me, cradling her face in my hands. My eyes trace the contours of her lips and I'm drawn to them once again.

"What took us so long?" I whisper against her lips before I claim them as mine. This kiss is so much more desperate, needing. We breathe each other in as our tongues dance together, pulling and entwining. I back away slightly so we can each take a breath. She laughs nervously and leans her forehead against my chin.

"I'm in love with you. Is it okay to tell you that?" I smile, pressing my lips into her hair.

"You just did." She laughs again. "Olive juice, too," she says through giggles.

I pick her up so our noses are touching, her feet a few inches off of the ground. "I want to hear it for real." Our eyes burn into each other.

"I'm in love with you, too. And yes, it's okay to say it."

I don't want her to feel guilt. Jeremy was such an important part of our lives years ago, and I know deep down that he was her first love. Hearing her reassure me that it's okay to share these feelings eases my own guilt for loving my best friend's girl.

"We should take things slow," I suggest, worried she may not be ready to rush into a relationship just four months after she and Ryan split.

"Seriously? We've known each other since fourth grade and you want to take it slow?"

"Jules, you know what I mean."

"I suppose so," she says, wrapping her arms around my neck. Her expression becomes tight, worried. "I made a decision that you need to know about."

"What is it?" I ask nervously, wondering what decision she could possibly have made in the few days that it's been since we last saw each other.

"I'm moving back to California."

chapter twenty-six

Juliet
Sausalito, California
Age 25

"I'M MOVING BACK TO CALIFORNIA," I say to him, worried about his response, hoping this doesn't change our recent declaration of love. I tense in his arms and bite my lip.

"Then so am I." His worried look morphs into a huge smile.

Relief floods my chest and I can't contain my excitement. "Really?"

"I want to come home, now that I feel that it *can* be my home again."

It breaks my heart to hear him talk like this, and I can't imagine how he felt all of these years away from his family. But knowing what I do about his relationship with his father makes me understand, to some extent.

"Sean and Tiff moved out of one of our properties in Russian Hill. He told me it's mine if I want it, and suddenly I do." He smiles and kisses me tenderly.

"San Francisco?" I ask, thankful it's close. "I'm moving back home, and Dad is so excited."

"Perfect dating distance," he jokes.

"Yes."

We make our way over to the pool area and sink into our own lounge chairs. We're holding hands across the span between us.

"Now I have something I need to tell you," he says hesitantly.

I turn to look at him and feel my eyes widen. "What?"

"Tiffany found Lily." His words hang in the air and I stop breathing. Just days ago I was adamant that I wanted to find her. Determined. But hearing that she's been found suddenly scares me.

"That was fast," I say.

"Well, I actually asked Tiffany to start her search when you were in the hospital." A guilty look washes over his face, and he shifts in the lounge chair.

"What? Why didn't you tell me?" *He's been searching for her for four months?*

"Honestly? I started the search when I thought you were going to die. I wanted to find her so she could feel the pain that I was feeling. That your father was feeling." I suck in my breath as his eyes plead with me for understanding. "I was desperate."

I pull my hand out of his grasp and turn to face him. "Have you spoken to her?" I'm trying to refrain from accusations, but I suddenly feel betrayed.

"No! God. No. Sean told me that Tiff found her on the flight here. I haven't spoken to her and would never do that without you." The tension leaves my shoulders, but I'm still concerned about his intentions.

"But you said you started looking back when I was in the hospital." I pause before I ask the next question. "What would you have done if you'd found her sooner?"

He sucks in his cheeks and breathes deeply through his nose. "I would have made her come see you in the hospital and witness what one letter can do to a person."

"I wish you would have told me that you started the search already," I say, feeling betrayed.

"I didn't want to get your hopes up or interfere with anything Dr. Grant was working on with you. I didn't want you to get obsessed with finding Lily and not focus on your own recovery." He stands up and moves to the edge of my lounge. My knees are pulled into my chest, and he eases my legs down onto his lap. "You have to know that I would never do anything to hurt you. Ever."

"I know."

"What do you want to do?" he asks, rubbing my knees.

"I—I don't know. Does my father know?"

"No. It's not my place to share."

My father always told me that when I was ready, he would help me find Lily. The adoption agency that my parents went through has her personal information sealed, as the adoption was considered 'closed.' My mother refused to accept that Lily would want it to remain that way and sent pictures and letters to the agency for years. We had assumed that Lily was receiving everything that my family sent, but my father confirmed that packages started being returned as 'undeliverable' many years ago.

"So, she's alive?" I ask.

"Yes."

"Where is she?" As soon as the words leave my mouth, my pulse begins to race. *Do I really want to know?*

"Portland, Oregon."

I gasp as soon as he says her location.

She's so close.

I remember the trip we took to Portland to celebrate my 'Adoption Day' so many years ago. That was also the first time I received a letter from Seth.

"I've been there. So many times." My mind races with scenarios of us potentially being in the same place at the same time and not knowing. *Would she have recognized me?*

"Let me know when you want the information. Tiffany suggested that it would be a bad idea for you to just show up on her doorstep. She offered to call her in advance, explaining the situation and that you'd like to arrange a meeting."

"But what if she says no?" I won't accept that as an answer.

"Then we think of another way that doesn't break any laws," he laughs, making me relax a little. "Realistically, I can't see her saying no. You're both adults."

"I can't do this alone," I state, trying to read his expression.

We both sit down on one of the oversized lounge chairs by the pool.

"I'll do anything you want."

"Come with me," I say immediately. "I want you there when I meet her for the first time."

"Are you sure?" He pulls me onto his lap and nuzzles into my neck.

"Absolutely. And thank you," I whisper into his cheek. He turns and brushes his lips against mine. I deepen our kiss, pulling his face closer.

"Why did we wait so long?" I ask him, repeating his question to me the other day.

"I'm still baffled by it." He smiles and hugs me close.

My heart twinges, because I know the answer to that question. *Jeremy.* He's been gone for years, but my heart and Seth's loyalty have both been with him. No matter how Seth felt about me when we were younger, I know he would have never made a move. I belonged to Jeremy, and Seth was his best friend.

"What are you thinking?" he asks.

"Nothing," I lie. I don't want him to think that I have any doubts now that we're building a relationship. But I can't shake Jeremy's image from my mind.

We sit silently as the voices from the main house bring us back to reality and the reason why we're here in the first place.

"I should get home. I'm anxious to tell my father about Lily." He nods in agreement and pulls me to my feet. He leans in, tucking a strand of hair behind my ear and kisses me deeply.

A man's voice startles us both and we flinch simultaneously. "Oh, I'm sorry, I didn't mean to interrupt!"

We turn toward the voice and see a familiar face, smiling at us.

"Well, it's about damn time," Jason Reed says.

My heart jumps, and I suddenly feel like I've been caught cheating, despite his cordial greeting. "Jason, I'm sorry…" I begin to apologize to Jeremy's older brother. Seth remains tense by my side.

"Sorry? What the hell are you apologizing for?" he says, laughing.

"In case you're wondering, this is exactly what it looks like," Seth adds and begins to laugh along with Jason.

"Man, I couldn't be happier to see you two together like this." I breathe a sigh of relief, but still feel weird that this conversation is happening and that Jason saw me making out like a teenager with Seth.

"Are you really okay with this?" I ask, looking between Seth and Jason.

"Are you kidding me?" Jason asks incredulously. "If there were two people meant to be together, it's you. But apparently you two are the last to figure it out."

"Thanks, Jason. That means so much coming from you." His kind eyes fill me with warmth.

"Chelsea told me that you're on a book tour, promoting your latest best seller. Congratulations," Seth says, reaching forward and shaking his hand.

"Yeah, thanks. The series that I started a few years ago has really taken off, and I'm on the fifth book now. I leave for Vancouver next week, and I'll be traveling for three months straight. My publisher is relentless with promotional appearances when all I want to do is lock myself in the house and write."

"It seems so exciting," I say, clasping my hands together.

"We have some exciting news too," Seth says, pulling me against his side "We're moving back home."

"That's great news," Jason says. "You know, my parents would love to see you both." He addresses Seth. "They send their condolences, by the way. They're on a cruise and aren't due home until next week."

"No worries. And thank you," Seth replies.

"We'll drop by in a few weeks when we each get settled," I say.

"Fantastic! I'm glad I ran into the two of you." He grabs Seth's hand and shakes it vigorously and then pulls me into a big hug.

"Congratulations again, Jason." I smile and hug him back.

He walks back toward the house and I feel tears form in my eyes.

"Hey, what's wrong?" Seth looks worried.

The tears spill over and I let them fall down my face. "I was thinking about Jeremy just before Jason showed up."

"What?" Seth asks, confused.

"It's not a rational feeling, but I think I needed that to happen. I needed someone from Jeremy's family to acknowledge you and me as an *us*." I feel ridiculous saying this out loud.

"It's not weird. I totally get it."

I grab his hand, leading him toward the house. "I want to say goodbye to your family before I go home."

After I say my goodbyes and we tell them that Seth and I are moving back to California, he walks me to the garage.

"Seeing you today, having you here, means so much to me. Thank you," he says, hugging me tight. "I don't want you to go."

"I'll call you as soon as I talk to my father. Wish me luck." I kiss him and quickly jump into my car.

"DAD?" I CALL OUT as I enter our home.

"In here," he calls from the family room. He stands from his chair, pulling me into a hug. "How are the Tysons?" He didn't come to the graveyard after the funeral mass, because he wasn't feeling well. I can see that he has a bit more color in his cheeks now, and I'm thankful he came home to rest. He's had the flu all week.

Considering I didn't mingle with a single person, I can't give too much commentary on how the 'party' went. I laugh a little. "I honestly don't know. But I did see Jason Reed, and he's getting ready to go on a huge book tour."

"That's great," he responds. "I saw his father at the club a few weeks ago, and he was excited to tell me that one of his books, *Covet*, has been optioned by a big Hollywood producer. You should have seen Janice. She could barely contain her excitement."

"A movie? Wow. That's amazing. He didn't mention it to Seth and me when we were catching up."

"I'm not surprised. Bill and Janice said that he's in denial over it. He never thought any of his books would reach anyone, but he's grown beyond his own comfort level."

Jeremy's family deserves happiness, and it's wonderful to see good things happen to them. I'm sure Jeremy's looking down on them with pride.

"Have you decided when you're moving back? You know, we need to make plans to get you packed and moved." My father is anxious to have me home as soon as possible. I know he's been lonely and has felt so far away during the past few months when I was hard at work fixing myself, learning to accept the effect that Lily's decision had on my entire life. He called me every night, but I could hear in his voice that he wished he could be in Philly to help me.

"I need to talk to my landlord next week and see if I can break my lease early. If I can't, Summer is looking to move into a bigger place, so she's agreed to sublet."

"Let me know how I can help. We can draw up an agreement between you and Summer pretty quickly."

"Sounds good. I think I can get everything packed by the end of the month."

His smile expands. "I'm so happy you're coming home."

"Me too."

I need to tell him about Lily, because I'm anxious to get the ball rolling on going to see her, if she'll even see me.

My heart is racing as I sink into the love seat against the window. "Dad, there's something else I need to tell you." My mood turns serious and I take a calming breath.

Concern sweeps over his face and he leans forward in his chair. "What?" I can tell he's bracing for something bad.

"I know where Lily is. I plan to meet her." I blurt it out, bracing for his response.

He hesitates for a moment and his shoulders drop. "I'm glad."

Relief floods my chest. "Really?" I truly want him to be okay with me seeing Lily, and I know he's been worried about my expectation of this meeting for years.

"Do you think you're ready?" he asks, his concern surfacing once again.

"I don't know if I'll ever be ready, but it's something I need to do. It's like it's the last step in putting my life back on track. I need to forgive her."

He raises his eyebrow. "Forgive? That's a huge step, and I'm really glad that you're finally ready to take it."

He's always been the one to be sympathetic toward Lily, where my mother tried to hide her feelings. Unwittingly, she fueled my anxiety, because she tried to protect me from Lily's words.

"This is good news, Jules, and I'm really proud of you. Regardless of what she did when she was sixteen, the decision she made gave us a gift, and gave you the opportunity to grow into a strong, independent woman."

I laugh a little. "Well, it took a while to get here, and a lot of obstacles." Depression, anxiety, suicide attempt—to name a few. I'm still on shaky ground, but I'm hoping meeting Lily will help me solidify my footing. I need to be completely whole for myself. *And for Seth.*

"I'm still trying to understand, Dad, and Dr. Grant has been wonderful in helping me see things differently. Remove the narrow visor that I've had on for years and see the good in the bad."

"Does Dr. Grant know that you're coming home?" Dad's so supportive of my therapy sessions and thinks that therapy is a cornerstone to my full recovery.

"Yes, she's already referred me to a colleague in San Francisco. My first appointment is already set up." He nods, thankful.

"So you're okay with me seeing Lily? Because I would reconsider if you voiced any major concerns." It would be hard to do, but I could try.

"Jules, if you feel that you need to do this, I would never stop you. Put an end to your curiosity and hear what she has to say. Be fair to her, and if you're really ready to forgive her, do it. And mean it."

Whoa. "Thanks, Dad. I will."

His eyes look heavy, and I know he needs more sleep. Before he drifts off, I feel the need to give him more reassurances about my upcoming trip to Portland. "Seth is coming with me."

"I would expect nothing less," he says through his smile. "That boy would go to the end of the earth for you, you know."

I do know.

He's everything to me.

chapter twenty-seven

Seth
Philadelphia, Pennsylvania
Age 27

"JULIET!" SUMMER SQUEALS from the stairwell outside Juliet's apartment.

"Hey, Summer. I'm sorry we're late. We hit traffic coming from the airport," Jules says as she hugs her friend. "This is Seth. He's an old... friend." She opens her door and we all follow her in. Summer looks back over her shoulder with a curious look on her face.

"I don't think we've ever met, but Jules has told me a lot about you. You're from California where she's from, right?" Summer asks.

"Yeah, we're grade school friends." I smile, not offering any more details. Juliet and I haven't even defined ourselves. *Are we something?*

We flew back to Philly together this weekend so we could get packed and moved back to California. Jules decided to sublet to Summer because she didn't want to go through the hassle of breaking her lease.

"Let's take care of business, shall we?" Juliet pulls the sublet agreement from her purse and places it on the table. Summer practically hops over to the table to sign on the dotted line.

"I'm so excited!" she screeches.

"We couldn't tell," Juliet says sarcastically.

"When can I officially move in?" Summer asks, looking around the apartment. She seems to be making mental notes about what she wants to do with the place.

"I should be mostly packed by tomorrow night. I'm leaving the furniture for you, and when you move out, you can take it with you or donate it."

"Thank you! I have some pieces of furniture I'm bringing from my old place, but I can put them in the spare room for the time being. This place is perfect as it is."

She hugs Juliet and says, "I'll get out of your way so you can pack." She stops in front of me, extending her hand to shake mine. "Nice to meet you, Seth."

The door closes behind her and Jules flops onto the couch. "I'm exhausted already. Can I just snap my fingers and have this place pack itself?"

I snap my fingers and say, "Poof!"

She laughs and gets up to go into her room. "I'm getting something more comfortable on. Something I can get dirty. I hope you have something to change into."

"Who says I'm staying to help?" I call after her.

"What?" she yells from her bedroom.

"Nothing. I was kidding. Yes, I have gym clothes I can wear." I grab my duffle bag and go into her bathroom to change.

After I get dressed, I follow the sounds of the ripping and pulling of packing tape coming from her living room. She has a few boxes already assembled, and she points to a roll of bubble wrap. "Can you get started on packing up the kitchen? I'm going to leave her all of my pots and pans, but I'm taking the dishes, glasses and silverware."

"Sure." She is totally in the zone, and I can tell that she wants to finish packing as soon as possible.

I start emptying the cabinets, carefully wrapping the breakable items. I watch her go through her bookshelf, neatly packing away her treasured collection. She stops every so often to rub the cover of a book, admiring some of her favorites. I catch her smelling a book and I joke, "Smell tasty?"

"Haven't you ever smelled a book?" she asks as if it's a normal practice.

"No, I can't say I have." I chuckle and continue packing away glasses and coffee mugs.

"Come here," she gestures. I look at her awkwardly, but put down the mug that's is in my hand and join her in the living room.

She places a book under my nose and says, "Close your eyes and then inhale deeply through your nose." She waits for me to close my eyes and then says softly, "Now."

I inhale and the slight musty smell from the book below my nose takes over my senses. It doesn't smell *dirty*, but a little dusty and old.

"Well?" she asks.

"It smells old," I say truthfully.

"Open your eyes," she says. She's smiling and shows me the book that she just had under my nose. It's looks old and dusty. The cover is worn and the spine looks like it's been opened many times.

"It's *The Stand* by Stephen King. I took this from my mother's bookshelf when I was about thirteen or fourteen. I didn't actually read it for the first time until I was sixteen, but I would look at the cover and wonder what the book was about. I know that my mother bought this book years ago, and I saw her reading it cover to cover on more than one occasion. It always intrigued me, and when I finally did read it, I understood why she read it so many times. It's a brilliant book." She places her treasured possession in my hands. "You should read it."

Our fingers brush against each other, and the warmth from her touch seems to spread up my arm, straight to my heart.

"I can't take this from you. It's you're favorite," I say. Her bright green eyes reflect the sunlight coming through the window.

"It's just a loan. Besides, I know where you live." She smiles and backs slowly away from me. "Now, back to work," she orders.

I find my gym bag and put the book in one of the pockets where I know it will be safe. Am I crazy to want to just want to sit and smell that book all night?

She turns on her iPod and the rooms fills the apartment with music. The song that's playing is familiar. "What song is this?" I ask her.

"'Take Back the City' by Snow Patrol. I've been listening to them a lot lately," she says as she seals one of the boxes containing her books.

I make a mental note to download all of their music immediately.

About an hour later, I have everything in the kitchen packed, sealed and labeled. She finished all of her bookshelves and packed the other knick-knacks in the living room and dining area.

"Just my bedroom is left," she says. Her arm brushes mine as she walks past me, and I do everything to restrain myself from pulling her back against me.

I follow her, and she has larger wardrobe boxes already standing in the room. "Where did you get these from?" I ask her.

"I had them shipped here last week, and when Summer came to check out the apartment, she set them up."

"What do you need me to help you with?" I ask, looking around.

"Can you pack up all of the pictures from my walls? We still have bubble wrap left, right?"

"Yes, plenty." I leave and return with the giant never-ending roll that is tempting me to drop it onto the floor and stomp all over it.

Packing her room goes much quicker than the kitchen and living room did.

She reaches into her closet, grabbing a small box. She takes it with her as she sits down on the bed.

"I haven't opened this since college," she whispers, and I'm not sure she's talking to herself or me.

I walk to the bed and sit down next to her. "What is it?"

She runs her hand along the top of it as if to dust it off and then slowly opens it. I see an envelope and other pieces of paper, as well as some pictures.

She takes out the envelope, and that's when I realize what this is. She sucks in a breath and holds the letter to her chest. "This letter had the power to completely destroy me, and it almost did. I swore to myself that I would never read this letter again. Never look at it again." She closes her eyes and breathes deeply.

"That letter has no power over you, Jules. Do you understand me?" I put my arm around her and pull her into my side.

She has been through so much therapy and counseling and knows that she can't give any power to these words from a sixteen year old girl. Dr. Grant has told her several times to reread this letter someday and try to picture herself as a scared teenager.

She places the letter back in the box and pulls out what looks like a plane ticket or boarding pass. "What's that?" I ask.

"It's a plane ticket to go home. Jeremy gave it to me right before graduation as a promise to keep the distance between us minimal. He bought this to fly me home for my birthday."

"You didn't come home that year? Why?" I ask, knowing she didn't use this ticket.

She sighs. "For so many reasons, but I didn't want to give this ticket to anyone to be stamped or torn. I needed it to remain whole, in the same state as when he gave it to me." She places the ticket back into the box, carefully tucking it under a pile of pictures that I assume are of her and Jeremy.

"I'm sorry, Jules." I kiss her on her temple and let my lips linger as I breathe in her scent. Lemons with a twinge of salty sweat. That's when I realize how hard we've worked this afternoon as I look around her room. Everything is almost completely packed, and we did it in less than a day.

She places the box on the nightstand and wraps her arms around my waist. "Thanks for helping today. And every day."

"I would do anything for you, Jules."

She yawns and moves away from me, laying down on her side. "I need a nap. My eyes are burning I'm so tired." She pulls the down comforter up to her chin and closes her eyes. Her breathing is soft and slow, and just like that, she's asleep.

How does she do that?

I remember the time she passed out in Jeremy's bed and was asleep in literal seconds, but I assumed that was because of all of the alcohol she drank.

I look around the room, trying to find something else to pack, fighting the urge to get into bed with her. But she looks so comfortable, and I can't resist. I could use a nap too. I gingerly slip under the covers and softly pull her against me.

Feeling her body moving in against mine and hearing her soft breaths begins to lull me into my own slumber.

As I drift off, I think to myself that this is something I've always wanted for her.

Peace.

chapter twenty-eight

Juliet
Philadelphia, Pennsylvania
Age 25

I'M PINNED TO MY BED and when I open my eyes, the room is pitch black.

How long have I been asleep?

Seth's arm is draped heavily over my side, and his chest is pressed tightly against my back. *And when did he get in bed with me?*

I lie still in his arms, trying to make sense of everything that's happened between us over the past few months. His voice was the only one I heard when I was in a coma. So many people came to see me and stay with me, my father included. But it was Seth's voice that made me come back to him. To everyone.

I wrap my arm around his and pull him tighter against me. He breathes heavily, and I know he's still asleep. What did I do to deserve a lifelong friend like Seth? And now that *we're something*, we're taking things slow.

He begins to stir behind me and pushes his hand against my belly. His body suddenly goes rigid and he says quietly, "You awake?"

"Mmm hmm."

"I'm sorry, I hope I didn't overstep by slipping into bed next to you. You just looked so peaceful." I pull his hand closer to my heart and smile.

"Did I thank you yet for coming with me to help?" I ask as I close my eyes again.

He nuzzles into the back of my hair. "Probably. But you can return the favor by helping me pack up some things over at my place tomorrow."

"Of course," I say, stretching my legs out. *What time is it?* I look around and realize that I packed my clock already. I reach for my phone and see that it's eight o'clock.

"Wow, I can't believe how late it got. When I fell asleep, it was still daylight," I say.

"I should get over to my place, maybe get a head start on packing so we don't have as much to do tomorrow," he says as he begins to pull his hand from my waist.

My breath hitches at the loss of his touch, and I say quickly, "You don't have to leave." I roll over to my other side, facing him.

He sits up on the bed next to me and stretches his legs in front of him, contemplating my statement. "Are you sure?" he asks.

I nod and place my head back down on the pillow.

"Are we still taking things slow?" he asks, and I tense up a little.

"Yes, I think so?"

"Okay." He turns his head toward me and smiles, rolling back onto his side so we're facing each other. Nose to nose. His warm breath tickles my mouth, and I part my lips to lick them a little bit.

"Okay," I whisper back, feeling the words pass from my lips to his.

He closes the short distance between us by pressing his lips onto mine, kissing me softly, tenderly. His hand brushes through my hair, fingers tickling the back of my head. I moan softly into his mouth and deepen our kiss. There seems to be an invisible barrier between the lower halves of our bodies.

Taking things slow.

I move my hand down his arm and under his shirt. He immediately tenses his abs as my fingers run over his warm skin, following the tight contour of his muscles. His hand remains firmly planted against the back of my head, massaging me, holding me in place so he can kiss me tenderly, sweetly. Our kisses turn hungry, frantic. My body aches for more, and I inch my hips toward his. As soon as my hipbone presses into his, he pulls away. Our noses are still inches apart, and I'm gasping for air.

"This isn't taking things slow, Jules," he says with a serious tone to his voice.

My chest is heaving as I try to regulate my breathing. I'm flustered. "I know."

He turns onto his back and pulls me against him so I can lay my head on his chest. "I'm doing everything in my power to restrain myself. You have no idea how much I want this. All of you." He runs his hand along my arm, grazing the side of my breast, causing shivers to travel down my spine.

"I didn't mean to tempt you like that," I say, trying to lighten the mood. We're so close to crossing a line that we can never hop back over. Once we go *there*, there's no turning back.

"I don't want to ruin everything, you know?" he asks.

"I'm afraid of the same thing," I admit. "But this feels so right. *Us*."

"It feels better than anything. Ever. And it is right, Jules, but we need to stick to our plan and ease into this with our eyes wide open."

"Okay," I say, closing my eyes again.

He tickles my arm lightly, up and down. His touch is lulling me back to sleep, and I welcome it. Suddenly, his cell phone starts buzzing and he slaps his hand on the nightstand to grab it.

He places it to his ear. "Hey, Tiff." As soon as I hear his sister-in-law's name, I perk up and turn my head to look at him.

"Okay, is that it? Thanks for following up. Tell Sean I said hey." He ends the call and places the phone back onto the night table.

"Tiff spoke with Lily." I hold my breath in anticipation of what may come out of his mouth next. The answer is no, she doesn't want to meet me. I prepare myself for the negative response and burrow my head into his side.

"She wants to meet you, and she's suggested sometime next month." I let out my breath and a sob escapes at the same time.

"She said yes?" I say through the tears that have already started falling.

He nods his head and his worried look returns. "Are you sure you're ready for this?"

"Yes, I need to meet her." He lifts his hand to swipe tears from my cheek and leaves his hand there.

"Promise me you'll give Dr. Grant a call while we're still in Philly?" His eyes search out mine, pleading.

"I'll call her, but tomorrow is Sunday. I don't think she has hours."

"Try, please," he implores. "I want to be sure she knows everything that's happened with finding Lily. With me. *Us.*"

"Okay."

"Let's get some sleep. Are you sure you want me to stay tonight? I don't want things to be awkward," he says.

"It would be awkward if you left." I smile and place my head back onto his chest.

"I don't ever want you to leave," I say as I begin drifting back to sleep.

chapter twenty-nine

Seth
Portland, Oregon
Age 27

JULIET IS FROZEN IN PLACE at the end of the sidewalk leading to a cozy-looking house on Lake Oswego. This is the house that belongs to Lily Todd, the same woman who gave birth to her and almost wrecked her. She's taking deep, calming breaths, and I know she's having second thoughts about going through with this meeting.

We arrived in Portland after leaving San Francisco early this morning. She didn't speak much during the short flight, and her silence worried me immensely. I needed her to talk through her anxieties about what she was about to do, so I could make sure she was going to be okay.

"I think I'm ready," she says, and I'm not sure if her words are directed toward me or if she's trying to convince herself.

"Are you sure you don't want me to wait out here?" I ask, unsure of the answer that I want to hear.

She grabs my hand tightly and says, "I need you with me. Please?"

"Of course. Let's do this." I smile and we walk toward the house.

The front door opens before we get there and a tall, striking woman opens the door. Juliet almost freezes midway up the sidewalk, but I urge her forward.

We reach the house, and Juliet and Lily just stare at each other, studying the other's faces and features. It's very clear to me that Lily is her mother. They have similar hair, eyes and noses. Lily's smile is tight, nervous.

"Juliet, it's so good to meet you," she says as her voice begins to waver. "Please, come in." We enter her home and see that it's just as cozy on the inside as it is on the outside. Warm colors and the scent of candles fill the house.

"Your home is beautiful," Jules says, breaking the silence as she looks around. "And I see that you have a wonderful view of the lake." She strains her neck to look through the back sliding doors.

"We love our home," she says.

When Tiffany spoke to Lily and explained the reason behind her call, after her shock over the news, Lily shared a few details about her family. She's married and has three children. Two girls and a boy. One of the girls and the boy are twins. Tiff shared this information with Juliet.

As my eyes scan the house, I see pictures of Lily's family everywhere. Smiling. Happy.

"This is Seth. I hope you don't mind that he came with me?" Juliet asks her.

Lily nods her head. "Of course. And it's a pleasure to meet you both."

They continue their small talk for what seems like forever, neither wanting to address the real reason why we're standing in her living room.

"I'm glad that you found me," Lily says, sitting down in an armchair by the window and gesturing for us to have a seat on the couch.

Juliet looks astonished and struggles for words. "Really?"

"Yes," Lily responds and folds her hands in her lap. "Where would you like to begin?"

I feel Juliet stiffen next to me, and I want to blurt out all of the questions that I know are burning on her tongue. I place my hand over hers to let her know that I'm here for her no matter how this conversation goes.

"I want to know everything," Jules states simply. Calmly.

Lily looks a little flustered but composes herself quickly. "I can tell you everything. Anything. But why don't I start at the beginning, with my pregnancy and what led me to make the decision to give you up." Her eyes fill with tears, and I'm suddenly terrified for Juliet.

I hope she's truly ready for this.

"That's as good a place as any," Jules says softly.

Lily takes a deep breath, and her eyes begin to dart around the room as if she's taking inventory of the pictures of her family that christen the walls of her home. Getting strength from her loved ones.

"I was young. Too young. *We* were too young. The year I turned sixteen was easily the hardest year of my entire life." She pauses and tries to gain her composure.

"My twin sister, Layla, killed herself on our birthday. She suffered from severe clinical depression from the time she was ten years old. Our parents tried to understand the reasons, and because we were twins, they put us both into therapy. Where I could cope with things, to a point, she spiraled out of control, making completely reckless and dangerous decisions. There were times when she was ecstatically happy and fun to be around. Those were the days that I remember as some of the best times with her. They were also the days that our therapist described as my sister's 'manic episodes.' Layla couldn't control her urges during these times, but our parents relished them as I did. Because we were happy and having fun."

She gazes toward a picture of two young girls on a hammock together, and I immediately assume it's Lily and Layla. Juliet stares at her, waiting for her to continue this sad story.

"After she killed herself, our family splintered. My parents put all of their energy into only remembering the 'manic' Layla, and not enough energy into making sure I was going to be okay. They started ignoring me and traveling to every end of the earth, volunteering with our church mission. They didn't know anything about me, and I was still alive and breathing. I had been dating Mason Holland since I was fifteen. Mason was two years older than I was, and I knew that he was going to be my escape from all that my family had become.

We got very serious, very fast. After Layla died, he was my support, my rock. He loved me passionately, or as passionately as a sixteen-year-old can even understand. My parents were away on one of their missions when Mason was driving me home from school. We were goofing off, tickling each other, which caused him to lose control of the car. We were going very fast, too fast, when we veered off the road and into a large tree. He died instantly."

Jules's breath hitches, and she brings her hand to her mouth. "I'm sorry," she whispers.

Lily brings a tissue to her eyes, dabbing the pooling tears. "I don't know why I didn't die too. I should have. The accident was my fault. I don't remember anything else, because I was unconscious at the time of impact. When I came to at the hospital, the nurse told me what happened to Mason. It broke me. It was then that I realized that I also lost my escape from my family and all of the sadness that we lived through. Mason was my light and my love, and he was gone. After running tests on me to be sure I was okay, they informed me that I was pregnant. At first, I didn't believe the nurse, but she walked me through the blood work, confirming for sure that I was. I begged her not to tell anyone. My parents hadn't yet arrived, and I was alone with this secret and alone with my intense grief.

My parents were detained during a layover, and my Aunt Cecilia came to the hospital to comfort me. When I was discharged, I went home with her. When my parents came home, they made sure I was okay, of course, but they retreated even further into their own world and virtually ignored my existence. I had convinced myself that I was too harsh of a reminder and that every time they looked at me, they saw my sister. Knowing I was pregnant, I had no idea what to do. I always stayed with my aunt when my parents were away, and I confided in her throughout my life. She was more of a mother to me than my own, especially when Layla and Mason died. When I finally told her of my pregnancy, she was comforting, promising to support any decision that I would make."

Juliet surprisingly interrupts her. "So you had someone who could help support you while you raised a baby?" Her voice is tight and accusing.

"Aunt CeCe was sick. She had terminal cancer and died a few months after you were born." She bows her head and pulls the tissue apart in her hands.

"Oh," Jules says.

After Lily composes herself, she continues. "I told Aunt CeCe that I couldn't keep my baby. I was too young, and I couldn't handle a reminder of what had become of my life and the loss of Mason. She promised me that she would support me, and even offered to help me terminate the pregnancy. That was something that I absolutely could not do. Mason's blood was running through my baby's blood, and even though I couldn't make the decision to parent, I couldn't kill a piece of him."

"I see." Jules turns to look at me, and I see tears threatening to spill from her eyes. I want to absorb all of her pain and sadness right now, make all of it go away, but I can't. She needs to hear this from Lily.

"No one knew that I was pregnant. I dropped out of school and my aunt helped tutor and homeschool me. My parents didn't even know. When they were home, which was rare, I avoided them and Aunt CeCe covered for me. She would make excuses about where I was, inventing fictitious friends. I was home alone when I went into labor, because my aunt was in the hospital, fighting for her life. My parents were out of the country again, and I literally had no one to call for help. I gave birth to your sister at home."

Jules and I both gasp and she says, "My sister? What are you talking about?"

Lily looks stunned. "Oh my God, I didn't tell you in the letter, did I?" She covers her mouth and shakes her head. "I'm so sorry if this is a shock. Please forgive me."

"Where is my sister?" Jules demands.

"Let me explain." Lily tries to calm herself as her voice shakes. "As I said, I gave birth to your sister at home. On Halloween. I was terrified and had no idea what I was doing. When she came out, she was a bluish gray color and didn't make a sound. I don't remember everything that I did—it was all a blur—but when I realized she wasn't breathing, I remember wrapping her in the first thing that I could grab and walking to the hospital. I was dazed and confused and had probably lost a lot of blood. University Hospital was about five or six blocks from my aunt's apartment, and I honestly don't know how I made it there. She was dead in my arms, and I was terrified." She covers her mouth again and starts sobbing. "God forgive me, but I just left her there. On the ground in the ambulance bay."

My heart jumps in my throat and I feel faint. Juliet cries along with Lily and my head is spinning. "What hospital?" I ask her to repeat herself.

"Why does that matter?" Lily asks, and Juliet turns to me.

Because that baby wasn't fucking dead!

"Lily, tell me where you left that baby," I urge, already knowing the answer.

"University Hospital," Lily says, looking thoroughly confused.

"Seth, what's going on?" Juliet asks.

I can't tell her what I know.

My voice wavers and I lie. "Nothing. Sorry, please continue."

Juliet squeezes my arm and I whisper, "I'm sorry, I didn't mean to interrupt."

But I'm dying inside right now. I *need* them to know. My mind is racing with all that this implies, and I feel sick.

"After I left her, I tried to go home. My sixteen-year-old mind didn't think straight and couldn't comprehend that I needed medical help. I didn't know that you were still inside me, because I didn't know that I was pregnant with twins. I must have wandered the streets for some time, because when I was coherent enough, I realized I wasn't even at my aunt's house. I collapsed outside a restaurant and a stranger took me to St. Joseph's hospital. That's where I gave birth to you."

Jules starts rubbing her hands on her jeans, and I know her mind is racing with questions needing answers. I want to shout out everything that I think I know.

"I was in bad shape and nearly died from the blood loss. I didn't tell them that I had given birth to your twin earlier that night, because

I didn't want to be charged with murder. In my mind, I thought that by giving birth at home, I had somehow killed her. The emergency room where I gave birth to you was a zoo that night, so it didn't even come up, and the intern who delivered you clearly didn't notice. It was terrifying and a relief at the same time. I didn't know how to mourn your twin, because I was so lost and distraught over my actions."

"I'm sorry, we need to get some air," I blurt out before I pull Juliet into the foyer.

Lily remains in the living room while Juliet looks wildly confused. "What the hell?"

"We need to go outside and get some air. *Now*," I insist.

"I'm sorry, Lily. We'll be right back," Juliet feebly apologizes as she follows me outside.

I begin to pace on the porch, pushing my hands through my hair. *How the hell am I going to tell her what I know?*

"What the fuck is going on?" Juliet laces into me.

"I don't even know how to tell you this. Holy shit." I stop pacing and pull her to a bench on the porch.

Her eyes are wide and she looks pale.

"I don't think your sister is dead," I blurt out, and her mouth gapes open.

"What?" She looks at me with disbelief and confusion. "How the hell would you *know* this?"

"Because I know her." *Holy shit.*

"Who do you know?" she demands.

"Your sister. I'm certain she's alive because it's... Tabitha." As the words leave my mouth, I almost vomit. *How can this be? How could I not have not known? Not seen it?*

I search her face for confirmation and I see the resemblance, although slight. Her eyes are wide, and I reach out to touch her cheek.

"Don't," she flinches and stands up. "How could you know this? This can't be true. You heard Lily yourself. She left a *dead* baby at that hospital. Dead! It can't be Tabitha." She's pale and looks like she's about to pass out. Her stare is tearing through me, and it's killing me to see her look at me this way.

"It's too much of a coincidence. Lily's story is an *exact* match to how Tabby was found at that same hospital, *on that same exact day*. It *has* to be her." Sisters? Tabitha and Juliet. My mind still can't grasp this reality.

The front door opens and Lily comes out onto the porch, lowering her head. "I'm sorry to interrupt. I know all of this must be so overwhelming, and I'm sorry if what I've told you is upsetting. I wish I could rewind the clock and do things differently. I was young and scared to death. I hope you can at least see that." Her voice is strained, begging for understanding.

Jules turns to face her, shaking her head, unable to speak. Lily looks defeated and withdrawn.

I need to do something.

"Can we go back inside?" I ask, applying light pressure to Juliet's back. "I think there's something else we need to discuss."

Lily opens the door, leading us back into the living room.

"Seth, I don't think you should," Jules says weakly.

Lily looks confused as she sits back in the armchair.

I ignore Juliet's comment, knowing this could be the end of us. The realization of who her sister is could destroy everything that we have.

"Lily, I don't believe Juliet's twin sister is dead," I blurt out as Juliet throws her head into her hands and Lily's eyes widen.

"What on earth do you mean?" Lily asks incredulously.

"I *know* her. Her name is Tabitha Fletcher, and she was born the same exact day that Juliet was and left in the ambulance bay at the same exact hospital. This can't be a coincidence."

"I can't—I mean this can't be." Lily's voice drifts off and she sobs quietly into her tissue.

Juliet turns to me. "I had no idea that Tabitha and I had the same birthday."

"I don't understand how it would have mattered in the past, Jules. I never thought anything of it until now."

"How can she be alive?" Lily is whispering. *"How?"*

I turn to see her holding a picture of a baby in her hands. "This is you, Juliet." She turns the frame so we can see. "If I'd known she was alive, I swear you would have stayed together. Please believe me when I tell you that. I have no idea how to react to what Seth just told me, but you have to believe me that I never would have separated you had I known she was *alive*."

Juliet rises from the couch and stands in front of Lily, taking the picture from her hand. "This was my second birthday." She touches the glass. "I was a butterfly." She hands the photo back to Lily and asks, "Why did you stop accepting pictures from my family?"

Lily places the photo back on the table, and I notice that there are three other children's photos. I assume they are the children that she has now.

"When we moved here to Portland, about ten years ago—this will sound terrible, and I apologize up front—but when my husband and I moved here, I wanted to leave everything that happened to me in Philly behind. I started my life over when we bought this house and had Grace. Then Brandon and Leah came along, and I realized that I could find happiness and keep it. I never forgot about you, and I've told my children about you."

As Juliet digests this additional information, bile begins to rise in my stomach as I recall the time that Tabitha spent in Portland was tortuous. And Lily was here at the same time. The irony is startling, and I shake my head and say without thinking, "Tabitha spent some time in Portland a while back." *I shouldn't have said that out loud.* Lily doesn't need to know the hell that Tabby went through, *or does she?*

"Really?" Lily and Juliet ask simultaneously. I decide to keep the details to myself and just nod my head. I've never told Juliet about all of Tabby's hardships, because it wasn't my story to tell.

"Yes," I pause. "A while ago."

"Tell me about them," Jules says to Lily. "Tell me about your family."

chapter thirty

Juliet
Portland, Oregon
Age 25

"TELL ME ABOUT THEM," I say to Lily. "Tell me about your family."

My family.

She opens a drawer in the end table next to her and pulls out a small box that was placed toward the back of the drawer. She puts the box on her lap and rests her hand on top of it. "First, I'd like to show you pictures of your father, Mason."

"Why don't you sit here, so you and Juliet can look at them together." Seth squeezes my hand and stands up, offering his seat to Lily.

"Thank you," she says, moving next to me on the love seat.

She opens the box and starts flipping through old photos. She finds the one that she's looking for and pulls it out. I'm apprehensive about seeing my birth father for the first time, and my nerves start to get the better of me. *What did he look like?*

"Mason was born to be outside." She shows me the photo and he's smiling ear to ear. From what I can tell, he towers over everyone else around him, at least six feet tall and more. He has shaggy, dark brown hair and his eyes are bright green. His arm is draped over a young girl, who I assume is Lily. "We were volunteering with our church for Habitat for Humanity. This was taken the year before he was killed. I was fifteen in this picture."

I take the picture from her hands and study it closely. *I can't believe I'm staring at my birth father.* He and Lily both look so happy and *so young.* I see that he and I have the same tone and complexion, and our noses are also similar.

"Mason's father was the pastor in our church. We spent a lot of time helping out where we could. His family sometimes traveled with my parents when they went on their missions around the world. Our families were very close."

"What else did he like to do?" I ask while staring at the picture some more.

"He loved life." She smiles as she flips through the box for more pictures. "There wasn't a sport he couldn't play or a person he didn't help." She lowers her voice. "Our parents didn't know about us and our relationship. Since our families were so close, and he was two years older than I was, they just assumed we were friends. My parents trusted him around me because they viewed him as an older brother to Layla and me. When Layla died, Mason was a constant fixture around our house until my parents took off to South America. He was there for all of us, but comforted me the most."

"He seems like a wonderful person."

She places a picture on my knee. "That's Layla and me when we were about twelve or thirteen." She suddenly sucks in her breath and begins to lose her composure.

"I'm sorry, for some reason, seeing this picture is upsetting me." She pulls another tissue from her pocket and dabs her eyes. "I hope you can understand that I'm still in complete shock that your sister is actually alive. Seeing Layla and me together during one of our happy times makes me incredibly sad for what you could have had with Tabitha."

I'm still trying to even process that I have a sister. I need to digest everything and figure out how to handle what I found out today. I look up and make eye contact with Seth, who is now sitting in the chair that Lily vacated. His eyes are worried and sad, as if he believes that what I found out today will destroy our future.

He was in love with my sister.

I know enough about Tabitha to know that she had a very difficult life. Seth never shared too much, because he was trying to protect her. He said that some of her secrets were dangerous, and now I need to know more.

"I'm still trying to process it myself, Lily. I can't believe that I have a sister." I pause and look at the smiling girls.

What would our lives have been like if we'd been adopted together?

Would we have been able to support each other through everything?

Would she have been able to help me through my tough times?

Would she have avoided her tough times?

Would we have been best friends?

She gestures toward the table with my picture on it. "This is my family now."

She stands up and grabs the picture of the five of them and brings it back to the couch. "I met my husband, David, about fifteen years ago. I was teaching in a private school outside of Philly, and he was an investment banker with a large brokerage firm in the city. A mutual friend introduced us, we hit it off immediately, and we married a year later. After a few years in Philly, we decided we needed a change from everything. I don't have the best relationship with my parents, and David's family lives in Seattle. We decided to move to Portland when David's company offered a relocation opportunity. Grace is ten, and the twins, Brandon and Leah, are eight."

"You have a lovely family," I say hollowly. I have siblings who are children, just babies. And I have a sister my age. Seth is glancing at all of the other pictures on the table, but I'm not sure how much more I want to hear. This is all so overwhelming and is beginning to feel like a dream. I instinctively rub my hands on my jeans, and Seth turns toward me with a worried look on his face.

"Jules, we have a flight to catch, but I can call Clark and let him know we're running late." Seth picks up on my body language, offering an exit strategy.

Lily quickly tucks the pictures into the box and covers it with the lid, placing her hand on top protectively. "I'm so glad you found me, Juliet." She places her other hand over mine, and her warmth settles me somewhat. "I'm not the same scared girl that I was when you were born. I learned to heal my wounds and allow someone to love me. I know it may be hard for you to hear, but I'm very happy."

"Would you go back in time and do things differently?" I blurt out, and pulling my hand out from underneath hers.

"That's impossible to answer," she says softly. "My life was different back then. I was lost. Alone." She takes a deep breath and continues, "I would like to say that I wish I could have that decision to make again, but I honestly don't think I would make a different choice. I'm sorry if that's not what you want to hear."

"No regrets?" I whisper.

She turns to face me and suddenly pulls me into her arms. "I have so many regrets, Juliet. But giving you a healthy and happy life with your parents is not one of them." I let her hold me for a few more seconds, and then we slowly let go of each other.

"Thank you for sharing everything with me," I say as Seth stands up to leave.

"I want to know about Tabitha," she says suddenly, and I turn to look at Seth. He looks at his watch and pulls out his phone, quickly sending a text.

He turns to me and says, "I told Clark to hold the jet for another hour, if that's okay?"

I nod in agreement. I too want to know as much about Tabitha he can share. We sit back down in the living room and Seth begins to tell Lily about his former love. I can tell he is holding back some details, because he doesn't describe in detail the hardships that Tabitha endured throughout her life, but he does tell her about her youth, and how her adoptive mother was killed suddenly, forcing her into the foster system at a very young age.

Lily is visibly uncomfortable and pained listening to Seth telling parts of Tabitha's story. "I wish I'd known that she was alive," Lily sobs. "Her life would have been so much different, better." She turns to me. "And so would yours. You would have grown up with your sister, as a family." She begins shaking her head and cries into her hands.

"I'm sorry if this is hard for you," Seth says soothingly. "I can tell you that she is married now and has a family of her own." I don't know why he omitted the fact that Tabitha gave up two children for adoption, but I suppose it's not entirely his story to tell.

"If you don't mind sharing, can you give me her address? I'd like to let her know who I am." Lily composes herself enough to grab a notebook from the desk and hands it to Seth.

He pulls out his phone and starts typing and scrolling. He scribbles onto the paper and says, "Here's the address of the bookstore that she worked in. I'm not sure if she's still there, but the owner will know how to get in touch with her. I'm sorry, but I don't have her current address."

"That'll do," Lily says as she stares at the paper. She says her name out loud. "Tabitha Fletcher Treadway. Thank you for this."

"Of course," Seth nods.

She turns to me and says, "Well, I've certainly made a mess out of many lives, haven't I?" She looks lost and sad.

"Thank you for making the choice that you did. You gave me a wonderful family." I smile, and for the first time, I truly mean what I say. I can't bring myself to tell her that my mother is dead. I can save that for another time.

Will there be another time?

"Please stay in touch with me?" she asks, reading my mind.

Without hesitating, I respond, "Of course." I take the piece of paper from her hand and write my email address on it. I don't know what to expect from future correspondence, but I can only hope that we learn more about each other. I'm not looking for a 'mom,' because I have one, in my heart and in heaven. Maybe keeping the lines of communication open between us will help us each grow stronger in our own lives.

"Thank you, Juliet." She hugs me again and turns to hug Seth as well.

"Ready?" He reaches his hand out toward mine and I instinctively grab it.

"Yes," I say, and we walk out the door. As we get closer to the car, I have the urge to turn back. I want to know more. *Would she tell me more about my grandparents? Do I have cousins? How much do her children know about me?*

"Are you okay?" Seth asks as we pull away from Lily's house. His voice is tight, and I can tell he's still worried about everything that happened today.

"Not really," I respond, looking out the window. "But I think I will be, eventually."

"I'm so sorry about everything that happened today. I'm just as shocked as you are about Tabitha. This is just…"

"Weird?" I complete his sentence.

"That's one way to describe it." His phone buzzes, and he immediately switches it to Bluetooth. "Clark, we're on our way."

"Mr. Tyson, I'm sorry, but we're grounded for the night. There's a storm coming and the airport is closing. They tell me we can get out first thing in the morning. Do you have the keys to the place downtown?"

Seth sighs and reaches to open the glove compartment, spotting the keys. "Yes, I'll call you in the morning, but I'm thinking we'll want to be in the air by ten." He turns to me and I nod in agreement.

"I'm sorry that we're stuck here for the night. I hope it's okay. The apartment downtown has several bedrooms, so there's plenty of room if you want your space. Or we could get you a room somewhere?"

As confused as I am by everything I found out today, I don't want to be alone. "The apartment is fine for me. We don't have any clothes or toiletries though." We left from San Francisco this morning, expecting to be back just after dinner. We clearly didn't plan for this.

"I'm sure I have some things there, like sweats and t-shirts. At least you'll have something to sleep in. We can stop to buy something if you'd rather not wear my clothes."

"No worries. I can wear this outfit home tomorrow and sleep in whatever you have. Thanks for the offer though." I smile. "I'm glad you're with me, Seth." I reach out and link my pinky with his, and he squeezes it back. There is no way I could have done this today by myself. It also occurs to me that neither Lily nor I would know about Tabitha. *But is that a good thing?*

We drive the rest of the way in silence as our little fingers remain linked.

chapter thirty-one

Seth
Portland, Oregon
Age 27

I OPEN THE DOOR to my family's apartment in downtown Portland, and I honestly can't remember the last time any of us were here. Jules follows me in as I turn on the lights in the living room. She throws herself onto the couch and kicks off her shoes.

We need to talk more about what we found out today, and I'm afraid to start the conversation. I place my phone into the speaker system and look around the room for the remote control. We need to relax, and maybe music will help.

"Am I anything like her?" Jules asks hesitantly.

"Like Lily?" I ask, unsure of who she's referring to. I sit on a stool at the bar, and I'm seriously contemplating having a drink.

She shakes her head and looks away from me. "No, like Tabitha."

I guess this conversation is going to happen.

"Now that I've made the connection, you have a similar look," I reply, worried where this is going. I still don't feel like I can share anything about Tabitha's troubled past with anyone. "You must be fraternal twins, because you're clearly not identical." I shift nervously.

"I don't care about looks. I want to know other things." She takes a deep breath and makes eye contact with me. She looks exhausted. "Was she ever depressed? Suicidal? Anxious?"

"Jules, I don't know what you expect to get out of finding out about Tabitha's issues. How is knowing any of this going to help you?" I get up from the stool and sit at the other end of the couch.

"I don't know. Maybe it'll help validate my own issues from when I was growing up. I never fully accepted my place in general. I was angry, sad and unable to accept that I was discarded, given away. *Unwanted.*"

"But you now know that's not the case. You heard Lily's story today. Would you have done the same thing in her shoes?"

She looks down at her hands and shakes her head. "I have no idea what I would have done. But isn't it ironic that my sister had to make a similar decision? She was able to give up her children just like Lily did. Is there some sort of inherent trait or gene that tells our brains to do these things? Are we unable to cope with big issues so we have to bail?"

I place my hand on her leg and rub gently. "You can't compare yourself to Lily and Tabitha. Their lives were vastly different from yours. They endured hardships that no person should ever have to endure. Their decisions were fueled by desperation and despair. You're *nothing* like them, in any way. You didn't have to live as they did, because Lily made sure that you were with a family who could take care of you in a way that she couldn't."

"I get it," she says, leaning her head into the couch cushion. I don't believe her.

"What do you want to know?" I ask her, preparing myself for an onslaught of Tabitha-related questions.

She hesitates. "Do you love me the same way you loved her?" This question stabs me in the heart. *How can she possibly ask me this?*

"I *did* love Tabby, but for all of the wrong reasons. I thought she could help me escape everything that I was running away from. My father. My mother's alcoholism. Meredith. I put all of my energy into making sure she could forget her own pain, and I mistook her appreciation for love. At the same time, I moved further away from the man my father expected me to be. I lived anonymously with her.

She was immune to everything the Tyson name held. I was starting over, and she was my starting point."

"It sounds like you were both using each other," she observes.

"To an extent," I admit, wishing it weren't true.

"Like I used Ryan," she confesses.

"She felt safe with me, for a while. I can't explain it, but I felt like I *needed* to be her savior. Maybe Dr. Grant was right in saying that I always have to be the savior. "

"Do you feel that way about me?" she asks quickly.

"It's different with you. It's so natural, real." I stretch my legs out so our feet are almost touching. "It's hard to explain, but Tabitha became a challenge for me. Not in a conquest sort of way, but her issues were so pronounced, I felt that if I could help her, I could help anyone." *Like my mother.*

"How bad was it for her?" she asks, slouching down and resting her head on the armrest. She looks exhausted and emotionally drained.

"As bad as it could get for one person to handle." I'm struggling with what I have the right to tell her. Tabitha's horrors should be forgotten forever by anyone who knew what she went through.

"The only happy time in her life until recently was when she was adopted by one of the nurses from the hospital where she was found. But it was short lived. Her mother died when Tabitha was seven and her life spiraled out of control after that. She bounced from foster home to foster home until she was a teenager, subjected to all kinds of neglect and abuse. She ran away and wound up in Portland and was psychologically and sexually abused by a man who eventually got her pregnant. She was forced to give up her child."

Jules's face drops and her eyes widen. "Was she raped?" she asks as tears pool in her eyes.

"Yes, multiple times." I don't want to linger on this, and I've already said too much.

"She's better now, though." I pause to remember her wedding day, the day that Jules tried to kill herself. Ironic that Tabitha's life had a new beginning that day as Jules's almost ended.

Jules looks pensive. "I'm glad she had you."

"Trust me, our relationship was far from perfect, but one thing I know for certain is that she and I were better off as friends." If I hadn't crossed that line with Tabitha, things could have been so different for her and Alex.

"But then Emily wouldn't have been born." Juliet tries to help make sense of the hopeless situation I was in with Tabitha.

"Emily isn't mine." As the words leave my mouth, I realize this is the first time since she was born that I've acknowledged what I truly believed inside.

"How could you know that? She could be yours."

"No. I don't believe she is. When I held her in my arms the day that I said goodbye to her, I saw it in her eyes. She's not my child."

I realize we've taken a very long and round-a-bout way to get to her original question, and I attempt to get us back on track.

"And to answer your question from before, no, I didn't love you both the same. Tabitha was desperate for love and security. More like safety. I tried to give her what I thought she needed, but she couldn't reciprocate. It was one-dimensional, one-sided and was doomed from the start." I shake my head, realizing the mistakes that we both made. "Like I said before, she and I would have been better off as friends."

"*We've* been friends since we were kids. Do you think we'd be better off staying that way?" Her voice hitches as she looks away. How do I tell her that I've never had a love like hers? She consumes my thoughts and has for years, even when she shouldn't have.

I shift on the couch, sitting up and pulling her legs onto my lap. She drops her head to the side and looks at me tentatively.

"You're my first love, and I never had the courage to tell you. My love for you is pure, ageless. I knew it the first time I saw you bob for apples at your ninth birthday party. I've known it all of our lives, and my love for you has grown as we've grown together, apart and back together again."

Her eyes fill with tears and I hold my breath. She knows that I love her *now*, but admitting that I've loved her for years feels like an admission of guilt. I loved her when we were with other people, when she was with my best friend.

"Seth," she whispers as she closes her eyes, forcing the tears to spill down her cheeks.

I pull her toward me, into my chest, placing my chin on her head. She sobs quietly against me and we sit in silence.

"Why didn't you tell me all of this back then?" she asks.

"You know why I couldn't tell you. Jeremy was my best friend," I state simply.

I know her mind is racing and playing through all of the 'what-ifs.' Maybe if I'd told her how I felt, Jeremy wouldn't have been in the car with her and her family that day. Maybe he'd be alive. Maybe I would have been in the car instead. I know her well enough to know she's torturing herself over my admission.

"You're the only person besides Jeremy that I've said 'I love you' to." Her voice is muffled against my shirt.

"If I remember correctly, it was 'olive juice,'" I joke, and she starts to shake against me.

I'm thankful to bring a little humor into the room. It's been such a long and emotionally draining day for both of us, but her especially.

"You're never going to let me live that down, are you?" She looks up at me and smiles through her tear-streaked face. "And *you're* the only one I've said *that* to."

I want to kiss her so badly right now it hurts to be this far away from her lips. The revelations from today still hang in the air between us, and I need her to accept all that she's learned.

She places her head back onto my chest, and I spot the remote control that I was looking for on the floor. I reach down, grabbing it and turning on the music system. "Chasing Cars" by Snow Patrol plays, and we both relax into each other as I program the song to play on repeat.

As she settles into me, I run my hand down her arm, entwining our fingers together, feeling her heat through her fingertips. There are four bedrooms in this massive apartment, and the only place I want to be is on this couch. With her.

Her fingers tighten around mine and she says, "As comfy as you are, I don't think I can fall asleep on the couch."

I stretch and stand up, pulling her with me. "You have your choice of rooms. Let me go find something for us to sleep in." She nods and follows me down the hallway, toward the room that I know has a dresser filled with some of my clothes. I find a couple of pairs of sweats and tee shirts. "Here, they'll be pretty big on you, but if you roll the top of the sweats a few times, they should stay on." The vision of her wearing my sweats rolled on her hips suddenly causes a shift in my own pants. I quickly move toward the door to give her privacy. "Why don't you sleep in here? The bathroom is over there." I gesture toward the door on the far end of the room.

She walks over to the bathroom and turns quickly. "I don't want to be alone tonight," she says in a low voice as her green eyes flicker, reflecting the dim light in the room.

"What do you mean?" I ask, moving toward her.

"Stay with me tonight, Seth?" she asks as she takes a step toward me.

I quickly close the distance between us and stop when our toes touch. My eyes search her face for something, anything. Permission for more. She stares at my lips and then up to my eyes. Her fingertips graze my hand, moving up my arm and over to settle on my waist. She tugs at my shirt lightly, pulling me closer to her.

Does she want this as much as I do?

When she drops her gaze back to my lips again, I don't wait for another cue. I move my hands to the sides of her head, pulling her mouth to mine. Our lips collide and my teeth scrape against hers. "Sorry," I whisper into her mouth, replacing my words with my tongue. She willingly accepts it as she twists her hands in my shirt, pulling me against her.

She begins to back up toward the bed, pulling me with her, our lips and tongues still connected, intertwined. We fall onto the bed, her underneath me. She raises her hips against me, and I press myself between her legs. I move my hands from her head and let them travel down her body as I shift my weight to her side. She gasps at the loss of contact between our lower bodies. She gasps again when I brush the side of her breast with my fingers. I slow down my assault of her mouth, pulling slightly away to look at her. Her hair is a mess, spread out in all directions on the pillow. Her green eyes shimmer in the dim light, and our eyes lock. "Don't stop," she begs, pushing her chest forward, heaving her breast into my hand. I run my thumb over her nipple and she moans softly. We're both wearing too many clothes, I decide, so I pull her shirt over her head. She sits up to allow me to unclasp her bra from behind, and she begins a trail of small kisses and nibbles down my neck.

I feel her tug at my shirt, and she pulls it up and over my head. I watch as she takes her bra the rest of the way off, her breasts spilling out. Her skin is flushed and pink, and her nipples are erect, begging for contact. I lean forward and pull her nipple into my mouth, teasing it with my tongue. She cries out and thrusts her hips toward me. Her hands leave my sides as she unbuttons her jeans and shimmies them down her legs, kicking them off the edge of the bed. She brings her hips up to meet mine again and presses her core against me. "God, Jules," I groan into her mouth. Her eyes pop open and her look is dark, needing. I find her mouth again with mine, and she softly bites my lip, tugging it between her teeth.

I push myself off of her and stand, quickly ridding myself of my own jeans. She watches me as I contemplate removing my boxer briefs as well. Her eyes widen and she smiles. That's the only cue I need, and I grab the waist of my briefs and pull them down, stepping out of them. I'm fully erect and exposed, needing the warmth of her body against me. She slides down, out of her panties, and I remove them the rest of the way.

She's beautiful.

I slowly climb back over her, lowering myself onto her body. "I love you," she pants from beneath me. My hands are back in her messy hair, and I kiss her again, this time less frantic and more passionate. Our bodies move against each other in unison, and her heat transfers to me from her breasts and between her legs. I rest my elbows on either side of her head, breaking our kiss so I can devour all of her.

"I love you," I say before taking her breast into my mouth. Her hands grip my hair, guiding me over to her other breast. My tongue encircles her nipple and she thrusts against my hips.

I want her now.

I swirl my hips against her as I find warmth, poised to enter her, needing to be inside her. I hesitate, breaking contact, and she immediately says, "I'm on the pill." As soon as the words leave her lips, I thrust inside and am immediately enveloped by her warmth. She cries out as I thrust a second time, completely filling her. I find her lips again and kiss her tenderly as our hips move perfectly together. She places her hands on my ass, applying pressure, as if begging me to go deeper. We fit perfectly, our bodies entwined, as I slowly glide in and out of her warmth, connecting us in a way that we've never been before. And it's perfect.

I feel her body stiffen below mine and her hips thrust harder. She begins to pulsate around me, drawing me in deeper and deeper. I reach down between us and press my thumb against her nub, circling slowly as our bodies move together toward bliss. Our breathing picks up as we pant against each other's mouths. Our kisses become clumsy as our breathing becomes uneven. She cries out with her release, and I ride her wave of pleasure until my own climax rips through me. I slow down my thrusts but remain inside her, not wanting our connection to end.

She opens her eyes, and her pink cheeks glow as she smiles wide. "Hey," she says softly, her lips swollen. I nip at them lightly and then kiss her deeply.

"Hey, yourself," I say, easing myself out of her. I immediately pull the covers over the both of us, pulling her against me to preserve our warmth, our connection.

"That was..." she says against my chest, her lips kissing my collarbone.

"Too soon?" I ask, worried.

She freezes in my arms and looks up at me. "No, silly." She playfully slaps my chest and says, "That was amazingly perfect."

I relax against her and kiss her again. I don't want to let her go or this moment to end. "I've been waiting my whole life for you to see me the way I see you. *You're* amazingly perfect," I smile. "I love you."

"Thank you for always being there, Seth. I've always felt your presence around me, even when it was through a letter or a computer screen. Thank you," she whispers before she tucks her head into my chest. I squeeze her tightly and listen to her soft breaths, feeling her warmth against me. She drifts off to sleep and I smile.

I want her like this forever.

chapter thirty-two

Juliet
Sausalito, California
Age 25

WE PULL UP TO MY HOUSE and Seth puts the car in park. "Sorry you had to wear those clothes for two days in a row." He glances at my outfit and I laugh.

"These jeans may walk off of me before I even get into the house," I joke. He raises his eyebrow and I realize what I just said. "I mean..."

He puts his hand in the air and closes his eyes. "No. Don't take that mental image away from me." He pops his eyes open and laughs. I pull his face toward mine and kiss him softly, tenderly. He wraps his arms around me and pulls away slightly. "Please tell me this isn't goodbye."

I gasp against his lips. "Goodbye?" I ask "After last night, how could you ask that?" We *started* something last night, something I never want to let go. There will be no goodbyes from me.

"So, are we?" he asks.

"Are we what?" I respond playfully.

"We have some things to deal with, together," he says, his mood turning serious. I know he's referring to the fact that he was once in a relationship with my sister. While it seems crazy to even try to comprehend, somehow it doesn't matter as much to me as maybe it should. We've both had our share of relationships and shared intimacy with others, but what matters most right now is that we're both in a better place, emotionally equipped to focus on us.

"To answer your question, we're an *us*."

He smiles and cradles my face in his hands. "As long as we're *something*, because I couldn't cope with the alternative."

"I love you," he says against my lips, kissing me with urgency then suddenly releasing me. "You need to tell your father about yesterday, so stop making out with me already."

I smile and back away from him slightly, leaving my hand on his cheek. "You're everything to me, Seth Tyson. I love you."

I reluctantly pull my hand away and open the door. "Are you sure you don't want me to come in?" he asks. During our flight home, we debated what would be the best way to tell my father everything. At first, I thought it would be great for Seth to be there, but then I realized that it would potentially be too awkward for him, especially when we discuss Tabitha.

"I'm positive. This is something I need to do on my own. Besides, I also need to tell him about *us*, and I think that might be a little weird for you to be there." I get out of the car and shut the door.

He immediately rolls down the window and says, "Please call me tonight. I need to know how everything goes. And that you're still okay."

"Of course I will," I say and reluctantly walk into my house. I don't want him to leave. I hear him pull away after I'm inside and shut the door.

"Juliet, is that you?" my father calls from the library.

"Yes." I drop my purse in the foyer and find my father at his desk, working. Papers are scattered everywhere and what looks like contracts are on the floor. "Whoa, it looks like a bomb hit in here," I joke.

"It's been a crazy week. The board has decided to sell off some real estate holdings that Ted had insisted we hold onto. After he died, Sean uncovered some sketchy deals that Ted made a few months back, and now I'm trying to unwind them and get them ready for sale."

"Oh no, I hope this isn't bad for the company."

"Actually, quite the opposite. Once we free ourselves of some of these properties, our liquidity will improve immensely, and we already have some lucrative investments on the horizon. Sean is determined to turn Tyson Industries into a better company than when his father was at the helm. He's also going to work on some philanthropic endeavors, so if you have any ideas, just let us know. He wants to invest money into local charities and small businesses."

I breathe a sigh of relief and sit in the oversized leather chair in the corner of the room.

"Do you have time to hear about our visit with Lily?" I ask, and he immediately pushes away from his desk and sinks into a matching chair across from me.

"I have all of the time in the world," he says.

"First, I'm sorry that we didn't make it home last night."

"Thank goodness you didn't fly home. The weather was horrendous. I'm glad they closed the airport. I'm glad you were safe. You were in good hands."

I was safe and in bed with Seth.

I blush a little and continue. "About that. Umm—I think Seth and I are kind of a couple now."

"It's about damn time," he says, repeating the same thing that Jason said to us.

"We're taking things slow." *Lie.* I smile and pull my feet underneath me.

"I've no doubt that you'll move at a comfortable pace. I couldn't be happier for you. Where is he?"

"I wanted to tell you about Lily on my own. We found out a lot of things yesterday that were really difficult for me to digest." A look of concern sweeps over his face.

"Tell me everything," he says.

And I do.

I talk non-stop for over an hour, barely coming up for air. My father sits silently through most of it, offering comfort when I get to the difficult parts. It's hard to tell him about what Lily went through with Tabitha's and my birth. He's shocked over the fact that I have a twin sister.

"Are you going to reach out to her?" he asks, interrupting my rambling.

"I don't know, Dad. I'm not even sure what I would say to her."

Hi. You don't know me, but I'm your twin sister who's dating your ex-boyfriend. And oh, by the way, our birth mother thought you were dead.

"I think that you're a truly special woman to meet her. That had to be the hardest thing you have ever done, going up there, not knowing what to expect. I'm so proud of you."

"Thanks, Dad. Yesterday certainly wasn't easy, but Lily and I were able to help each other understand the various decisions we've made. She has no regrets though. She would choose you and Mom for me all over if she had to do it again today."

"I'm so sorry for everything that you've gone through and all that you've struggled with internally. I don't need to tell you again the impact you've had on our family. You belonged with us from the day you were born."

I stand up and walk across the room. I give him a huge hug and a kiss on the cheek.

"I have a surprise for you," my father says through his grin.

"I don't like surprises," I joke.

"I think you'll like this one. C'mon, follow me." He gets up and walks toward the basement door. I haven't been down there for years. We have a large informal living space, pool table, bar, exercise room and a theatre. The last movie I watched in there was *The Princess Bride* with Jeremy.

I follow him toward the back of the basement where the door to the theatre is. I look at him strangely as he opens the door and says, "Ta-da!"

I look around and don't see anything different. This place is exactly as I remember it.

"Dad?" I ask curiously, unsure of what he's trying to show me.

He pulls me toward the cabinet that houses our movie collection. "I had something made for you. For us." He pulls open one of the drawers and takes out a DVD that looks custom made and hands it to me.

The title of the DVD is "The Olivers," and there's a collage of pictures on the front. Pictures that I know my mother took over the years.

"What's this?" I ask, my voice cracking. Seeing all of our smiling faces when we were younger makes me feel nostalgic. When I see my mother's bright eyes and smile, tears come to my eyes.

"It's one of twelve DVDs I had made for us to enjoy. It's a home movie and the story of our lives."

"Dad, this is amazing," I say, swiping at the tear that rolls down my cheek.

"How about movie night tonight?" he asks.

I immediately say, "Yes!"

I reach out and pull him into a huge hug. "Thanks, Dad. This is exactly what I needed today. I love you."

"I love you too, sweetheart."

"HEY," I SAY TO SETH. I hold my phone with my shoulder as I strip off the jeans I've had on for two days and change into something more comfortable.

"Hey, yourself," he says, and I can hear his smile through the phone. "I've missed you."

I pull on my yoga pants and flop onto my bed. "It's only been a few hours." My heart swells and my belly tingles, thinking about last night. Making love with Seth was amazing. "Did last night really happen?" I ask.

"I don't know what you're talking about," he jokes. There wasn't a moment today when I didn't long for his touch, his breath on my neck. "Of course it happened." His voice turns serious and I relax. "It was the best night of my life."

"Mine too." I pause to think about how weird it was telling my father about our meeting with Lily yesterday.

"How did everything go with your Dad?" he asks, reading my mind.

"It went well. I told him about everything, including Tabitha."

"How'd he take it that you have a sister?"

"Good, actually. It broke his heart to hear about her troubled life, and I could tell that he wished we would have been adopted together. He knows that he and my mother would have given her the best life possible, just like they gave me."

He's silent, contemplating what could have been, I'm sure.

"My dad asked me if I was going to reach out to her."

"Tabitha?" Seth asks, sounding distant.

"Yes. And I didn't know what to say. I'm not sure if I should."

"Do what feels right," he says, and I know he means it.

"When can I see you again?" I ask, changing the subject. I want to focus on us.

"Always," he says, and I smile. "You can see me whenever you want. How about you come to my place tonight?"

"How about tomorrow? I want to stay home with Dad tonight. He and I actually planned a movie night." I'm looking forward to seeing the home movies that Dad had made, eating popcorn and just being together.

"Movie night? Sounds fun. Anything good?" he asks.

"Yes, Dad had home movies made from when I was younger. I'm actually looking forward to seeing them and seeing Mom." My heart hurts a little bit, thinking about the tears that will surely come tonight, but it's time for me to see my past play out before me and embrace the happiness that I had when I was younger. Somewhere along the way, I lost pieces of myself to Lily's letter. I let an inanimate object control me in such an unhealthy way. It nearly killed me, and I need to experience my youth through different eyes.

"It's going to be wonderful," he says. "What time am I picking you up tomorrow? I want to take you out on a date."

"A date? Hmmm, let me look at my calendar to see if I'm free..." I joke.

"Wear something comfortable."

"No hint as to where we're going to go?" I ask, knowing he's not going to tell me.

"Nope. But if you want to bring something to stay over at my place, don't hesitate." He chuckles.

"Maybe," I say, teasing, and then, "Goodbye, I love you."

"Olive juice, too," he says, and I huff.

"Jules," he says softly.

"Yes."

"I love you."

"Goodnight," I say before I hang up reluctantly.

I look at the clock, and I still have about an hour or so before movie night starts. My Dad had to drop off some contracts at the office and then he said the rest of the night is mine.

I sink onto my bed and close my eyes. I see the picture that Lily showed us yesterday of her and Layla. I wonder what Lily's life was like growing up with her sister, despite Layla's issues with depression. The picture showed two giggling girls, happy and without a care in the world. It was like they had a secret they were keeping between them, and the confidence in their eyes that they would be together forever.

What would my life have been like if Tabitha had been here?

Everything I know about her life devastates me and completely breaks my heart. I wish things had been different for her, and the loss that I feel over never having known about her begins to tear me up inside.

What if...?

I reach into my night table and pull out my journal. I flip through the pages and see years of thoughts, happy and sad. I stopped writing in my journal after Mom and Jeremy died. I didn't want to acknowledge my feelings in writing, fearing that it would document the truth.

I find a blank page and smooth it out with my hand. My favorite pen is in the drawer and I grab it, hoping it still works.

I gather my thoughts and try to decide what I want to write. The words don't come immediately, so I just put the pen on the paper and begin.

Dear Tabitha...

epilogue

Juliet

Five Years Later
San Francisco, CA
Age 30

Dear Juliet,
We've known each other practically our entire lives. I can't believe I was just ten years old when I wrote my first letter to you. I'll never forget how awkward it was, but as time went on, our interactions became more and more real.
I longed to hear your 'voice' through your words. I longed for your support through all of the difficult times with my family. Through the ups and downs with my mother.
I longed to comfort you during times of sadness. Through your growth as you yearned to find your true self.
While our experiences have been difficult, to say the least, we've always found our way back to each other. To comfort each other.
You've truly been my best friend for as long as

DEAR JULIET

I can remember.
I love you, Jules.
With all of me.
So this letter is from all of the 'Seth's' that you've grown up with:
> a curious ten-year-old who found his first long-term pen pal
> an ambitious but sad pre-teen who seemingly had everything going for him, but had to learn the hard truths about addiction and depression
> a confident but nervous teenager who was terrified to leave his family and friends behind while he attempted to make something of himself in college
> an independent but disheartened adult who tried desperately to find his way and create a future for himself
But I've always found my way...
Back. To. You.
Back. To. Us.
We belong together—we just didn't know it or see what was right in front of us for so many years. I guess we had to grow separately and experience everything that we did in order to find each other one last time.
Let's not waste any more time.
Let's make 'us' forever.

Yours,
Seth

P.S. Please open your door.

I taste the familiar flavor of my salty tears as I watch them drip from my chin onto the handwritten note that Seth wrote to me five years ago.

The day he proposed to me.

When I opened my door, he was standing there with a piece of paper with the words Marry Me scrawled on it. My doubts always plagued me when it came to relationships. *Did I deserve to be with someone forever? Would anyone ever really 'want' me? Was I destined to be alone?*

Seth helped me find out so much about my past and myself. His shoulders absorbed the countless streams of tears that I cried for my Mom, Jeremy, Lily and my past. He supported me through some of my toughest, saddest times. He was with me when I met Lily, and he helped me fill in the blanks that had burned on the branches of my family tree.

He'd always been here for me.

Always.

But could I give all of myself to him?

As I remember that day and all of the conflicted moments in my life that led me to that moment, I picture Seth standing outside my door, dropping to his knee and taking my hands into his own. He was committing to us and to our forever. I remember the thoughts that swirled through my mind that day. *Could I do the same? After everything that we had been through together and separately? Could I commit to giving myself fully to this man?*

I fold the letter carefully, putting it into its special place in my nightstand, and try to claim what feels like inches on the edge of my bed.

Our bed.

I look over and see that Seth is barely clinging on to his side of the bed as our three-year-old twins are stretched out between us. Cassie's elbow is shoved into the back of her father's neck, while her face is planted between his shoulder blades. Tommy is perpendicular to his sister, his feet dangerously close to kicking her in the belly, while his head is burrowed into my side.

I said yes.

Yes to the ten-year-old boy who wrote me my first pen pal letter.

Yes to the pre-teen who had to grow up in the shadow of addiction.

Yes to the teenager who not only lost his best friend, but realized he also loved his best friend's girl.

Yes to the adult who made terribly difficult choices because he didn't want to be anything like his own father.

Yes to the man who gave me this wonderful life along with my past, present and future.

I gingerly turn onto my side and face the family beside me. I reach across and place my hand on top of Seth's head. His free hand quickly covers mine and squeezes softly.

"I love you," I whisper through happy tears.

"Olive juice, too," he replies, and I flick his ear playfully.

He grabs my hand again, squeezing harder this time, and says, "I love you, Jules."

I drape my other arm over our beautiful children and feel my heart swell. This is exactly where we are supposed to be. Together.

We've found our Forever Family.

The End

Do you miss the band, Epic Fail?
Dax, Tristan & Garrett?

The Epic Fail Series
Epic Sins
Epic Lies
Epic Love

Available Everywhere

note to my readers

If you or someone you know has been raped or abused, please urge them to seek help. Please beg them to tell someone.

No means no.

Do something and say something.

For more information about how to help yourself or a loved one, please visit one of these important websites or call the toll-free hotlines.

RAINN (Rape, Abuse & Incest National Network)
www.rainn.org
1-800-656-HOPE (4673)

Safe Horizon
www.safehorizon.org
1-800-621-HOPE (4673)

If you or someone you know has feelings of suicide or depression, please urge them to seek help to prevent a tragedy.

For more information about how to help yourself or a loved one, please visit one of these important websites or call the hotlines below.

National Suicide Prevention Hotline
www.suicidepreventionlifeline.org
1-800-273-8255

The Kristen Books Hope Center
www.hopeline.com
1-202-536-3200

If you or someone you know needs help dealing with alcoholism and addiction, please visit this important website or call one of the hotlines below.

AL-ANON Family Groups
www.al-anon.org
1-757-563-1600

acknowledgements

*may contain spoilers

Ah! THIS BOOK! I really had to dig deep to find the voice I needed to write this book. It went through so many re-writes as characters literally changed completely, died or became non-existent. This story was my albatross for almost a year. I just couldn't find my way. Then I dug deeper.

In a convoluted way, I needed to write this story for Tabitha. Her birth mother, in my mind, needed to be redeemed. Be somebody 'good.' She had to have good intentions, because Tabitha deserved something good from her horrible ordeal. Yes, she got her happily ever after in Dear Tabitha, but something was missing, and I needed to find her birth mother. Thus, the creation of Lily and Juliet. They've completed the puzzle for me of Tabitha's life, and I was able to create a new world with new characters.

I also couldn't have finished this book without Seth's voice, and when I finally heard it, the story began to tell itself. His voice paved the way for the closure of Juliet's questions as well as opened the door for Tabitha to complete her happily ever after.

So, my first acknowledgment is to those precious voices inside my head. Thank you for finally coming to life and guiding me toward the story that I was meant to tell. Cheers!

My family has, once again, endured a long Christmas. At least most of our decorations are down before Easter this year. Thank you to my husband for constantly encouraging me to just sit down and write and for always covering the housework when I get into 'the zone.' Your support means the world to me, and I'll say this over and over again: "Olive Juice." My children are a constant inspiration for my stories and I love them with all of my heart. Thank you to my special 'Irish Twins.'

Amanda Maxlyn: Thank you for believing in me when I stopped believing in myself. Our frequent chats are a source of strength for me, and it feels great to have you on speed dial. You're my lifeline and I love you so much.

Rebecca Shea: Thank you for always keeping it real for me. Your advice is invaluable and your friendship is treasured. I know that every single time I talk to you or ask you for your opinion, you always tell me the truth—which is exactly what I need to hear. I love you!

My BETA girls: Thank you for understanding that I had to take a slightly different direction and approach with this book and remaining patient with me as I pulled it all together. You all contributed in your own ways in helping make this story the best that I could tell. I love you girls so much.

To one of my anonymous Betas: You have been an incredible source of strength for me and helped push me along in writing this book, even when I didn't want to. You listened to various plot lines and tried to throw your own crazy twists in here and there. (No. Just. No.) You helped me stay true to the story that I wanted to tell. Thank you. I love you so much!

Murphy Rae: I can't thank you enough for all of the work that you've done to synthesize the voices across all three of my books. You've helped give Dear Emily and Dear Tabitha a burst of energy and light while helping mold Dear Juliet into the story it is today. You challenged me to be a better writer and made me look at my technique in a whole different way. Thank you so much.

Brandee Veltri: Your constant support throughout all of my blitzes and releases is truly amazing. Thank you so much for all that you do to pull all of my promotions together and making them a success. I love you!

Becca Manuel: Your trailer for Dear Tabitha made me cry hard. It was beautiful and fit the story perfectly. Your trailer for Dear Juliet took my breath away. Perfection. True perfection. Your talent is truly amazing.

Stephanie White: Thank you for creating this beautiful cover. As you know, it's my favorite of the series and you truly captured the essence of what I wanted for this book. Flawless, as usual. Thank you!

Elaine York: Just like the outside cover, the inside of a book needs to look perfect. Thank you so much for giving the interior of this series a makeover.

To all of my wonderful friends in the Forever Family Facebook group. I absolutely love that I can jump in the room at any time just to say hi. I feel safe and happy with all of you. Thank you for always putting a smile on my face and for patiently waiting for my next release. Your support is unwavering and I love you all for that.

I'm once again overwhelmed by the incredible support that this awesome blogging community has given me. I still feel like a newbie in this sea of amazing and talented authors. Every single time you sign up to support a blitz, release and post a review, I'm truly humbled. For you all to spend just a little bit of time supporting me and my books is amazing, and I wouldn't be here without you.

To all of my peers. I'm thrilled when I see my author friends succeed in this industry. I cheer each and every one of you on as I watch your works of art climb the charts. I can't thank you all enough for the support that you've shown me over the past year and a half. We are a great community of wonderful people. I'm proud to call myself an author and stand among your ranks.

And finally, thank you, readers! You continue to trust in me and take a chance on these stories. Thank you for being patient and embracing The Forever Family Series. Stick with me, and I promise to continue giving you emotionally gripping stories.

Cheers!

other books by trudy stiles

The Forever Family Series
Dear Emily
Dear Tabitha
Dear Juliet
Sincerely, Emily (coming soon)
Forever Sara (coming soon)

The Epic Fail Series
Epic Sins
Epic Lies
Epic Love
Epic Holiday (coming soon)

Links to all of her books can be found on her website:
http://trudystiles.com/books/

about the author

Trudy Stiles is a USA Today Bestselling Author, writer of New Adult Romance, mom to two beautiful children, and married to the love of her life. She's the author of the bestselling **Forever Family** *series including* **Dear Emily, Dear Tabitha,** *and* **Dear Juliet.** **Epic Sins, Epic Lies** *and* **Epic Love** *are the first three books in the* **Epic Fail** *series and will continue with at least one more standalone novel,* **Epic Holiday.** *She plans to write many more stories about some of the characters you've already met, and maybe a few new ones. Emily will get her own story,* **Sincerely, Emily**, *to be released in 2017. Sara will also have her own story,* **Forever Sara,** *also to be released sometime in 2017.*

She's also a contributing author to the USA Today Bestselling anthology, F*cking Awkward, a hilarious group of short stories sure to make you cringe, laugh and everything in between. All proceeds from this project benefited The Bookworm Box and its charities.

Trudy is a music junkie and you'll know that she's writing when you see her plugged into her laptop with her earbuds in. Her playlist is unique and is a must for her writing sprints.

When she's not writing, she's carting her children to their various activities while avoiding any kind of laundry or housework. She also loves to run along the boardwalk of the beautiful New Jersey shore.

She celebrates Wine Wednesday almost every day.

To learn more about Trudy, visit her website here:

http://trudystiles.com

Email:authortrudystiles@gmail.com

Facebook: www.facebook.com/authortrudystiles

Goodreads: www.goodreads.com/trudy_stiles

Twitter: @trudystiles

Instagram: https://instagram.com/trudystiles/

CPSIA information can be obtained
at www.ICGtesting.com
Printed in the USA
BVOW06s1844040417
480298BV00008B/358/P